VOIDSTALKER

JOHN GRAHAM

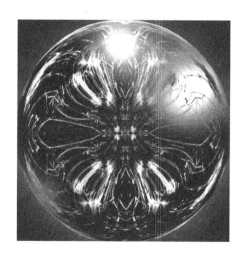

KDP

Published by KDP

ISBN: 978-1-7290-6725-3

Typesetting services by BOOKOW.COM

Contents

THE FAMILY

Real nightmares are rooted in memory, and this nightmare was no different. The door to the depressurised chamber opened and he felt a spike of adrenaline pierce his heart as he was ejected into the cold and lonely void. Twisting and spinning through space with his sense of direction thrown into confusion, he felt like he was suffocating as he hyperventilated from sheer panic.

He had to force himself to slow his breathing, taking shallower and shallower gulps of air until his pulse had settled and he was no longer panicking; then he extended his limbs and relaxed. Without an EVA jetpack, there was nothing else he could do, and by the time he had calmed down, the vessel that had carried him there was already gone.

The darkness that surrounded him was so thick he could almost touch it. Save for the countless tiny points of light that dotted the background, the distance between himself and the stars was a never-ending expanse of pure emptiness, extending in all directions. The sheer immensity of space made him feel like a grain of sand in a vast ocean, or a speck of dust floating in a planetary atmosphere.

Worse still was the sheer nothingness of it all. At least in the ocean or the atmosphere, you could feel the currents making their presence known and their power felt, buffeting you back and forth, reminding you constantly that it surrounded you. In the vacuum of space, there truly was nothing, not even gravity. The eternal abyss exerted no push or pull, no awesome reminder of its infinite power, because there was nothing there to exert such power. To be trapped in space was to be just another particle drifting forever.

But perhaps worst of all was the total loss of orientation. There was no direction in the omnidirectional void. No up or down, no left or right, no forwards or backwards; even the points of light were too indistinct to provide a sense of direction. Nor did his spacesuit have any sort of navigation equipment installed, leaving him with absolutely no sense of direction. All he could do was float and stare out into the abyss, and the longer he stared, the more the abyss seemed to swallow him.

The panic returned.

His pulse began to race and his breathing began to accelerate as if sucking up more of his precious oxygen would soothe the maddening sense of nothingness. Flailing in the dark, he felt himself sinking further and further into the blackness, and even the barely visible stars seemed to fade beyond vision, like tiny gems submerging into a tar pit. The sheer absence of anything, the infinite abyss of pure nihilism was slowly devouring his mind ...

* * *

Gabriel awoke with a start.

Another nightmare. At least, he knew that most people would call that a nightmare; and yet he felt none of the physical signs that a nightmare ought to bring. He felt no cold sweat, he wasn't gasping for air, and his heartbeat rapidly subsided to normal. Nor did he feel any horrible sense of panic that he might fall back into the nightmare. Whatever feeling of terror he might have had evaporated almost as soon as it came.

Now, he felt only clinical acknowledgement of the fact that he was awake.

Gabriel lay his head back on the pillow and tried to return to sleep. But he was no longer tired enough to close his eyes and just doze off, and after staring at the ceiling for a while, he headed to the bathroom. The light-strip atop the mirror awoke at his presence, and he splashed some water on his face, the icy cold liquid refreshing the nerves under his skin and washing away any remaining traces of drowsiness.

Gabriel looked up at the mirror, and his reflection looked back with minimal expression. His face was clean-shaven, with an angular jaw, and a head of short dark hair. He was naked from the waist up, the toned, powerful musculature of his chest and arms resembling chiselled marble. Though barely visible under the light, the slightly pale skin across his body was covered with faint scar tissue, their precise, symmetrical patterns giving them away as the marks of numerous surgical enhancements.

Most distinctive of all were his eyes. The irises were a shimmering, emerald green, almost luminescent under the light. Many people assumed they were bionic implants or garish contact lenses; but they were definitely his actual eyes, staring back at him with hard, emotionless authority. That was the way he usually looked to the world: cold and stern.

He cracked a well-practised smile in the mirror. It looked sincere and convincing enough, but it felt unnatural, like putting on a clever disguise that was uncomfortable to wear. It was fake, and he stopped from embarrassment. That well-practised smile was only something he showed to those closest to him, to reassure them that he wasn't a sociopath.

The soft sound of footsteps entering the bathroom reached his ears, and a petite pair of hands slid across his body, pulling him into an embrace.

"It's hard to sleep when you can't," Aster said, her voice weighed down by tiredness.

"I can sleep," Gabriel reassured her, reciprocating the embrace with one arm, "I just need less of it than the average person."

"Thanks to the people who put this thing here," Aster said, reaching up as she spoke.

She pressed her thumb against the back of Gabriel's neck and traced it across the skin. The action caused a symbol to appear: a capital S intertwined, serpent-like, with a capital V.

"Is there something wrong with it?" Gabriel asked as the symbol faded from view.

"Is there something wrong with the fact that you have a glorified cattle brand on the back of your neck?" Aster asked rhetorically, a note of tension creeping into her voice.

"You get it when you join," Gabriel reminded her, ignoring the slightly barbed tone of her voice, "And you join for life."

"I get that much, and I can accept that much," Aster replied, resting her chin on his chest, "but the nightmares are a different story."

She gazed up at him with her light brown, puppy dog eyes. Gabriel placed a hand on her head, stroking the shoulder length brunette curls with their blonde highlights. But the gaze had a question in them, demanding an answer.

"I can't tell you."

"Why not?" Aster demanded, slipping into her native colonial accent.

"They're classified," Gabriel replied matter-of-factly.

"How the fuck can your nightmares be classified?" Aster shot back angrily.

"Keep your voice down," Gabriel hissed angrily, "the children are sleeping."

"I know that," Aster hissed back in an angry stage whisper, "what I don't know is why you can't tell your own wife about the nightmares you have every week, or why the fuck they make you put that thing on your head before you go to sleep."

Gabriel gingerly touched the skin-coloured gel-strip adhering to his forehead, causing the invisible circuitry to light up in response. It seemed like a silly question when the answer was so obvious: to monitor his neural activity when he was asleep.

But of course, what she really wanted to know was what was done with the data. Even he didn't know that, and even if he did he couldn't tell her. The data collected by the gel-strip, and the uses to which it was put, were classified.

Aster knew all of that, and she showed what she thought of that by reaching up and giving the gel-strip an irreverent flick.

"Don't touch it," Gabriel warned her, flinching in irritation.

Aster replied by defiantly flicking the gel-strip again.

"I said don't touch it," Gabriel's tone hardened, "you might damage it."

"It's a wireless electroencephalographic monitoring strip, not an egg-shell," Aster retorted, making clear that she knew more about the technology than he did, "your lords and masters will still get their pristine data feeds."

She emphasised the point by giving the strip another sharp jab.

A rush of anger swept through Gabriel's chest, and he angrily seized Aster's wrists and pinned her against the wall, not tolerating her provocations any longer. Aster inhaled sharply, taken aback by his outburst of aggression.

"Which part of 'don't touch it' do you not understand?" Gabriel hissed angrily, piercing her eyes with his own as he spoke.

He was hissing at Aster through gritted teeth to suppress the volume of his voice but inadvertently ended up with a menacing, wolf-like snarl on his face.

Aster didn't respond, but the emotion in her eyes wasn't fear. They were chest to chest, their lips only inches away from each other. Gabriel's gaze drifted down from her eyes to her button nose and slightly open lips, then down across the soft skin of her neck, converging downwards into a V-shape. He could feel the warmth of her body against his own, and the closeness of their bodies caused another feeling to stir in his chest, quenching his anger.

As Gabriel's anger subsided, he realised he was physically pinning his wife to the wall. Self-consciously, he relinquished his grip on her wrists and took an apologetic step backwards. Aster used her now free hands to pull his head back towards her own. Their lips connected, and she held him there for a long moment before breaking the kiss.

"Don't pull away," she whispered to him.

Aster pulled him in for another kiss, this time allowing his tongue entrance. As they continued to lock lips, Aster ran her fingers through his raven-black hair and wrapped her arms around his neck. Gabriel's own hands slid down her back towards her butt, cupping her cheeks in his palms. Then he reached down further and placed his hands behind her knees, hoisting her effortlessly into the air. Her body felt warm and exciting, and she wrapped her legs around his waist in response, hugging him close.

"We should get back to bed," she whispered into his ear.

* * *

Even after their nocturnal exercise session, Gabriel still wasn't tired enough to fall asleep, and he lay awake for the rest of the night, spread-eagled on his back, staring at the ceiling in the dark. His stare was blank, but his mind was abuzz with thoughts.

Revealing details of past operations, let alone present ones was strictly forbidden, even if those details were filtered through dreams and nightmares. Secrecy was central to what he did. Aster hated the secrecy, and it was a constant source of tension between them. But it was nothing that couldn't be defused in the bedroom.

Aster was lying face down on top of him, curled up around his chest for comfort. Her skin felt so soft and warm against his own; just feeling her body warmth was enough to rekindle his arousal. Gabriel planted his hand on her shoulder and ran his palm down the curve of her back to her butt, cupping the cheek in his palm.

"Someone seems ready for round two," Aster murmured with a smile.

She lifted her knee a little higher and slid her body up closer to him. From her rear, he reached down a little further to the place below.

Gabriel's smartphone chimed suddenly, interrupting his ministrations. Gritting his teeth in annoyance at the interruption, he reached over and plucked the device off the bedside table, finding a single message in danger red, block capitals displayed on the holographic screen: '*REPORT TO DGNI'S OFFICE, 9 AM*'.

"Another assignment?" asked Aster, perching her chin on his chest and looking up.

"No comment," Gabriel replied laconically.

"Of course," Aster said with a sigh.

Gabriel could sense how weary Aster was of all the secrecy.

"It was a flashback, by the way," he said, abruptly changing the subject, "they're all based on memories from past assignments. That's why I can't tell you about them."

That semi-cathartic disclosure wasn't necessarily wise, even though he hadn't strictly speaking revealed anything classified.

"Listen, I know you can't talk about these things," Aster said hesitantly, "but–"

"The flashback happened during training," Gabriel uttered suddenly.

"…what happened?" Aster asked, wrong-footed by Gabriel's sudden confession.

"They leave you in space for 24 hours," Gabriel replied nonchalantly, "If your sanity is intact by the time they pick you up, you pass."

"Isn't zero-g combat part of basic training?"

"It is," Gabriel confirmed, "but that involves learning how to navigate in space using EVA suits. In the training I underwent, they throw you into the void with just a basic suit and 25 hours' worth of oxygen, enough to get you through the exercise. But there's no thruster pack, no safety tether, and no retrieval team for those who want to quit early."

"That sounds awful," Aster said, horrified.

"Worst of all is the toll on the mind," Gabriel continued, "The sheer emptiness around you. It's the worst kind of isolation, and you just have to endure it."

Aster was silent as she processed his surprise honesty. Gabriel was even more surprised that he had done it. He hadn't technically revealed anything operational, but that certainly wasn't something the average civilian needed to know.

"I'm glad you told me that," she said at length, snuggling closer to him, "I hate that the Masterminds know more about what goes on inside your head than I do."

"You wouldn't like what you find in there," Gabriel warned her.

"Maybe not," she answered, "but I'd rather know than have you shut me out altogether."

"Also, would you mind not swearing so much?" Gabriel changed the subject again, "I don't want the children waking up and overhearing it."

"Oh, do accept my humblest apologies, Mr Gabriel," Aster replied in a mock, upper-class accent, "I would hate to sound like a 'fleeking', uncouth colonial."

Gabriel's smartphone chimed a second time. The holographic screen displayed a plain message from a different sender: '*Morning drinks at Ellipsis, booth 39. See you there.*'

Gabriel scowled at the message. An invitation to drinks at an elite club for the rich and pampered was one thing; an invitation phrased as an instruction was downright condescending. Then again, it was typical of the sender to do that.

"Another message from work?" Aster asked.

"No, it's a drinks invitation," Gabriel said darkly.

"I hope it's not from a mistress of yours," Aster poked him playfully.

"I don't have anyone on the side," Gabriel replied in complete seriousness, "but I do know the sender. One guess who it is."

Now it was Aster's turn to scowl.

"Give her my regards," she said with barely concealed contempt, "or don't."

"Understood," Gabriel replied.

"And take that fucking thing off your head!" She snapped, reaching over and ripping the gel-strip off his forehead.

Gabriel neither flinched nor complained.

* * *

Gabriel preferred the shower cold, the better to hurry up and start the day. Aster, however, insisted on a warm shower so they could take their time. The water ran in soothing rivulets across their bodies, and a cloud of vapour filled the intimate space. There was enough space for two people, though not enough to avoid sharing some skin.

"So what are you doing at work today?" Aster asked as she washed her hair.

"Probably just tests and refresher drills," Gabriel lied.

Aster responded by sliding a hand down to Gabriel's crotch. Her grip was gentle enough, but it made him stiffen up in more ways than one.

"Don't lie to me, dear," she admonished.

"What makes you think I'm lying?" he asked.

"You always get a message from work before disappearing," Aster replied as she held him under the water, "they don't call you in that early in the morning for routine stuff."

"I don't know what I'll be doing at work today," Gabriel answered, "and my security clearance would prohibit me from saying anything, anyway."

"Of course, I understand," Aster said, looking up at him, "besides, all that hazard pay you rake in puts food on the table."

"Actually, my hazard pay is enough to buy us a small spaceship," Gabriel replied.

"It's an expression, idiot," Aster said, flicking his temple with her finger, "If you're this slow at work, your hazard pay probably isn't worth the risks you take."

"You do know that my hazard pay is on a pro rata basis, don't you?"

"Yeah, I know, the longer you're on deployment, the more you earn," Aster answered, "That's probably the only thing that makes up for you being away so much. Otherwise, my salary is more than enough."

"I need to get ready for work," Gabriel said.

* * *

Breakfast consisted of flavoured nutrient juice, with Gabriel downing an entire bottle to the dregs before changing into his midnight-black uniform. Once he was ready, he headed straight for the front door; but before he could leave the house, he was ambushed by three little figures still in their nightclothes.

"Morning, daddy!" His children chorused as he squatted down to greet them.

They weren't quite peas in a pod, but they all had their father's distinctive electric green irises, and some of his features. The oldest, seven-year-old Orion, was already a few inches taller than his two sisters and, apart from his mother's curly hair, almost resembled a clone of his father. Rose, the older of the two little girls, managed to lift herself onto Gabriel's knee before making an adventurous attempt to climb aboard her father's shoulders.

"Sorry, sweethearts," Gabriel plucked his five-year-old daughter from her perch and placed her carefully back on the ground, "daddy has to go to work."

Couldn't his children just get up earlier and greet him *before* breakfast instead of when he was on his way out the door? As nice as this little morning ritual was, it was holding him up and could make him late. The director-general hated unpunctuality, and so did he. In fact, being delayed at all was downright irritating.

Somewhere in the back of Gabriel's mind, it occurred to him what a cold train of thought this was to have about his own children. All they wanted to do was say good morning to him. Even so, was it too much to ask that they do it earlier in the morning?

His aspiring mountain-climber daughter reached up and irreverently poked her father in the nose with her tiny finger. Gabriel flinched in annoyance. He wanted to scold Rose, but he looked down and saw the cheeky grin on her face, and the shimmering emerald eyes she had inherited from him. He pursed his lips, then tapped her nose back in playful retaliation. She wrinkled her nose and giggled in response.

Why in Terra's name did he expect his children to know or care about routine and schedule, or punctuality? They were just happy to see their father every morning. They knew even less about what he did when he was away than their mother. And unlike Aster, they wouldn't understand what had happened if he never came back.

Every morning they had together could be their last.

On an impulse, Gabriel pulled all three of them in for a group hug, squeezing them close. His children squeezed him back, happy for their father's affection. This really could be the last time he saw or hugged them in person, and Gabriel's annoyance melted away as he savoured the moment of familial closeness.

He looked up and saw Aster standing at the far end of the hall, their fourth and youngest child dozing in her arms. Their eyes connected and Aster smiled at him. Gabriel smiled back as he squeezed their children close. Then he remembered.

"Their monthly check-up is today, by the way," Gabriel reminded her.

"At eleven o'clock sharp, I know," Aster responded, "I'll get them fed and drop them off at the medical centre, then I'll go to work."

"So what are they having you build today?" Gabriel asked out of curiosity.

Aster's warm expression turned into a frown.

"You're not the only one with a security clearance, you know," she responded seriously.

Gabriel understood, and he dropped the issue.

* * *

It was standing room only this early in the morning, with over a hundred people huddled together in each carriage of the mag-train. Some were engaged in hushed conversation, others stood in silence as they watched the news on the holographic viewing screens or occupied themselves with their smartphones. A few passengers cast wary glances at the towering figure in their midst, dressed in a night-black military uniform, stern and motionless.

Gabriel stared out of the window, ignoring everyone. He didn't mind the wary glances or the nervous stares directed at him, as long as they stayed out of his way. He did sort of mind having to be around so many people, especially the background din of frivolous chattering. But he had to take a detour before reporting for duty, and his destination was best reached via mag-train. He would just have to put up with it for now.

The magnetic rail was built as an extension from each sky-scraper's superstructure, snaking from tower to tower, and occasionally splitting or converging at various junctions. The mag-train itself moved at incredibly high speeds, taking it to the centre of the city in very little time. Its path also took it several hundred stories above the ground, giving the passengers a view from the carriage window which never ceased to amaze.

Asgard was named after a heavenly realm from the legends of ancient Earth, and with its gleaming forest of spires stretching far away into the distance, the city more than lived up to the moon's mythical namesake. Asgard City was a megacity of over 80 million people, an urban nerve centre connected to count-less smaller settlements across Asgard's surface, and serving as the administrative and economic capital for the entire sector.

The gas giant Odin seemed to hover directly above, looming large through the artificial ozone haze, an enormous blue sphere beside the bright white orb in the sky. The local star bathed the moon of Asgard in a flattering radiance, with Asgard City as its crown jewel, beaming under the morning light. And to think that this was just one hub-world among many. One could only imagine what Terra itself must be like.

Looking down revealed a rather less glorious sight. Just visible in the shade, occupying the lower tiers of the city and woven in between the skyscrapers' foundations, was a vast, multi-layered complex of warehouses, factories, and housing. It was called the Undercity, where most of the city's industrial base was located; it was also the sprawling home of the vast majority of the city's inhabitants, stretching deep underground and hiding most of it from view.

The Undercity was far less prosperous than the fabulously wealthy upper tiers of the city, an area known as the 'Clouds'. Nor was it lost on anyone that the economic activity in the Undercity was what made the luxury of the Clouds possible, almost as if wealth were lighter than air. Most of those who lived in the Clouds had never been down to the Undercity, and the few that had didn't care to return.

Gabriel had been down there many times.

* * *

The mag-train pulled into the central transport hub in the Ellipsis Commercial Tower. The enormous, shimmering monument of steel and glass was a marvel of engineering, reaching over a kilometre into the sky with foundations that reached at least that far underground. As well as one of the biggest mag-train stations in the city, it also housed the city's main financial hub as well as the homes of most of its elite.

The doors opened and the passengers poured out onto the platform, dispersing down the various corridors and elevators of the enormous station. Heedless of his fellow passengers, Gabriel strode straight down the middle towards the main elevator, the crowds parting before him like a shoal of frightened fish.

Taking the elevator up to the top floor, Gabriel stepped out into the entrance hall of an exclusive, private club, perched at the top of the tower like a nest of luxury. An elaborate water feature, forged in the shape of a pair of mythical sea monsters, dominated the cavernous lobby. White and gold support beams arched over the entire complex, intertwining like the branches of a bird's nest, with the natural light of the local star shining down through the glass in between the branching beams.

The super-elite came and went with their Human and android attendants, dressed in the latest and gaudiest fashions. Some of them paused briefly to stare at the intimidating figure marching down the hall towards the reception desk as if he belonged there. Gabriel knew how out of place he looked, and he didn't care.

The Human receptionist was looking down at his desk, so Gabriel snapped his fingers to get his attention. The receptionist looked up, then flinched in shock.

"Um…only club members and their guests are allowed to pass beyond this point…sir," the receptionist stammered.

"I *am* a guest," Gabriel replied with an impatient scowl, "Scan me."

The receptionist raised a trembling hand, pausing uncertainly between activating the biometric scanner and pressing the button under his desk.

"If you alert security, you'll be dead before they can get here," Gabriel said to the man dangerously, "now stop wasting my time and scan me."

The receptionist did as he was ordered and activated the biometric scanner, flash-scanning Gabriel's eyes and bringing up a profile on the receptionist's computer screen. The receptionist narrowed his eyes as the system denied him access to Gabriel's biographical information, then he turned pale when he saw why.

"Am I cleared to enter?" Gabriel asked menacingly.

"Yes…please go in," the terrified receptionist replied, buzzing open the doors.

Gabriel marched through the doors into Club Ellipsis without another word.

The receptionist must have been brand new to the job. Normally, non-member guests had to be screened before being allowed in – for reasons having less to do with security and more to do with maintaining the club's 'exclusiveness' – but anyone else at the desk would have known to wave Gabriel straight in after seeing the uniform.

Come to think of it, why have a Human manning the reception desk at all? An android could handle the job with far more efficiency and courtesy than that dolt. Perhaps the club wanted to guarantee employment for a member's son or grandson or nephew or perhaps having an actual Human at the front desk enhanced the club's prestige by providing a 'Human' touch. Or maybe it was both.

Club Ellipsis itself was an extravagant, multi-level palace in the Clouds, complete with a bar and restaurant as well as numerous open and private booths with crystalline-glass tables and chairs. Antigravity platters flitted back and forth overhead with food, drinks, and stimulants to serve the guests and their scantily clad 'companions'.

The sheer decadence on display was eye-watering. The carpet was blood red – no doubt woven from bioengineered fur – and every wall was covered with pieces of expensive art. Some of the paintings and sculptures had clearly required genuine skill to produce, but others were vapid ego-statements by the artist – one of these pieces of 'art' was just a blank canvass with the artist's signature on it.

How original.

The most extravagant piece of decoration, however, was suspended from the ceiling: an actual chandelier made from thousands of custom-forged diamonds suspended from a carefully manufactured frame with innumerable arms. Each diamond had been polished to a smooth finish and refracted the sunlight out across the club in a kaleidoscope of rainbow colours. It must have cost a fortune.

Gabriel ignored everyone and everything, moving with purpose past the tables and private booths. The tables' decadently dressed occupants paused their frivolous conversation to gawp at the menacing-looking military officer, this visibly out-of-place interloper, marching through *their* private club.

Out of the corners of his eyes, Gabriel could see their expressions – ranging from curiosity to alarm, and everything in between – frozen on their stupid faces. But no one dared cause a fuss, let alone call security or the staff, and Gabriel ascended the stairs to the next level unmolested. He approached booth 39 and waved his hand across the scanner to open the door, walking straight into an argument.

"You slippery bitch!" one booth occupant bellowed as Gabriel entered.

The shouter was a stout man dressed in a smart blue suit with a frilled, white shirt and collar. He had a bushy black moustache and his finely combed, dark hair was styled with parallel streaks of white dye. His angry expression remained frozen on his face as he turned around to see a uniformed soldier walking into the booth.

"Gabriel!" the other booth occupant beamed, "good of you to join us, have a seat."

The angry shouter turned back to face the 'slippery bitch', his anger now tinged with a mixture of outrage and disbelief.

"Jezebel…" the shouter's bellowing voice had been reduced to a shocked murmur, as if she had just committed some unforgivable faux pas, "I would have thought even you recognised that politics and security don't mix."

"Politics and security?" Jezebel scoffed derisively, "I thought we were just talking about business, your failing business, to be exact. And, by the way, it's 'Madam Jezebel' to you, *Mr* Darius. We're not *that* friendly."

Mr Darius turned on his heel and confronted Gabriel, his eyes narrowed to suspicious beads. It was a brave thing to do, considering that Gabriel stood a head taller than he did. Gabriel could smell men's perfume on the man, an overpowering scent of tropical flowers that made him want to gag.

"Gabriel, was it?" Darius asked, employing the tone of a lord disciplining a servant.

"Colonel," Gabriel replied flatly, not inclined to give away his full name.

"How in Terra's name did you get into Club Ellipsis?" Darius demanded imperiously.

"Through the front door," was the cool reply.

"Ah," Darius sneered, disliking the sarcastic nature of the response, "so if I were to have a word with your commanding officer–"

Darius never got to the end of his sentence as Gabriel wrapped his fingers around the man's neck, lifting him clear off the ground with one arm and squeezing the rest of his threat out of his throat in the form of a choking noise.

Darius struggled and gasped, tugging in vain at the ironclad grip on his throat. His previously narrow eyes were now bulging with surprise and panic, and his cheeks were turning red with effort as he hyperventilated.

"Mr Darius," Gabriel said, his soft tone making him sound far more menacing than he could have done by shouting, "Believe me when I tell you that you should hope *never* to meet my commanding officer."

With that said, Gabriel relinquished his grip on the man's neck, dropping him to the floor. Darius fell to his knees, clutching his throat and gasping for air for a full minute. Once he had recovered his breath, he moved to salvage his dignity by making a swift exit. The booth door sealed behind him, leaving Gabriel alone with Madam Jezebel.

"Quite a performance!" Madam Jezebel smirked, sipping from an ornate glass.

"I'm leaving," Gabriel informed her, turning towards the door.

"Oh, don't be so antisocial," Madam Jezebel said, waving him back over, "I hardly get to see you anymore. Sit down, have a drink with me."

Gabriel's normally impassive features were crinkled ever so slightly into a scowl. He didn't want to spend a minute longer in this woman's company than absolutely necessary; nonetheless, he did feel a sense of obligation that was strong enough to over-come his reluctance. Slowly, he turned away from the door and took a seat directly opposite his hostess.

Madam Jezebel was a slim, elegant woman dressed in a snow-white fur coat; an item of clothing with no practical use in the temperature-controlled booth, but no doubt very chic – what-ever that meant. Her eyes were a hazel brown colour, looking somewhat dark compared to the luminescence of his eyes, and her dark hair was styled with parallel blonde stripes and was tied into a corn-braid.

She exuded an aristocratic presence with traces of a superior smirk perpetually playing at the corners of her blood red lips. Her relaxed demeanour stood in stark contrast to Gabriel's rigid posture and stone-faced expression.

"Why am I here?" Gabriel asked with an undertone of impa-tience.

"Is there something wrong with talking to my son?" Jezebel Thorn asked innocently.

"In principle, nothing," Gabriel conceded out of respect for logic.

"Well then presumably that's why you're here," Madam Jezebel replied as she took another sip, "Now lighten up and talk to me."

Mother and son shared the same grammatically flawless speech and cadence of the upper classes. But whereas Gabriel's time in the military had rendered his accent and pronunciation textbook-standard, Madam Jezebel retained the flute-like pitch and inflexions which her son had long since shed.

"So, you didn't just double-cross yet another business partner and summon me here to send a signal that you have friends in high places?" Gabriel asked suspiciously.

"You know better than I do that interference in security matters is illegal," Madam Jezebel brushed aside the accusation without explicitly denying it, "not that you spook-types seem to have a problem lording it over the rest of us."

Gabriel eyed her distrustfully, dissatisfied with her answer.

"Although, if you must know," Madam Jezebel continued, "a joint venture between Darius and myself recently fell through and he was unhappy that I shorted his stock."

"I thought you no longer fleeced colonists for profit," Gabriel said with disdain.

"I have indeed left the colonial investment business which paid for your expensive upbringing here amongst the Clouds – for which you're welcome, by the way," was his mother's breezy riposte, "so stop projecting your dear wife's bitter feelings onto me. Speaking of which, how are my grandchildren getting along?"

"Very happy and progressing well," Gabriel replied as if delivering a field report, "Orion will have mastered elementary algebra before he turns eight."

"Hmm, cramming several millennia worth of knowledge into such tiny little heads," said Grandma Jezebel pensively, "call me a Luddite, but I'm not sure sticking them in front of a holo-screen for seven hours a day is good for them."

"Call me rude, but I don't think that's any of your business," Gabriel retorted.

"You're rude," Jezebel countered smoothly, "unless you can tell me why my own grandchildren are none of my business. When are they next coming over to visit?"

"If Aster has anything to say about it, never," Gabriel replied.

"Of course. You know, I could get them accepted into one of the top engineering academies," Grandma Jezebel offered magnanimously.

"Their father and mother both succeeded without a nepotistic leg up," Gabriel answered, flatly declining the offer, "they can as well."

"Well, that first part isn't strictly true," Madam Jezebel answered, unfazed by her son's brusque tone, "But the offer remains open, nonetheless."

Gabriel's smartphone chimed, reminding him that it was almost 9 o'clock. Without a farewell or an explanation, he got up from his seat.

"Have fun at work," Madam Jezebel waved him off with a smile.

Gabriel left the private booth and went back the way he had come.

Madam Jezebel Thorn had mastered the elegant, unassuming smile that she presented to the world, but it concealed a sociopathic contempt for others around her, particularly if they couldn't help her schemes succeed. One wouldn't know it from a single meeting, but she had made a sizeable fortune as one of the most ruthless colonial venture capitalists in the industry, providing the seed money for numerous outposts on the frontiers before pitilessly squeezing them for everything they were worth.

'Vulture Capitalists' they were called, ready to seize export or import shipments to compensate for late payments or slash security meant to defend against corsair raids. Colonial outposts that were desperate enough to turn to vulture capitalist funders were effectively signing themselves into debt slavery.

Walking past the throngs of pampered parasites as they exchanged vapid gossip on the latest goings-on, Gabriel was reminded that many of them had made or inherited fortunes from similarly immoral lines of business. Not all of them, to be sure; he also recognised the faces of tycoons in mining, robotics, shipbuilding, pharmaceuticals, heavy engineering, and consumer electronics. But there were more than a few vulture capitalists here – glorified loan sharks rubbing shoulders with the other sharks.

Here they all were, wallowing in self-indulgent decadence and luxury, feasting on the fruits of what were mostly other people's labours; living in this well-feathered nest in the sky while tens of millions toiled in the squalid depths below. All of them were perfectly capable of stabbing each other in the back – and sometimes the chest – and had no doubt done so on multiple occasions in order to stay on top.

Gabriel felt few emotions at all. But there was one in particular that made its presence felt in his chest all the way back through the entrance hall.

It was disgust.

THE DIRECTORATE

EVERY tower in the city tall enough to poke above the cloud line gleamed with pride, basking in the glorious rays of the bright white star like conifers in the winter dawn. Every tower was a monument to the success of interstellar capitalism, a glorious testament to the incredible wealth which had financed their construction.

Every tower except one.

Amidst the shining towers of Asgard City, some distance away from the hyper-opulent city centre, stood a sullen fortress jutting out of the ground like an iron spike piercing up through the soil. The 'Spire' was surrounded by a half-kilometre-wide dead zone of barren ground that was empty of comparable structures as if to keep the gaudy neighbouring towers at a respectful distance.

The surface of the Spire was made from a dark material which absorbed virtually all the light that touched it, adding to the dour contrast with the surrounding towers. Across the entire tower, not a single window was installed; such a frivolous sign of civilian comfort was a structural weakness, unsuitable for a building from which all intelligence activities in the sector were coordinated.

The headquarters of the Directorate of Naval Intelligence couldn't be reached by public mag-rail. For people without clearance, it couldn't be reached at all. Gabriel's air-taxi touched down on an extendable landing pad, allowing him to alight before quickly returning to the skies. The biometric sensors flash-scanned Gabriel's eyes, and the half-tonne door retracted silently into the wall to allow him access, sealing again once he was inside.

This section was called the 'Office Block', a bad in-joke by the architects since it was a literal block of space in the middle and upper sections of the Spire given over to offices for analysts and other personnel. For a building with a staff of over 75,000, there were very few people to be seen in the concentric rings of hallways. Most of them were support staff flitting between offices; all of them gave Gabriel a wide berth.

Near the top of the Spire, Gabriel headed down a short corridor towards the spine of the building, stopping in front of a reinforced door emblazoned with the acronym 'D.G.N.I.'. Passersby who caught a glimpse of the acronym double-timed past it. The biometric sensors flash-scanned Gabriel's eyes and the blast door slid open, granting him entrance to the most powerful room in the city.

The office of the Director-General of Naval Intelligence was part-office, part-command centre, part-throne room. It was a hemispherical space with a desk and a throne-like chair, surrounded by holographic screens, set atop a dais opposite the front door. The person behind the desk was reviewing a video file on one of the many screens, with the audio playing through the speakers so that Gabriel could hear.

"…*my facility goes dark and the first thing you do is short my company and cash out?!*" Gabriel recognised Darius's voice bellowing in anger at his mother.

"*Of course,*" said the recording of Madam Jezebel Thorn, "*you would have done the same if a project of mine 'went dark' without explanation.*"

"*It didn't 'go dark', thus far it's nothing more than a temporary communications loss–*" Darius tried to splutter out an explanation.

"*'A temporary communications loss', 'a fault in the uplink array', 'space weather', 'regular weather', 'an act of the divine',*" Madam Jezebel sneered, "*I've heard countless variations on all those excuses, and they're always made up by incompetent fools to cover up the fact that they couldn't keep their business under control."*

"*You're just trying to cut the venture off at the knees at the first sign of trouble!*" Darius angrily accused his erstwhile business partner, "*You think you can short my company and leave ME with the fleeking mess!?*"

"*You came to me for seed money for this little off-world facility of yours, and I gave it to you,*" Madam Jezebel calmly reminded Darius, winding him up without raising her voice, "*I even let you have full control over the facility's activities, which is just as well, seeing as you probably didn't register it.*"

"*Mind your fleeking tongue, or I might have it cut out!*" Darius snarled dangerously, perhaps conscious that the walls might have ears.

"*In any case,*" Madam Jezebel continued, "*the facility was always yours to own, and so are the consequences of whatever might have happened there. So I suggest you man up and stop making such a scene.*"

"*You slippery bitch!*"

The recording paused at the exact moment that Gabriel had walked into the booth. The individual seated in the throne-like chair dismissed the video with a flick of her fingers and swivelled round to face Gabriel. He stood to attention and saluted, respectfully fixing his gaze on the opposite wall as he waited for her to speak.

The director-general wore a midnight-black uniform similar to Gabriel's, except that it bore a gold admiral's insignia on the lapel, whereas Gabriel's uniform had no insignia or identifying markings. She wore her raven hair in a tight bun and her face appeared locked into an expression of complete indifference to the world.

Her most eye-catching feature, however, was her right eye. It was a bionic implant, with a bright, laser-red iris, in stark contrast to her biological, hazel-coloured left eye. The obvious nickname

'Red-eye' had stuck, though no one with a sense of self-preservation dared utter it within earshot of her.

"Your integrity is beyond question," the Director-General of Naval Intelligence said matter-of-factly, "the same cannot be said of Jezebel Thorn or Darius Avaritio."

"I presume you want me to investigate Avaritio's facility?" Gabriel asked.

"That is correct," the director-general confirmed, "It's a standard IRS operation. Check in with the medical staff and get yourself suited and ready. Your operational briefing will be forwarded to you on the way."

"Understood," Gabriel replied, waiting to be told why he was there.

Most DNI employees dreaded the prospect of being called into the director-general's office, not least because of her rumoured delight in playing underhanded mind games with her subordinates – like playing recordings of supposedly private conversations just to make them squirm with embarrassment.

Gabriel knew better. It was just a rumour; the director-general only called people into her office for important matters. She rarely summoned people to her office to give them their orders in person, and she certainly didn't summon them to her office just to embarrass them. She had better things to do with her time.

"There is one other thing," the director-general added, "For this deployment, I'll be placing you in command of a squad of five operators."

Gabriel blinked, thinking he might have misheard.

"Normally you would be sent in alone, of course," the director-general continued, "but given the size of the facility, I believe the support of a full squad is warranted."

"…Understood," Gabriel answered stoically.

"Expressing dissent is acceptable," the director-general said, almost reassuringly.

"No it isn't," Gabriel contradicted his superior, "I've been given a mission and a set of parameters, and I intend to complete that mission within the stated parameters."

"So you have no problem at all with working with a team?"

"None," Gabriel lied.

"Understood," Red-eye noted with a faint smile, perhaps noting the lie, "Dismissed."

* * *

Whilst most of the Spire's levels were devoted to regular office space, the lower levels were given over to research laboratories which formed the core of the DNI's in-house tech empire: the 'Rand Block', as in 'R&D'. Most DNI employees were restricted to certain areas of the Spire, but the biometric scanners granted Gabriel access to almost every part of the building, including the Rand Block.

Gabriel took the elevator down over a hundred floors to a special preparation chamber. Once he arrived, he stripped down to his underwear and lay down on the horizontal examination slab that awaited him. The robotic medical arms descended from the ceiling and bathed his body in sensory light, scanning him from head to toe. When the scan was complete, a holographic screen materialised in front of him.

"*Voidstalker-1707*," said the doctor on the other end of the line, "*Colonel Gabriel Thorn. All of your enhancements are functioning within normal parameters. No physical or cellular anomalies detected, although your REM sleep patterns last night were erratic.*"

"It was another flashback," Gabriel explained, "this time from void-exposure training."

"*I see*," the doctor noted, glancing down at his chart, "*and how is family life?*"

"Clarify," Gabriel said with narrowed eyes.

"*Last night, after you awoke from your nightmare you experienced a brief spike of anger followed by a round of sexual activity*," the doctor explained clinically.

"Clarify why that is any of your concern," a note of danger crept into Gabriel's voice.

"*I ask because it appears that you had a mildly physical argument which was subsequently…resolved*," the doctor explained, unconcerned with the personal nature of the question, and unfazed by the threatening undertone in Gabriel's voice.

"That is accurate," Gabriel confirmed through gritted teeth, "what of it?"

"*There is a clinically acceptable range of emotional coldness*," the doctor explained, "*but it cannot be allowed to degenerate into sociopathy towards your loved ones. It is possible that Mrs Thorn goads you into these arguments in order to elicit affection from you.*"

"Leave my family out of this," Gabriel warned in a raised voice.

"*Unfortunately, I can't do that*," the doctor replied sympathetically, "*Maintaining a stable and healthy family life is important for ensuring maximum effectiveness in the field, particularly for voidstalkers. And since aggression and arousal are the only two emotional responses which are not suppressed, it is a delicate balancing act.*"

"I can handle my own personal life just fine, thank you," Gabriel responded icily.

"*The directorate has a direct interest in that being true*," the doctor replied.

"So, are we finished?" Gabriel asked, his defensiveness turning to abrasive impatience.

"*Yes*," the doctor answered, "*Good luck on your next mission, Colonel.*"

With that said, the holographic screen deactivated and a new set of procedures began, starting with the foot of the examination bed pitching downwards until it stood at a perfect 90-degree angle. Gabriel stepped away from the vertically angled slab, and forward onto a small platform, standing perfectly still.

A set of nozzle-equipped robotic arms descended from the ceiling and sprayed a gel-like substance across his skin from his ankles up to his neck, avoiding his feet, hands, and face. Gabriel resisted the urge to shiver with discomfort as the substance congealed into a light blue under-suit that hugged his skin.

Once the under-suit had fully congealed, a pair of armoured boot soles were placed on the floor in front of Gabriel, and he planted his feet on the cushioned soles, digging his toes into the material until he had settled comfortably into them. Once his feet were firmly in place, the robots did the rest.

The robotic arms put on the secondary armour skin first. Made from flexible dull grey plates of carbon nanotubing, providing a full body layer of protection over the gelatinous under-suit, including covering his feet and hands. This layer of armour was for absorbing and dispersing the effects of energy weapons as well as providing an extra layer of protection against extreme temperatures and excessive radiation.

Finally, the primary armour was installed. Instead of flexible carbon nanotubing, the primary armour plates were totally rigid and were manufactured from custom-forged metallic composites strengthened with carbon nanotubing, increasing the tensile strength and impact resistance by an order of magnitude.

The armour had to be fitted piece by piece, each part interlocking with the others until it formed a vacuum-proof suit of armour covering Gabriel's entire body all the way up to his neck. Apart from his head, he was now virtually invulnerable. A robotic arm politely handed him his helmet; he took it without looking and attached it to his belt for later.

Now that he was dressed for battle, a holographic video image of Gabriel appeared in front of him, acting as a mirror. His armour was a deep crimson colour with black trim; traditionally, the colour scheme would be some form of khaki, eschewing any sort of easily identifiable colour. But in an age of advanced sensors and combat armour that could turn an ordinary man or woman into a walking tank, camouflage was a quaint concept.

Gabriel had no sense of vanity of which he was aware, but he looked like the angel of death with a Human face.

* * *

Below the Rand Block was the 'Under-block': a maze of bombardment proof chambers and corridors stretching dozens of levels below ground. It had various purposes, many of them pertaining to various doomsday scenarios, but one of them was to house much of the DNI's massive stockpile of weapons, munitions, and other essential supplies.

The Under-block also housed a mag-rail station for the exclusive use of the military, with high-speed lines running directly to various key facilities in and around the city. Gabriel linked up with the squad of DNI operators he would be commanding, and together they took the mag-tram from the Spire's station to the military terminal of Asgard's main spaceport.

The sight from inside the tunnel wasn't as impressive as the sky-high view from the public mag-rail, but the DNI's mag-tram system was no less a marvel of engineering. Unlike the public mag-trains, the DNI's mag-rail tunnels were almost completely evacuated of air, minimising air resistance and maximising speed. Travelling at close to half the speed of sound – and in a straight line – meant they would reach the spaceport in a fraction of the time.

Gabriel stared out through the wall-sized observation window at the front of the mag-tram, his own train of thought circling back around to the previous night. He couldn't tell Aster what the DNI did to his body and mind, let alone where he went or what he did on his missions. The secrecy made perfect sense to him, and the children were blissfully ignorant either way, but it clearly hurt her. Even so, what his family didn't know wouldn't hurt them.

So what in Terra's name gave the DNI doctors the right to bring them up in the first place? What possible right did they have to help him 'maintain a stable family life'? He could manage that perfectly well without their interference. It would be myopic to complain about the DNI techs monitoring his neural activity

– that was part of being in the programme – but what business did they have asking about his private life?

That really was myopic. Of course monitoring his neural activity gave the DNI an insight into his family life, however indirect; and yet being questioned directly about it angered him even more than the actual monitoring. After all, he had volunteered for all of this and thereby agreed to have his neural activity monitored. His family hadn't volunteered for any of that, and that was what angered him.

Then again, it was the DNI which supervised the children's medical check-ups.

Gabriel stared out into the shadowy distance, watching the ceiling lamps zipping by so quickly that they seemed to form a continuous stream of light. As he stared, a new question came to mind. The whole point of the Voidstalker Programme was that a single voidstalker could be sent in to deal with the most difficult assignments without the need for backup. Red-eye's decision to place a squad of operators under his command made no sense.

There was something else about having 'backup' foisted on him that bothered Gabriel, but he couldn't pin down why. It certainly wasn't pride. If Red-eye doubted his abilities, he wouldn't be a voidstalker in the first place. Nor did he doubt the abilities of the operators. They were part of the DNI's Special Operations Division. Not as deadly or versatile as voidstalkers, but perfectly competent.

"Colonel Thorn, sir?" someone interrupted Gabriel's train of thought.

Gabriel turned to face the speaker, recognising him as Captain Bale, his nominal second-in-command. He was a veteran operator with a weather-beaten face and a Marine Corps buzz cut so short he almost looked bald.

Gabriel had already read each operator's profile and absorbed their contents on his way to meet the squad. They would also have been given his profile to read – the unredacted parts, at least – so there would be no need for frivolous introductions.

"Do you have the mission briefing?" Gabriel asked.

"Yes sir," Bale activated a holographic screen on his wrist-top computer as the other operators gathered round for the briefing.

All five operators were kitted out in Marine Corps combat gear, albeit with DNI modifications and without any identifying markings. Their armour had the same deep crimson with black trim as Gabriel's armour, and their helmets were off so they could all speak face to face. They looked positively diminutive next to Gabriel, who stood a head taller and wore armour custom-manufactured for him by the DNI's scientists.

"Darius Avaritio's company, Jupiter Engineering Co., has been running an unregistered lab on the moon of Loki," Captain Bale explained, "Not many resources, and no official settlements nearby, but most of J.E. Co.'s recent products were based on its research."

"Until it went dark?"

"Yes sir," Bale confirmed, "According to DNI sources, J.E. Co. sent in one of its in-house security teams to investigate. That was almost 24 hours ago."

"How big is this facility, exactly?"

"It has about 1000 staff," Bale answered, "It's built into a natural cave system, and the nearest suitable landing site is a landing pad 20km away."

"Pretty brazen to run a facility that big in a major system," said another operator with the pale look of an Undercity dweller, "how the frick did this pass under the DNI's radar?"

Gabriel recognised him as Lieutenant Viker, a breaching specialist and a skilled driver.

"Good question," Gabriel replied, "but at least it's not too long of a trip."

"Respectfully sir," asked a third operator, "why is this even a concern for us?"

"Clarify," Gabriel ordered, subjecting the operator he recognised as Lieutenant Ogilvy, the squad's hazmat specialist, to an icy stare.

"I mean if some bigshot company's R&D lab has an accident," Ogilvy tried to clarify, "why can't we just let the corporate fleeksters clean up their own mess?"

Gabriel didn't care about Ogilvy using the classist term 'fleekster', even though the term technically applied to him. He did mind the idiocy of the question.

All of the Special Operations Division's operators were recruited from the Marine Corps, so by definition, they were all veterans. But Lieutenant Ogilvy had only recently passed the DNI's selection process, making this his first mission as a DNI operator; most people might excuse his beginner's naivety.

Gabriel was no such person.

"When a 'bigshot company' starts to produce top-of-the-line products that massively outstrip those of its competitors," Gabriel explained sternly, "it usually means that the company has been trafficking in xenotechnology, hence the hidden and unregistered nature of the facility. It also means that J.E. Co. has probably violated the second of the three Prime Laws: 'no unauthorised contact with alien species'."

Ogilvy was already smarting with embarrassment at having posed the question at all, but Gabriel wasn't finished with him.

"Furthermore," Gabriel continued, cutting his subordinate no slack, "If this facility really was carrying out experiments with xenotechnology, it also means that J.E. Co. has violated the first of the three Prime Laws: 'Humanity first and foremost'. *That* is why this is a concern for operators like you: because the corporates can never be trusted to clean up their own messes. Is that understood?"

"…Yes, sir," Ogilvy acknowledged sheepishly.

The squad members looked awkwardly at each other but kept their mouths shut. Ogilvy had more or less brought it on himself with his silly question, but it wasn't clear that his naivety warranted an outright scolding.

"Is anyone else unclear as to the necessity of this mission?" Gabriel demanded, looking around at the squad with a stern glare.

No one replied.

* * *

The mag-tram slowed to a halt as it pulled into the DNI's private station beneath the main spaceport. Gabriel and his new squad exited the mag-tram and reported to the armoury. A team of weapons technicians was already there, fine-tuning the firearms and other equipment that the squad need, including a back-mounted hazmat detection kit, a door-breaching plasma torch, and a variety of grenades and explosives.

Gabriel approached a separate stall, set up specifically for him. The technicians handed him his primary weapon, a hefty light machine gun with much more stopping power than the standard service weapon used by DNI operators. Its size made it overly cumbersome for most soldiers, but this particular weapon was designed for Gabriel's personal use. Only someone of his size and height could use it comfortably.

Gabriel examined the weapon, checking each setting before giving a nod of approval. The technicians then set up a private two-way video link for Gabriel and each of the operators before politely departing. A final communication with loved ones before deployment was mandatory for all operators, a requirement that Gabriel found oddly personal. Did the DNI really have to micromanage details like this for the sake of operational effectiveness? If it weren't mandatory, he would have made a call like this anyway.

The video link took a few seconds to connect before Aster appeared on the screen, sitting on a couch in some kind of waiting room.

"*Hi there, stranger,*" Aster greeted him.

"Are you at the medical centre?" Gabriel asked.

"*Yes, Colonel,*" Aster replied, irritated by the stern, military tone of his question, "*we've been sitting here for the past half hour waiting for the children's appointment.*"

"That's not what I meant," Gabriel said through gritted teeth.

"*I know, I know, I'm sorry,*" Aster replied, defusing the argument before it began.

"What's wrong?" Gabriel asked.

"*I don't know what you see on your screen,*" Aster explained, "*but I see your face against a computerised background with your superiors' logo; which means you're in one of their facilities about to deploy on another mission.*"

"I'll only be gone for a few days," Gabriel tried to reassure her.

"*Ooh, you'll be in-system?*" Aster noted.

Gabriel flinched, blanching internally at the inadvertent disclosure.

"I didn't say that it was," Gabriel said defensively.

"*You didn't need to,*" Aster replied innocently, "*If you're only going to be gone for a few days, you're going somewhere close enough to not need a Q-engine.*"

"I have no comment on that," Gabriel answered.

"*You shouldn't have married an engineer,*" Aster said with a playful smirk.

"I don't regret that at all," Gabriel replied.

"*Well, that's reassuring,*" Aster said appreciatively, "*because, neither do I.*"

Gabriel smiled in spite of himself.

"*Hold that smile, would you?*" Aster told him as she disappeared briefly off-screen.

Their children appeared on the screen. Their oldest son Orion occupied the centre whilst his two younger sisters, Rose and Violet, jostled to be in front of him. The youngest, Leonidas, was hoisted up within view of the screen by his brother.

"*Hi, daddy!*" they chorused happily.

"Hi, sweethearts," Gabriel said smilingly to his children, "Daddy's going to be gone for a few days, but I'll be back soon, ok?"

"*Are you going to fight monsters again?*" three-year-old Violet asked.

"That's what daddy does to keep you all safe," Gabriel answered.

"*What monsters do you fight?*" five-year-old Rose asked.

"Really scary monsters," Gabriel replied teasingly, "with lots of eyes and tentacles."

"*Eww!*" Violet said with disgust, "*I hate tentacles!*"

"*Can we come fight the monsters with you?*" Orion asked hopefully.

"Sorry, Ori," Gabriel replied, "Only grownups can go out and fight monsters."

His firstborn pouted in disappointment.

"How are you, Leo?" Gabriel asked Leonidas, who smiled at having his name called.

"*It's noisy here,*" Leo observed with a giggle.

The video link muted out all background noise from the other end, but the children were probably being driven to distraction by the chattering and noise in the waiting room.

"Daddy has to go, now," Gabriel told them, "take care of your mother while I'm gone."

"*Mommy sometimes cries when you're gone,*" Rose blurted out.

A spike of emotion pierced Gabriel's heart as Aster hastily took back the camera before the children could say anything else.

"*Their appointment should be soon,*" Aster informed him in an unconvincing attempt to brush off Rose's unauthorised disclosure.

"Ok, I'll see you in a few days."

"*Yes…*" Aster replied, her sentence trailing off.

"Aster," Gabriel asked, "don't cry."

"*I can't promise that,*" Aster replied, wiping away a tear.

"Goodbye, then," Gabriel waved at the screen.

"*Goodbye,*" Aster waved back, turning the camera to include the children in the shot, "*say goodbye to your father,*" she instructed.

"*Bye, daddy!*" they choroused, waving goodbye at the screen.

"*Goodbye, sweethearts,*" Gabriel waved back as the call ended.

Gabriel continued to stare at the blank screen for the longest time, wondering – not for the first time – if it was fair to burden his loved ones with the possibility of his death.

* * *

Once the doctors had come to collect them, Aster said goodbye to her children and departed for work, taking the public mag-train from the medical centre to the other side of the city centre. She knew for a fact that she would see them again, and soon. Such certainty was impossible whenever Gabriel deployed.

After a ten minute ride, the mag-train arrived at one of the largest towers in the city, gliding to a smooth halt before disgorging its passengers onto the platform. Splitting off from the streams of people, Aster made her way to the elevators at the opposite end of the station, overshadowed by a holographic corporate logo of a gas giant.

Aster stepped into the elevator and stood in front of the biometric scanner to confirm her identity. The automated security system granted her access and she descended to the lower levels. Once the elevator doors opened, Aster passed through an automated security checkpoint – checking her smartphone into storage – then stepped out into the entrance hall of Jupiter Engineering Co.'s main R&D complex.

It was deserted.

"Hello?" Aster called out, puzzled.

The whole place ought to be thronged with people at this time of day, but there was nobody to be seen. No alarms had been triggered, no warning lights were flashing, and there had been no instructions not to come into work, or that anything unusual would be happening today. So where was everyone?

Aster crossed the hall to Workshop 1-A, the doors sliding open as she approached. Once inside, the mystery of her colleagues' whereabouts was solved. They were all huddled together in the breakroom surrounded by DNI agents clad in jet-black body armour, side-arms strapped to their thighs, and retractable combat helmets partially concealing their faces.

"You," one of the agents pointed at Aster as she walked in, "are you Dr Aster Thorn?"

"Scan me," Aster answered back.

The agent obliged, and his suit sensors confirmed Aster's identity.

"Come with me," he ordered gruffly.

Confused and suspicious, Aster followed the agent past the crowd of colleagues into the corridor outside. She realised he was leading her to her office.

Waiting outside the door to Aster's office was the senior agent in charge of the raid, leaning against the wall with arms folded and visor retracted; she looked as though she'd been waiting for a while. The senior agent looked at Aster with a stern, impatient glare and nodded in the direction of the door, not deigning to verbalise the instruction.

"Good morning to you too," said Aster sarcastically as she turned to face the scanner.

The scanner confirmed Aster's identity and the door slid open; the two agents showed themselves inside, gesturing for Aster to follow. Aster followed them into a spacious office, featuring a desk equipped with a holographic display screen at one end, and a mini-lounge with a coffee table and a couch at the other.

The senior agent pointed at the couch and snapped her fingers.

"What about the couch?" Aster demanded, her patience finally running dry.

"Take a seat," the agent instructed.

"Then why don't you open your mouth and say so instead of waving your hands about?" Aster said, imitating the agent's hand gestures, "that's how you order around a pet animal—"

"Sit down!" the agent snapped, evidently not used to ordering around a civilian.

Rolling her eyes, Aster obliged.

The other DNI agent pulled a fist-sized object from his belt and tossed it into the air. Staying airborne under its own power, the scanner drone bathed the wall in a sensory light and methodically circumnavigated the office. Aster drummed her fingers impatiently – as if she would plant listening devices in her own office.

Once the bug sweep was complete, the scanner drone returned to its controller, having detected nothing suspicious. The agent plucked the drone from the air and put it back on his belt before leaving Aster alone with the senior agent, who stood over her like a disapproving schoolteacher. The agent adjusted her helmet visor and pulled up Aster's personnel file on her wrist-top computer before beginning.

"Dr Aster Thorn," the agent read off the screen, "Tertiary specialisation in electrical engineering. Quaternary specialisation in Q-physics engineering with a minor specialisation in fusion reactor design. Doctoral specialisation in applied fusion reactor physics."

"Is this an interrogation or a job interview?" Aster asked.

"All of your colleagues named you as the project-lead," the senior agent deftly ignored Aster's sarcasm, "and I want to know what that project is about."

"That's subject to corporate privilege," Aster shot back bluntly.

"Are you the project-lead or not?" the agent demanded.

"Yes, I am," Aster confirmed, "Now, are you going to tell me why the DNI is snooping around a private company's labs?"

The agent appeared to mull it over.

"Fine," the agent replied, "we are indeed from the Directorate of Naval Intelligence. Specifically, we're from Division 3, as in the 3rd Prime Law."

"'Politics and security don't mix'?"

"The actual wording is 'civic and security don't mix'," the senior agent corrected her, "and unauthorised acquisition, possession, modification or usage of xenotechnology definitely crosses the line between security and civic matters."

"You're seriously accusing us of trafficking in xenotech?"

"Yes, we are."

"Maybe you should speak with our chairman–"

"I wouldn't worry too much about Chairman Darius if I were you," the agent interrupted, "Right now, I'm asking you: what is the nature of the project that you lead?"

"…We're working on a new, ship-worthy fusion reactor," Aster replied hesitantly.

"Incorporating xenotech?"

"No!"

"Is there a J.E. Co. facility on Loki?" the senior agent abruptly changed tack.

"Yes," Aster confirmed, "It's a small R&D lab."

"How small and what was its purpose?"

"A couple of hundred staff were stationed there to carry out experiments which couldn't be safely conducted here on Asgard," Aster explained.

"To your knowledge, did any of these experiments involve xenotechnology?"

"Of course not!"

"How do you know?" the senior agent pressed, unconvinced.

"What do you mean 'how do I know'?"

"I mean exactly that: how do you know that your colleagues at the Loki facility were not conducting experiments involving xenotechnology?"

"Ok, suppose I give you two cups of coffee," Aster explained, doing her irritated best to sound patient, "one made from hydroponically grown, hand-ground coffee beans, the other synthesised in a lab. How would you know which was which?"

"Ok, how would I know?"

"You wouldn't, because both are cups of fucking coffee," Aster said in exasperation, "there's no way to tell which process was used to make the cup of coffee because both would taste exactly the same. Unless you can prove that there's a single scrap of xenotech anywhere in this building, you're wasting your time."

"Have you or anyone on your team ever visited the Loki facility?" the agent asked.

"No, I haven't, Dr Lawrence Kane is the one with liaison responsibilities."

"'Liaison responsibilities'?" the agent cocked an eyebrow.

"He's the one who visits the facility regularly to liaise with the on-site researchers."

"How frequently?"

"You're the almighty DNI, for Terra's sake," Aster's impatience was boiling over again, "can't you just access the records to find all of this out?"

"We can, and we did," the agent replied, "and, funny thing, there's no record of a facility of any kind registered on Loki."

Aster's irritation evaporated into incredulity.

"What...what do you mean?" Aster asked, hesitant to find out.

"You just told me that Dr Kane was 'liaising' with the staff of an R&D facility," the agent repeated, "a facility which, apparently, doesn't exist. So either our records are woefully out-of-date, or you just revealed the existence of an illegal research facility."

The agent paused to let that information sink in. Aster had no answer.

"I...I..." Aster's voice began to falter.

"You...you..." the agent replied in a vaguely mocking tone, "You, of course, had no idea that your employer would break the law and lie to its own staff. Although, given that you're the project-lead, it's a little hard to believe that you or your staff could be left so completely in the dark about a 'small' R&D lab with several hundred staff."

"Ok, fuck you," Aster exclaimed, rising from her seat as her patience finally ran out, "I'm going to make a call."

"To a legal advocate?" the agent raised a hand to stop Aster from leaving.

"Actually, to someone a lot more senior than you are," Aster retorted, swatting the senior agent's hand away from her chest.

"Oh, you mean the man who put that lovely ring on your finger."

Aster froze up.

"I saw the shared surname in your file," the senior agent continued, "and *his* file is off limits to pretty much everyone except the Masterminds. I mention that because a family connection to the DNI would make any charges against you *more* serious, not less."

"Do you get off on this whole routine?"

"If you're asking me if I enjoy putting corporates in their places," the agent answered with a smirk, "we all do. If you found an alien doomsday weapon, you'd auction it off to the highest bidder without a second thought. Profit over people, now and always."

"'Corporates' funded most of the civil research and space exploration over the past 500 years, and they still do," Aster shot back defensively.

"That's awfully high praise from a colonial," the agent retorted.

Aster's eye began to twitch. This DNI bitch had just crossed a very sensitive line.

"I hear some of the corporates really sucked the life out of a lot of their 'investments'," the agent remarked with barely suppressed smugness, "I'm curious, how did someone who grew up at the mercy of the corporates end up working for them?"

Aster swung her fist at the DNI agent as she lunged forward. The agent deftly caught Aster's wrist and twisted it behind her back, pinning her face-down on the couch.

"Relax, sweetheart," the agent said as she straddled Aster's back.

She pressed Aster's wrist firmly against her back with one hand whilst holding her head down with the other, then spoke into her comm. piece.

"Did you get all of that?" she asked the person on the other end.

"You fucking government pig!" Aster snarled.

"Understood," the agent said, ignoring Aster, "I'll let her go."

The senior agent leapt off the couch, releasing Aster's wrist in the same motion.

"What the fuck was that about?!" Aster demanded, climbing off the couch.

"Physio-Behavioural Analysis," the agent explained calmly, "it's the most effective, non-invasive field-interrogation technique we have."

"So all of that was just to bait me into a response?" Aster demanded.

"Pretty much," came the nonchalant reply, "You can re-join the others now."

Visibly fuming, Aster stormed out of the office.

She was still fuming as she returned to the breakroom. What business did that DNI bitch have taunting her about her colonial background? Like it wasn't bad enough being threatened with career-ending criminal charges.

Even so, she had nepotistically tried to invoke her high-ranking husband as some sort of trump card, like the DNI didn't already know everything about her. Amidst the anger and confusion, it occurred to her that she had potentially put his credibility on the line, a short-sighted and selfish thing to do.

The DNI agents directed her back to the breakroom where they still had her colleagues under guard, surrounding them like a holding pen made of black body armour.

"Did they put you through the PBA questioning as well?" Felix asked.

Still fuming with residual anger, Aster brushed him away without an answer.

"I'm guessing yes," his expression revealing that he too had been put through the process, "look, the thing works by pushing your buttons and reading your responses to see if you're lying or hiding something. If you were in trouble, you'd know it by now."

"I don't care, Felix," Aster hissed back.

Felix let the issue go, giving her a few moments to cool down.

"Did you secure all the data?" Aster whispered, her anger giving way to a clearer head.

"Yes," Felix whispered back, "All the project data and research notes were backed up to one of the offsite servers. Even the DNI can't touch it."

"Good," Aster replied, breathing a little easier, "If I'd known the DNI was going to raid the building, I would have taken the whole day off."

"And leave us to face the music alone?" Felix asked, miffed.

"That's my prerogative as your boss," Aster replied jokingly.

They chuckled, covering their mouths to smother the sound.

"Is something funny?" one of the DNI agents demanded sternly.

"Nothing," Aster replied, stiffening up.

She and Felix waited until the agent had moved on before continuing their conversation.

"Have the DNI taken Lawrence or anyone else in?" Aster whispered to Felix.

"Not that I know," Felix replied, keeping a wary eye on the watchful DNI agents, "plus, Lawrence was still at the Loki facility. He wasn't due back until tomorrow."

"I guess we can't help him, then," Aster said resignedly, "The rest of us will be lucky not to get blackballed for this."

THE MOON

DEATH was all around, and plenty of blood too. It stained the floor in semi-congealed pools and was spattered across the bullet-riddled walls in violet stains. Freshly murdered corpses were strewn across the darkened hallways, the flickering of the half-dead lights giving briefly illuminated snapshots of the slaughter. The din of an alarm was just audible, barely registering through the deathly silence.

Gabriel stepped over the bodies, the sickly squelching noise his boots made puncturing the morbid quietude as he walked down the corridor, surveying the grisly scene before him, the nightmarish aftermath of an ambush. By the time the crew had realised they were under attack, it had been too late to escape. Some had died fighting, others while fleeing, unable to find a hiding place in time.

But there was at least one survivor. Gabriel heard a scrabbling sound from around the corner, and he followed it, taking care not to trip over the corpses. He turned into a side chamber where the ship's escape pods could be accessed. The straggler was there; he had found an unused escape pod and had his back turned, frantically jabbing at a control panel to get the pod's door to open. It was too late.

The sound of footsteps entering the chamber made the straggler freeze up in cold terror. He turned around to face the sinister figure that had been stalking him, his silhouette just visible through the shadows. Gabriel stood in the doorway and raised his weapon, taking aim squarely at the target's head, ready to fin-ish what he had done. The straggler stared back, the certainty of his imminent death evident in his eyes.

Or 'its' eyes, rather. Despite the expression of palpable fear, they were still the beady eyes of a cold-blooded reptilian xeno-type with inhuman, slit-shaped pupils. There was no reason to anthropomorphise or empathise with it.

Gabriel felt nothing as he pulled the trigger.

* * *

Gabriel awoke with a start. Just like usual, the cold sweat was absent, and the panicked drumbeat of his heart quickly subsided as the seconds ticked by. But unlike the previous night, there was a lingering feeling present; an undercurrent of uneasiness about the memory. Aliens came with many different faces, but fear looked much the same on each one. It never bothered him at the time, so why would it bother him in his dreams?

He was laying down on a set of cargo boxes in an inconspicu-ous corner of the vehicle bay, an excellent place to have a power nap, being quiet and out of the way. Also, when the time came to depart for the mission, he and the squad would do so from here, anyway. There wasn't much in the vehicle bay, apart from the two Wolverine-class APCs secured to the ceiling, most un-necessary cargo having been cleared away.

Looking around, Gabriel noticed the operators gathered at the opposite end of the vehicle bay. They were holding an im-promptu bench-press competition to pass the time, taking turns lying down on a set of boxes and lifting a weighted bar. They were even using actual weight-disks, instead of an artificial grav-ity-assisted set-up.

"…8…9…10!" the squad cheered as one of the operators com-pleted his set and strained to put the barbell back on the rack above him. Sweating buckets from the workout, the operator lifted himself up off the boxes and took a water bottle offered to him, draining it in one go before wiping his face down with a cloth. As he rejoined the others, another operator took his place, laying down on the boxes and preparing to lift the heavily weighted bar.

Gabriel watched them as they steadily upped the weight on the barbell. Everyone's combat armour had to be attached and removed using special machinery, so they couldn't take off their armour to make it a fair measure of their actual strength. Gabriel's own armour and physical enhancements were far superior to those of his squad, so heading over to join them with two unfair advantages was out of the question.

No matter. The whole thing was a pointless exercise. Even with armour, the resulting muscle strain and soreness would negatively affect combat performance, even with delayed onset. Furthermore, each operator's combat armour, combined with surgical enhancements, significantly boosted their physical strength, thus limiting the need for intensive bodybuilding regimens, let alone idiotic displays of muscle power.

Gabriel decided to keep that to himself; telling them what he thought of their competition wouldn't be good for unit cohesion. After all, they were about to embark on a high-risk mission with a good chance that one or more of them wouldn't make it back. As silly as they were, he understood that these little bonding rituals were important for squad morale, not unlike the morning group hugs with his children...

Why did he even need a squad to accompany him?

The question re-surfaced unbidden in his head, still unanswered. Voidstalkers were lone-wolves trained and equipped to operate without support for long periods of time in the most hostile areas. Not needing a squad to back you up – or slow you down – was the whole point of voidstalkers. And yet, that wasn't what bothered him about it.

The director-general must have had a good reason to put him in charge of a squad of operators for this mission – or so he assumed and so he wanted to believe. She always had plans and schemes churning in her mind – that was her job after all – and trying to discern what they were was about as useful as tarot card reading. Perhaps he should have asked her reasons when he'd had the chance.

The operators finished another set of weight-lifting, their cheering interrupting Gabriel's speculations about his superior's motivations. Their competition wasn't just frivolous, it was wasting time. His squad members weren't children, they were grown men who needed to get ready for the mission ahead.

He also needed to get his own equipment pack fitted.

"This is VS-one-seven-zero-seven," Gabriel radioed the bridge, "what's our ETA?"

"*We'll be landing in fifteen minutes, sir,*" the ship's captain replied.

"Understood," Gabriel jumped off the cargo boxes and left the vehicle bay through a side door which brought him to the ship's armoury.

The walls of the armoury were lined with racks of assault weapons, sidearms, metallic ammunition blocks kept in sterile cases, and assorted explosive ordnance. At the other end of the armoury was a special platform and frame equipped with robotic arms for fitting equipment modules to the back of a suit of armour. The rest of the squad had had their equipment modules fitted back on Asgard. Gabriel's own module had to be installed separately.

The armoury technicians were expecting him. Without exchanging a word with them, Gabriel stepped onto the platform and turned his back to the frame. A cylindrical object was extracted from a special storage safe by a pair of robotic arms and mounted onto the slots on the back of Gabriel's armour. Then a complicated set of mechanical locks on the cylinder interlocked with those on Gabriel's armour, locking the module in place.

Then came the delicate part. The chief armourer opened up a second safe and removed a key with a complicated geometric arrangement of teeth. Then with the utmost care, he opened up a slot on the bottom of the cylinder and inserted the key. Once it was all the way inside, he turned it 180 degrees clockwise, causing the light to change from green to red. Then with equal care, he removed a tiny sub-key from inside the primary key and returned it to its safe, the slot on the cylinder sealing itself automatically.

"Command module online," one of the techs said as he consulted a chart, "all suit systems are fully functional. You're good to go, Colonel."

"Thank you," Gabriel replied, stepping out of the frame and leaving the armoury.

The squad of operators was still engrossed in their silly weight-lifting competition by the time Gabriel got back. They were wasting time.

"Wrap it up," Gabriel ordered them gruffly as he approached, "we're dropping down to Loki in fifteen minutes, so I want everyone ready to go well before that."

The operators looked surprised and more than a little disappointed, but the killjoy was in charge, and they duly obeyed. The barbell was replaced on its rack and the operators began checking and double-checking their armour, ensuring that each piece was locked and sealed in place before readying their weapons. Gabriel checked his own weapon before using the vehicle-bay controls to lower one of the Wolverine APCs to the floor.

The Wolverine had quite a sleek chassis for such a large vehicle, with a V-shaped underside, and a rounded nose. It resembled a bullet with wheels; six monster-sized wheels with knobbles and grooves for off-road travel. Its skin had been treated to a fresh paint job with a grey camouflage pattern, made somewhat redundant by the emblem on the underside of the nose featuring a stylised image of its snarling namesake. The top of the cockpit was also crowned with a multi-barrelled gun turret for fire support.

"Mount up, everyone!" Gabriel ordered.

* * *

The director-general put on a pair of VR glasses and inserted the attached earpieces. As she activated the glasses, a two-way link was initiated, projecting an image of a dozen other individuals seated around a virtual conference table. They were scattered across the city using similar setups, but they all saw the same simulated conference room, complete with surround-sound and holographic images of each participant.

Those seated at the table included the great and the good of the city: representatives from various industrial lobbies, departments of the civilian bureaucracy as well as members of the elected governing council. As per protocol, the mayor was chairing the meeting, but it was clear they had all been waiting for the director-general to join them. Even in hologram-form, they looked apprehensive; as well they should be, given the situation.

"Well, now that our illustrious spymistress has joined us, perhaps we should call this meeting to order," the mayor announced.

The ghost of a wry smile flickered at the corners of Red-eye's mouth. 'Spymaster' would have been acceptable to her; no doubt he was trying to be polite.

"Can you tell us more about what happened on Loki?" the mayor asked.

"The Directorate is still investigating," Red-eye replied coolly.

"Does that mean you don't know, or you don't think we ought to know?" the Interplanetary Shipping Consortium representative asked suspiciously.

"It means that we do not *yet* know, but will keep each of you appraised according to your respective concerns," Red-eye answered.

"So what *do* you know about the situation?" the Justice Ministry's vice-minister demanded, "or, at least, what do you know that you can tell us."

"Jupiter Engineering Co. was operating an unregistered research facility on Loki with which they recently lost contact, whether due to a communications failure or something more serious is unknown at this stage," Red-eye answered with the tone of a newsreader, "However, given that the facility was unregistered, it must have been engaged in illegal research."

"Xenotechnology research?"

"Almost certainly, although we have yet to confirm that," Red-eye replied, "More importantly, there is no alien threat to Asgard or to the wider system. This appears to be purely an incident of corporate malfeasance."

"What assets have you deployed to investigate this?" asked the economy minister.

"The details of ongoing operations are classified," Red-eye rebuffed him.

"It's a simple, fleeking question—" the economy minister pressed in exasperation.

"An answer to which you are not entitled to receive," Red-eye coolly cut him off.

"But if reports come out in the news—" he began to splutter.

"Nothing will appear in the news as long as there are no leaks to the news," Red-eye shot back, the volume of her voice rising ever so slightly.

Although Red-eye's words were directed at the economy minister personally, they carried a subtle but stern warning for everyone listening. They all understood the importance of information and its concealment – or its selective disclosure – so if they really wanted to keep this under wraps, all they had to do was keep their own mouths shut.

"Beyond that, I have nothing to add," Red-eye concluded politely.

"Then, I suppose that concludes your contribution to this meeting," the mayor said, "We trust you'll keep us appraised of the situation as it develops?"

"Of course," with that said, Red-eye deactivated the VR link.

* * *

The image faded to black and Red-eye removed the headset, placing it back on the table. She noticed two pending communication requests on the screen and opened a three-way conference link with both callers. The video images of two senior agents appeared on the screen, a man and a woman, each vid-linking from their respective wrist-top computers.

"*Director-general,*" the female agent spoke first, "*we've finished interrogating the staff at J.E. Co.'s headquarters. They all appear to be clean.*"

"*Jezebel Thorn's company offices and records have all been searched,*" the male agent reported, "*Nothing in her records mentions J.E. Co. at all. PBA-assisted interrogations of her staff also turned up nothing.*"

"*J.E. Co.'s records are still being searched,*" the female agent said, "*But anything sensitive will have been moved to an offsite server that we can't reach.*"

"No matter, then," the director-general reminded her subordinates, "our only concern is xenotechnology, not the data potentially derived from it. Forward your findings to our Civil Liaison Office, they can pass on whatever is relevant to the Justice Ministry."

"*Understood,*" the male agent acknowledged, "*But I recommend we sic a surveillance team on Jezebel Thorn until the situation on Loki is resolved.*"

"Permission granted," the director-general said, "Make the arrangements."

The male agent nodded and deactivated his comm. link.

"*All other tasks and preparations at J.E. Co. were completed,*" the female agent said.

"Good," Red-eye said, "in the meantime, consider the researchers to be active leads. We still don't know how much they knew about the facility on Loki, or if there was any corporate espionage going on."

"*But I just got done interrogating them.*"

"A calm liar with a high degree of self-control can fool the analysis," Red-eye replied coolly, "and the best moles, by definition, can and will pass most attempts to detect them."

"*Understood,*" the agent acknowledged, "*what about Dr Aster Thorn?*"

"What about her?"

"*Her PBA score was 91%, barely a passing mark,*" the agent explained, "*But she threatened to call her husband during questioning, and she believed the Loki facility only had a few hundred staff. Should we be concerned about her?*"

"Keep an eye on her along with the others," Red-eye instructed, "but unless something new comes to light, she's just another active lead."

"*Understood,*" with that said, the video link was terminated.

* * *

Loki was a barely visible dot in the shadow of the deep blue gas giant Odin, a dark and diminutive dwarf orbiting in gloomy contrast to the hub-world of Asgard with its sprawling and shimmering metropolises. Loki's surface looked barren from orbit, but it was actually crisscrossed with a complicated network of valleys and ridges, and its open plains were pockmarked with craters from aeon's worth of meteor strikes.

The DNI ship slipped quietly into the moon's atmosphere, its sleek and stealthy hull absorbing almost every ray of light that touched its matte-black surface. It was similar to the material which covered the Spire, and it could defeat almost all known forms of sensor technology. No one and nothing would know it was there.

Just as their intelligence had indicated, the landing pad was 20km away from the actual facility. Concealed in one of the many shallow craters that dotted the moon's surface, it was equipped with an uplink array and an automated crane system for handling cargo. Officially, there were no settlements or facilities of any kind on Loki, but the landing pad seemed big enough to handle trade for an entire town.

Swooping down low, the DNI ship slowed to a halt above the landing pad and opened the vehicle bay doors on its underside, dropping the Wolverine APC from inside. The antigravity plating on the vehicle's underbelly glowed faintly, slowing its fall to a safe velocity. As the Wolverine touched down on the landing pad, bouncing gently on its suspension, the DNI ship sealed the vehicle bay's doors again before firing its engines and disappearing back into Loki's twilit sky.

The 40-tonne armoured vehicle rolled forward and down the landing pad's ramp onto the moon's surface. The perfectly smooth surface of the landing pad made it difficult for the Wolverine to move forward on its knobbly wheels, but they found much better purchase on the moon's crooked terrain. The vehicle began to trundle forward up the side of the crater, following a well-worn path made by countless automated cargo shipments.

The Wolverine's interior was definitely not built for comfort. Four of the operators – Doran, Ogilvy, Cato, and Bale – were squeezed into the seats, two on each side, facing each other with their weapons secured to their chest plates. The fifth operator, Viker, was in the cockpit guiding the Wolverine along the bumpy path while Gabriel squatted down behind him, holding onto the safety rungs on the ceiling to steady himself.

"ETA: 30 minutes," Viker announced, "assuming these coordinates are right."

"And if they're not?" asked Lieutenant Doran, a heavy-set man with a blond buzz-cut.

"If not, we'll be driving around in circles until the fuel cell runs out of power," Viker replied, before adding, "in which case, ETA: one decade."

There was a round of chuckling – which Gabriel didn't join – followed by silence as they reached the edge of the crater and climbed up over the ridge. The Wolverine emerged onto a vast plain where it began to pick up speed as it travelled across the empty moonscape, following the indicator in the cockpit's display. The journey was uneventful until one of the wheels hit a rock, jolting the vehicle's passengers without warning.

"Ok, I'm taking the wheel on the way back," Doran complained, "because Viker fucking sucks at driving this thing."

"Fine by me," Viker replied, unfazed by the criticism, "as long as I'm the one who gets to bitch in your ear when you crash."

The squad laughed. Gabriel didn't. There was silence.

"Speaking of bumpy rides," Ogilvy broke the silence, "you'd think the DNI could afford to lend us a decent antigravity tank like the Marine Corps has."

"No good for a mission like this," Gabriel said, breaking his usual taciturnity, "The antigravity cushion generated by a skimmer-type vehicle is easily detectable. Plus, antigravity levitation beds consume far too much power for a mission like this, they're also prone to damage and breakdowns. A rolling chassis is far more durable and reliable."

There was a pause as everyone took this information on board.

"Our very own Mastermind has spoken," Cato remarked with an amused smile, eliciting chuckles from the rest of the squad.

"The colonel's right, by the way," Viker informed the squad, "I trained on the scout-skimmers and rapid-assault tanks in the Navy. Fricking fast and agile, but they burn through huge amounts of power just to stay off the ground. And the whole piece of levitation tech that keeps them in the air is incredibly fragile; one knock to the underside can short out half the cells. If that happens, the only way forward is straight down."

"So, it's good you're behind the wheel of a tank with wheels," Bale quipped.

"Easy on the jokes, Captain," Viker replied, "I can't drive if my sides are splitting."

The squad laughed again. Gabriel remained silent.

"Why do we say the word 'wheel' like that?" Ogilvy pondered aloud, pointing to the holographic interface in the cockpit, "I mean phrases like 'take the wheel', 'asleep at the wheel'. It doesn't make sense since it's not an actual wheel."

"It's a classical reference," Gabriel explained, "Primitive vehicles on ancient Earth used a kind of wheel in the cockpit which had to be physically turned by the driver in order to steer. The technology changed, but the metaphors endured."

There was another spell of silence.

"Don't remember learning that in school," Cato remarked, "Just a standard education in between chores around the outpost; then it was off to join the Navy."

"You're a colonial too?" Captain Bale asked.

"I think we're all colonials in here, aren't we?" Doran wondered.

"Not me," said Viker proudly, "Asgard Undercity, born and bred. First time I ever left Asgard was to ship out for basic training."

"You don't talk like an under-dweller," Ogilvy remarked.

"Well, I can if y'ask me," Viker replied in Undercity dialect.

"I didn't understand a word of that."

"Neither do my fricking in-laws," replied Viker, eliciting another round of laughter.

"…What about you, Colonel?" Captain Bale asked, "If you don't mind me saying, your accent sounds very…standard."

"It wasn't always standard," Gabriel responded, "I used to talk like a 'fleeking' flute."

Gabriel's response raised eyebrows.

"You're from the Clouds, sir?" Doran asked, picking up on Gabriel's word choice.

"Originally, yes," Gabriel replied.

There was another long spell of silence as the Wolverine made brisk progress across the plain. Instead of a windscreen, the cockpit featured an all-encompassing holographic view of the vehicle's exterior, giving the visual impression of an open-air cockpit looking out on the starry sky and surrounding landscape. Ahead, the ridgeline loomed large, and a gap in the rocks became faintly visible; a canyon entrance of sorts from which a tiny speck emerged.

A yellow icon began to flash on the holographic interface, signalling the approach of an unidentified object. It was the same speck visible in the distance.

"Contact, dead ahead!" Viker announced, tapping the icon, "looks like a freight truck."

"A freight truck?" Bale asked suspiciously, "why would the base still be getting supplies if it's out of commission?"

"Supply runs are all automated," Gabriel pointed out, "If something happened to the staff, then there wouldn't be anyone around to cancel the shipments. Keep driving."

Viker kept a steady speed as the speck grew larger and more distinct. It was indeed an automated freight truck – an AI-controlled sixteen-wheeler flatbed with a single, large cargo container clamped onto the back; Jupiter Engineering Co.'s company logo visible on the side. The freight truck hurtled past the Wolverine apparently without incident.

"Good," Gabriel said, echoing everyone's relief, "just a freight truck."

"Sir, that truck pinged our IFF as it passed!" Viker dampened everyone's relief.

"Why the fuck would it do that?" Asked Doran with alarm.

"No idea," Viker replied, "but whatever system it's connected to knows we're here and it knows we're not with J.E. Co!"

"Secure your restraints, everyone!" Gabriel ordered as he locked his own armour down and squeezed the ceiling handles, "Viker, double-time it to the objective!"

"Aye, sir!"

The Wolverine's wheels kicked up a conspicuous cloud of dust as it picked up speed. The vehicle's suspension minimised the bumps and shocks as much as possible, but with the element of surprise apparently lost, nobody cared to complain about the rough ride.

Two more icons appeared on the display. Red ones.

"Contacts, behind us!" Viker announced as he tapped the icons, "two Vulture-class patrol drones. Readying the turret now!"

"Negative!" Gabriel countermanded him, "save our ammo."

"But sir, they're closing in for–"

"The support turret is useless against fast-moving aerial targets," Gabriel shouted back, "we need to lose them in the canyons!"

"Aye, sir!"

Viker gunned the accelerator for everything it was worth and the Wolverine roared forwards, passing 200kph. The gash in the ridgeline loomed large and welcoming on the visual display even as the rear-view image in the corner showed two menacing, dark shapes swooping low over the open plain like birds of prey chasing down a frightened rabbit.

"Firing up the ECM module," Viker said as he swiped the activation switch.

"Electronic countermeasures won't work at point-blank range!" Doran shouted.

"1000 credits says they will," Viker shouted back, "and if I'm wrong, I'll pay up later!"

Leaving a billowing cloud of dust in its wake, the Wolverine vanished into the canyon entrance without another second to spare. Both patrol drones opened fire, sending two energy-seeking missiles streaking across the plain towards their intended target. One missile struck the ridgeline above the canyon entrance, vaporising several tonnes of rock in a ball of flame, while the other flew straight over the Wolverine.

Viker was right. The Wolverine's ECM module saturated the surrounding air with junk data, blinding the missiles' guidance systems. The patrol drones, however, weren't fooled or dissuaded.

Their onboard computers could scrub most of the junk readings even if the missiles couldn't, and they flew straight in after the Wolverine.

The canyon itself was only one part of a bewildering maze of geological troughs and gorges, carved out by a long-since dried up network of ancient rivers, and squeezed between numerous, steeply angled escarpments and sheer cliff walls stretching hundreds of feet above. The Wolverine zoomed along the edge of the valley like a plump sports car on a racetrack with the patrol drones in hot pursuit.

"This terrain is killing the suspension!" Viker shouted to make himself heard over the sound of the Wolverine's violently vibrating chassis.

"Better it than us!" Gabriel replied, echoing the rest of the squad's thoughts, "Keep pushing into the canyons! If we can find one narrow enough, we can lose them!"

Aided by the low gravity, the Wolverine rocketed forwards along the half-pipe shaped trough as the patrol drones followed close behind. One of the drones opened fire with a chin-mounted laser turret, scorching the ground with a near-infrared beam of blazing hot light.

The beam briefly made contact with the Wolverine's outer hull, releasing a hissing cloud of dark smoke as a layer of the vehicle's ablative armour skin was boiled away, but leaving the vehicle itself unharmed.

Viker swerved hard to the right, crossing the middle of the trough at high speed to evade the laser beam and confuse the patrol drones. It didn't work. The drones soared high, flying abreast of one another to cover each side of the trough as their fast-moving target zig-zagged between the piles of rocky debris in the middle of the canyon.

"We can't keep this up forever!" Viker shouted over his shoulder, "They probably have onboard maps of the entire area!"

It was a wonder Viker could talk at all as he tried to navigate a natural obstacle course at dangerously high speeds, all while keeping an eye on the hostile red icons harassing them. The Wolverine's onboard computer assisted with the driving, but it was still a hell of a multitasking challenge for just one person.

"There!" Gabriel said, pointing at the screen, "Try that fork up ahead!"

Viker drove the Wolverine towards the right-hand fork before lurching left at the last second. The patrol drones – themselves flying at high speed – were caught off-guard by their target's surprising agility. One of the drones swerved hard and lost valuable time flying up over the top of the canyon wall before swooping back down into the left-hand fork to catch up with its quarry. The other drone kept flying down the right-hand canyon.

"We lost one!" Viker shouted as one of the red icons vanished off the edge of the screen.

Gabriel doubted it. The chase had plunged his mind into a hyper-focused combat fugue, blurring the distinction between wariness and paranoia. Viker was probably right about the drones having onboard maps of the region, and so there was no way that an AI-piloted combat drone would simply give up the search.

Ahead, the trough itself veered even further to the left, but the sheer rock wall was broken by a steep natural ramp on the right-hand side, leading straight up and over the ridge into the right-hand canyon. Viker turned right and drove the Wolverine up to the ridge as the pursuing drone closed in low behind them, ready for a point-blank kill.

Near the top of the ridge, the other red icon suddenly reappeared.

"The other one's back!" Viker yelled, "Dead ahead of us!"

"Swerve! Now!" Gabriel barked.

Viker slammed the brakes and brought the Wolverine around in a full, screeching circle – not a safe thing to do at breakneck speed – right as the other drone reappeared in their path, popping up from the right-hand canyon below to ambush them. The timing couldn't have been better as the pursuing drone jetted over the top of the escarpment at maximum speed, overshooting the Wolverine and slamming into the other drone.

The two drones collided in spectacular fashion, each one devoured in a mutually encompassing ball of flame and mangled debris. The collision sent thousands of flaming fragments raining down across the landscape like a localised meteor shower. The now stationary Wolverine's shielding flashed, deflecting incoming shards of debris as the flaming wreckage of the drones went spinning down together into the canyon below.

The squad was ecstatic.

"Two-for-one kill without firing a shot!" Viker shouted triumphantly, "Frick yeah!"

"I take it back, Viker," Doran exclaimed, "You should've been a racer!"

"Get your heads together, everyone," Gabriel poured cold water on their celebrations, "Those can't have been the only two drones out there."

Sure enough. Two more red icons appeared on the screen, closing in from behind.

"Two more contacts!" Viker yelled as he hit the accelerator.

He brought the Wolverine speeding down into the right-hand canyon, zig-zagging between the rocks and wreckage as two more patrol drones flew over the ridge from behind and swooped in after them.

"I doubt the same trick will work twice!" Captain Bale shouted.

"Agreed!" Gabriel shouted in response, "Ready the support turret!"

"You want us to try shooting them down?!" Viker asked incredulously, toggling the turret's fire-control system.

"Not yet!" Gabriel replied, "Wait for the right moment!"

The canyon was starting to grow narrower and straighter. The Wolverine had to count more and more on sheer speed as it weaved in between the rock piles within the confined halfpipe of a riverbed. The patrol drones closed in like a pair of hunting hornets, staying just above the top of the canyon as they chased their prey into a kill zone.

"Prime the turret!" Gabriel ordered.

"Primed!" Viker said as he highlighted the red icons, "hostile targets designated!"

The drones were flying at too high an angle for the turret to hit…yet.

"Keep the turret locked forward!" Gabriel added, "I have an idea!"

The canyon wasn't just getting narrower and straighter, it was also sloping downwards. The drones were about to lose their quarry, so one of them swooped down into the narrow gorge, where there was just enough space for it to fly through with room to manoeuvre. As the drone closed in from behind, it readied its missiles.

"It's got line-of-sight!" Viker said, panicking, "the ECM won't save us this time!"

"Brake, now!" Gabriel barked.

Viker slammed the brakes, causing the Wolverine to decelerate violently. The drone overshot its target before it could open fire, bringing it into the turret's crosshairs.

The turret released a deadly spray of armour-piercing rounds into the drone's vulnerable rear, puncturing its armour and mangling its engines and internal systems. The damage inflicted caused it to falter like a wounded bird before crashing to the ground, the impact igniting its weapons and releasing a dramatic flurry of flames and debris.

"Three down!" Viker yelled triumphantly as the squad celebrated.

"There's still one more drone out there," Gabriel reminded everyone soberly.

"Right," Viker stopped his premature celebrations and hit the accelerator again.

Sure enough, just as the Wolverine was picking up speed, the fourth patrol drone swooped down in front of them, unleashing a barrage of missiles.

"Woah!" Viker yelled in a panic and slammed the switch for the antigravity plating.

The antigravity plating was meant for landing safely on a planet's surface, not aerial acrobatics, but the trick worked. Aided by momentum, the Wolverine was lifted clear off the ground, causing the incoming barrage of missiles to undershoot the Wolverine and saving it from certain destruction.

The Wolverine's wheels hit the ground rolling as it shot forwards to escape.

"Nice one, Viker!" Ogilvy shouted.

"Thank me when we're in the clear!" Viker shouted back as he swerved to avoid the wreckage of the third downed drone.

"These drones learn from every tactic we use!" Gabriel shouted, "We'll need cover!"

"The objective isn't far from here!" Viker replied, noting the path on the map.

"Then that's where we're going!"

There was precious little room to zig and zag in the tiny gorge, but the upside was that the remaining patrol drone had to pull up to avoid getting squeezed between the rock walls. It would have to catch its target out in the open again.

Eventually, the narrow pathway took a leftward turn and widened out. The Wolverine emerged into a vast impact crater, resembling an amphitheatre-like basin whose surface sloped down into what looked like a sinkhole at the centre. Viker steered clear of the sinkhole and circled around the outer edge of the basin as fast as he could.

"The facility's entrance is on the other side of this basin," Viker said as he navigated around the edge of the basin, "but it'll be a dead-end once we get there."

The patrol drone reappeared above and swooped down low towards the Wolverine, firing its laser turret and leaving a blackened trail as the beam chased its target. Viker brought the Wolverine back around and drove through a gap in the rocks towards the research base, exiting the basin with the drone in hot pursuit. Up ahead at the base of a sheer cliff-face was a man-made structure: a vehicle ramp leading up to a set of loading bay doors. It was the entrance to the facility. Like Viker had said, it was also a dead-end.

"Last stand!" Viker shouted, switching the turret's fire control system to AI control.

Just shy of the doors, Viker brought the Wolverine swerving around just as the patrol drone opened fire with its laser turret. The laser beam boiled away part of the Wolverine's ablative armour coating as its turret swivelled round and returned fire.

The drone's armour couldn't withstand the blizzard of bullets, and it burst into flames as it came tumbling from the sky, bouncing along the ground like a burning bowling ball before smashing straight through the loading bay doors. A huge tongue of flame spewed out from the entrance as the flaming wreckage of the downed drone ignited whatever was being stored in the loading bay, reducing it to smoke and burning debris.

The squad watched the images in silence. They were all glad to be alive, but they hadn't intended to actually demolish the front door.

"At least we don't have to knock," Gabriel quipped wryly.

* * *

Viker drove the Wolverine up the vehicle ramp, through the flames and smoke, and into the loading bay itself, then he brought the vehicle around before bringing it to a complete halt and killed the engine. The squad secured their helmets, checked their weapons, and made sure their armour was sealed; then Gabriel moved to the vehicle's rear and hit the release button. The rear-door unfolded into a boarding ramp and the squad poured out of the vehicle with their weapons raised, fanning out to secure the area.

In fact, there wasn't much of an area left to secure. After smashing through the doors, the drone had kept on going until it hit the back wall, flinging flaming fragments at high speed in all directions, and shredding most of the cargo modules stored there. Dozens of small fires blazed around the area, diminished slightly by the thin air and automated sprinklers, and an emergency klaxon could be heard blaring in the background. Any threat that might have been waiting for them hadn't survived the drone's spectacular entrance.

Doran walked over to the burnt-out frame of the patrol drone to examine it. Its outer skin was riddled with pockmarks from the Wolverine's turret, but the frame itself had been blown open by the crash, exposing the damaged electronics inside which flickered and sparked from the residual power.

Doran gave the downed drone a vindictive kick.

"*Pretty crappy armour,*" he sneered over the comm.

"*You say that like it's a bad thing,*" Ogilvy remarked.

"*Hey, I'm not complaining,*" Doran replied indifferently, "*I'm just saying you'd think these rich corporates could afford to equip their drones with proper shielding.*"

"*Evidently, they didn't expect their targets to shoot back,*" Gabriel said.

"*Um, speaking of shielding,*" Viker interjected with a note of concern, "*the Wolverine's defences took some damage back in the canyons.*"

"*How much damage?*" Captain Bale asked.

"*To the vehicle itself, none,*" Viker clarified as he scanned the Wolverine's exterior, "*but about 40% of the thermal ablative paint is gone. If we have to run that hawk-and-rat race again, it'll be a lot harder getting back in one piece.*"

"*But the shields are ok, right?*" Asked Cato, concerned.

"*They are, but they're only good against bullets and shrapnel,*" Viker responded, "*Against lasers, particles beams or plasma, not so much.*"

"*One problem at a time,*" Gabriel said, "*Someone find us a way down.*"

"*Found it!*" Doran said, accessing the door panel for a personnel elevator, "*This elevator leads straight down to the main lobby.*"

"*Pretty obvious place for an ambush,*" Ogilvy pointed out.

"*Well if you prefer, we can always take the cargo elevator down,*" Doran explained, "*if you don't mind getting lost in the guts of the supply network.*"

"*Personnel elevator it is, then,*" Ogilvy conceded.

"*I've set the Wolverine's turret to auto-defend,*" Viker informed the squad, "*it'll gun down anything that comes back up this way; except for us, of course.*"

"*Good,*" said Gabriel, "*everyone, move out.*"

The squad filed into the elevator and waited as the doors sealed shut behind them automatically. A set of nozzles released a fine spray, filling the space with a translucent white cloud of anti-hazard chemicals which circulated around the enclosed space for a minute before being sucked out again by the nozzles. Once the decontamination process was complete, the elevator began to slide downwards on a diagonal rail into the depths below.

"*Remember,*" Gabriel reminded the squad, "*this is an IRS op. Investigate the facility, retrieve any useful data, and scrub any threats. Survivors are potential intelligence assets, but ultimately expendable.*"

"*Understood,*" the squad chorused.

"*What do you think we'll find down there, Colonel?*" Cato asked.

"*If I knew, we wouldn't be heading there in the first place,*" Gabriel replied before adding gravely, "*but usually these sorts of ops are glorified police raids. Teams of regular agents storm the place, cuff everybody, and seize anything of interest. If the DNI is sending us in, it's because everybody's already dead.*"

"*How much resistance is there usually?*"

"*Well, no one wants to be arraigned on xenotech possession charges,*" Gabriel replied, "*That's a reasonable incentive to shoot back. But like I said: if we're being sent in, whatever experiments they were conducting must have gotten them killed. Any survivors will gladly take a prison cell in exchange for safety.*"

"*Well if they are stupid enough to shoot at us, we'll kill them first!*" Ogilvy said.

"*Damn right!*" Doran added his own bravado.

The squad's morale was high heading down towards what could be certain death. High morale was a good thing, technically. But listening to their bravado made something click in Gabriel's mind: the real reason he was uncomfortable leading a squad.

Their camaraderie, their banter, their bonds of friendship; it mattered at least as much to them as the mission itself, if not more. Furthermore, all of them undoubtedly assumed that he felt the same level of commitment to the unit as they did.

He didn't. A voidstalker was a lone wolf, there was no room for bonds of comradeship. If Gabriel were forced to choose between the squad and the mission...

He would leave them all to die.

THE FACILITY

Eventually, the DNI agents completed their search, departing as quickly as they had come. No arrests were made, no equipment was seized, no areas were cordoned off, and no court summonses were issued. They simply finished what they were doing and left. Once they were gone, all the staff were summoned to the breakroom for a meeting with the chief legal officer.

J.E. Co.'s chief legal officer was a tall, slim woman, seemingly devoid of emotion or the capacity to overreact; the virtual opposite of the short, stout, irascible man who chaired the company. Aster disliked her intensely. Apart from her cool and stilted attitude, she looked like Jezebel Thorn without the smile, right down to the black-and-gold hair colouring.

"Let me begin by assuming that each and every one of you adhered unwaveringly to your employment contracts, and especially to the non-disclosure clauses stipulated therein," she began, the force of her implied threat smothered by her dull tone and legalistic phrasing, "and let me finish by reminding you that as long as you fulfil your obligations to the company, the company will fulfil its obligations to you."

"All the project data was secured to an offsite server before the DNI raid," Dr Felix Kessler reassured everyone, "they won't have found anything by searching the computers here, and it's subject to corporate privilege, anyway."

"Good," said the legal officer.

"Like that would matter to the spooks," somebody snorted cynically, "just like the phrases 'due process' and 'probable cause'."

"Corporate privilege means that such data is deemed inadmissible as evidence during litigation proceedings unless specifically requested through the process of legitimate legal discovery," the legal officer explained dryly, "A raid by the intelligence services does not constitute legitimate legal discovery."

The scientists stared at her blankly.

"That means even if the DNI somehow got hold of the data, it cannot be used against you in a court of law," the legal officer translated.

"Has there been any information from the board?" Aster asked.

"Regarding what, specifically?" the legal officer asked.

"Instructions, guidance, advice, anything to show some leadership or direction?" Aster clarified, frustrated by the stonewalling and that annoyingly blank look.

"The board is still assessing the company's position regarding the DNI raid," the legal officer replied, "once that assessment is complete, new instructions will be provided."

"What about the Loki facility?" someone shouted from near the back, "we heard that something happened up there, is that true?"

"That's a confidential matter," was the blunt response.

"But we've all heard rumours that—"

"Nothing happened at the facility on Loki about which any of you need to be concerned," the legal officer said in a sharply dismissive tone, "New information and guidance will be communicated to you as and when it becomes available via the company intranet. Until then, go about your day as normal."

With that perfunctory statement, J.E. Co.'s chief legal officer abruptly departed before the heckling could begin in earnest, leaving the assembled staff standing in confused silence. Apart from a vague and veiled threat about not betraying the company, they still had no idea what was going on or what to do next.

"As project-lead, I say we continue our simulations," Aster announced, breaking the awkward silence, "No live testing until the board says otherwise."

"I heard a rumour that the DNI arrested Chairman Darius," someone declared.

"There's no proof of that," Aster responded, "and rumours won't help the situation."

"But that's how these things start," someone else cut in, "first the executives are arrested or skip town, then the company gets raided–"

"I don't know if anything at all has happened to the chairman and neither do you," Aster shut him down, "right now, the most we can do is go about the rest of the day."

"All the DNI agents wanted to know about Lawrence Kane," one of the engineers spoke up, "But I didn't see them search his office."

"They did search his office," somebody else called out, "I saw them go in. Maybe they were looking for something Dr Kane might have gotten hold of?"

"It doesn't matter what they were here for," Aster interjected, "what matters is that nobody is in trouble. And I'd like to keep it that way."

"What about the Loki facility?" another engineer asked.

"What about it?" Aster pursed her lips at the question.

"She wouldn't tell us what happened up there."

"And what makes you think I would know?" Aster demanded impatiently.

"Well, it's just that we heard there was a big accident–"

"Maybe the board doesn't yet know what happened," Aster cut him off, "and besides, there are more urgent things for us to worry about right now."

"But if something happened over there," the scientist went on, "then shouldn't we–"

"Shouldn't we do what, exactly?!" Aster exclaimed, her voice rising to shouting level, "rent out a shuttle and head over there to investigate ourselves?"

"But those are our friends and colleagues over there; *your* friends and colleagues!"

"For whom nothing can be done!" Aster shouted, her patience evaporating, "In case you've already forgotten, the DNI was here raiding our offices; so if something did happen on Loki, everyone over there is either dead or under arrest."

Everyone fell silent. Aster had said openly and bluntly what they were all thinking, and it sounded a lot harsher coming from her mouth than from the chief legal officer.

"That's not me being cold or heartless," Aster continued resolutely, "that's a cold, hard fact that you all need to accept. Flailing around in anguish helps no one, and the less we involve ourselves in whatever the fuck may have happened over there, the better."

More silence. But this time, people were nodding in reluctant agreement. As worried as they were about their colleagues on Loki, nobody wanted to be slapped with a criminal complicity charge. It didn't matter how uninvolved they actually were; the Directorate of Naval Intelligence took a dim view of ignorance and those who pled it.

"If there's nothing else, it's time to get back to work," Aster concluded, "Rerun your simulations and diagnostics, and report back to me before the end of the day."

* * *

The elevator took the squad a quarter of a kilometre below the moon's surface before finally trundling to a halt. The heavy blast door unlocked, sliding open and causing a rush of air to flow into the partially depressurised space. Gabriel and the squad stepped out, weapons primed and ready to shoot on sight.

There was no lighting or power, leaving the room pitch black; but through the visual enhancement filters in their helmets, the squad could see that they were in an atrium. Aside from pristine rows of leather seating and an unattended front desk, there was nothing else to see. More importantly, nobody jumped out to ambush them.

"*No environmental hazards detected,*" Ogilvy said through the comm., using his wrist-top computer to adjust his suit's hazmat module, "*Radiation levels are normal too.*"

"*There should be a security station behind the front desk,*" said Bale.

"*Secure it,*" Gabriel ordered.

As the squad weaved in between the rows of seating, covering every corner, Doran reached the front of the atrium and vaulted over the front desk, stowing his weapon and accessing the holographic computer controls.

"*Everything's been shut down,*" Doran said as he brought everything back online.

"*You don't say,*" Viker replied sarcastically.

"*No, I mean somebody deliberately powered down the computers,*" Doran clarified, "*There was no power failure or emergency shutdown that I can see.*"

As Doran powered up the system again, the ceiling lights glowed faintly before slowly brightening, re-illuminating the atrium. It wasn't just deserted, there was no sign that anything out-of-the-ordinary had happened at all. No bodies, no physical damage, no signs of battle; nothing unusual except the lack of people.

"*Ogilvy,*" Cato said warily, "*are you sure there aren't any hazards in here?*"

"*I'm pretty sure,*" Ogilvy replied, "*seeing as I'm using top-of-the-line equipment.*"

"*That's not all, by the way,*" Doran said as he searched through the computer system, "*There's nothing in the logs to show that anything strange happened. No contamination alerts, no containment breaches, no evacuation order, not even decent encryption.*"

"*Just because there aren't any logs, doesn't mean there wasn't an accident,*" Gabriel pointed out, "*or that other parts of the facility aren't contaminated somehow.*"

"*So what's our next move, Colonel?*" Bale asked.

"*Find us a map of the facility,*" Gabriel ordered, "*We'll explore this whole place room-by-room, corridor-by-corridor until we find out what's going on.*"

"*Done,*" Doran replied, "*I've downloaded the facility schematics to the squad-net. There's a tram line circling the facility, it can take us wherever we need to go.*"

As if on cue, the double doors swung open. The squad snapped back to attention, aiming their weapons at the lone figure who walked in.

"FREEZE, NOW!" Viker shouted at the man, the voice-modulating speakers in his helmet making him sound demonic.

Confused yet strangely calm, the man obeyed, raising his hands above his head as Viker and Ogilvy closed in on him with weapons raised.

"ON YOUR STOMACH!" Ogilvy shouted, "PALMS FLAT ON THE FLOOR!"

The man did as he was told, lying face down on the ground and spreading his limbs as the rest of the squad joined Viker and Ogilvy. He was wearing maintenance overalls and despite being held out gunpoint, he didn't seem terribly frightened.

"Identify yourself," Gabriel ordered the man.

"Uh, Teller. Marcus Teller," the man replied hesitantly, "I'm a junior technician."

"What happened here and where is everyone?" Gabriel demanded.

"Well, I can take you to the rest of the facility staff–" Teller offered.

"That's not what we asked you," Bale interrupted him sternly, "what happened to this facility and where is everybody else?"

"Nothing happened," Teller replied calmly, "a perimeter breach was detected, so we went into a soft lockdown and evacuated everyone to secure parts of the facility."

"What the fuck is a 'soft lockdown'?" Doran demanded suspiciously.

"A soft lockdown gets initiated in case of a perimeter breach," Teller explained, "no alarms are triggered, no event logs are registered; just a partial lockdown until the breach is resolved. I just came to get everything up and running again."

The squad processed the man's answers, such as they were. Ogilvy switched off his own helmet speakers, remotely deactivating the rest of the squad's helmet speakers so that their captive wouldn't overhear them.

"*I bet he's lying,*" Ogilvy said.

"*Agreed,*" Cato seconded, "*who goes into 'partial lockdown' for a perimeter breach?*"

"*There was no intelligence on the security protocols used by this facility,*" Gabriel pointed out, "*he could be telling the truth.*"

"*So what do we do with him?*" Viker asked.

Gabriel reactivated his helmet speakers and turned back to their captive.

"Get up," Gabriel ordered him.

The hapless junior tech slowly got back on his feet and dusted himself off.

"So, I'm guessing you guys are DNI, huh?" Teller asked.

"Correct," Gabriel answered, "And I'm sure I don't need to tell you that it's in your best interests to cooperate with us. This facility is suspected of illegal xenotech research. We need to access this facility's computer mainframe to find out."

"Well, the corporates don't pay me enough to say no to armed commandoes," Teller replied nonchalantly, "Follow me, I'll take you to central operations. If you want to access the mainframe, that's the place to go."

With his guests holding him at gunpoint, Teller led the squad back through the doors and down a flight of steps to the deserted tram station.

"So, you guys really think there's xenotech down here?" Teller asked congenially.

"You work here," Bale pointed out, "you tell us."

"Hey, I'm just a junior technician," Teller replied defensively, "Masterminds know what the scientists get up to in their labs all day. I just keep the machinery running."

A mag-tram was already waiting, and Teller waved everybody aboard. Once the doors had shut, he keyed in their destination.

"The tram goes to central operations," Teller explained as the tram began to trundle forward, "But to be honest, you guys are the most interesting thing that's happened here."

"*The intel brief said that J.E. Co. first lost contact with this place several days ago,*" Doran said over the squad comm., "*Now this guy's telling us nothing strange happened except for us showing up? Not even a banal communications loss?*"

"*We'll get our answers once we're at central operations,*" Gabriel replied.

"*The brief also said that J.E. Co. sent in its own in-house security team to investigate this place,*" Cato added his own doubts, "*think he forgot to mention that as well?*"

"*Maybe,*" Gabriel replied sceptically, "*None of this adds up.*"

"*Permission to put a bullet in his head just to be safe, Colonel?*" Viker half-joked.

"*Denied,*" Gabriel replied seriously, then added, "*For now.*"

The facility's tram glided along at a steady pace, moving slowly enough to see the station names. The squad stood in patient silence whilst keeping a watchful eye on Marcus Teller, who seemed unusually calm for a man effectively being held hostage.

"How long have you worked here?" Bale asked Teller through his helmet speakers.

"About six months," Teller replied amicably, "They don't let you go home that often, long-term rotations and all. But still, this place is sac…such a great place to live and work, I mean," Teller apparently corrected himself, "So much to do, so much to learn…"

"*What the frick is this guy talking about?*" Viker wondered over the comm.

"Here we are," Teller announced as the tram glided into the station. The holographic sign above the platform read: 'Hydroponics'.

Ogilvy grabbed Teller by the collar and threw the man to the ground.

"Do you think we're fucking stupid?" Ogilvy yelled at the man, aiming his weapon at Teller's head, "You said we were going to central operations!"

"We *are* going to central operations," Teller replied, displaying his bare palms to the squad, "you just have to pass through the hydroponics bay to get there."

"He's telling the truth," Doran informed the squad as he consulted a holographic map.

"Look," Teller said as he picked himself up off the ground, "you guys asked me to take you to central operations, that's what I'm doing."

"It might have helped if you'd told us the route beforehand," Gabriel said suspiciously.

"It's up the stairs, straight through the hydroponics labs, and on to central operations," Teller clarified, "once you're there, you can do whatever you want."

The tram doors opened and everyone disembarked, following Teller through the deserted station, then through another atrium before finally arriving at the hydroponics labs.

The squad found themselves at the top of a huge, multi-storey complex covered with greenery and filled with steam, like an indoor tropical rainforest without the trees. The walls were lined with rack after rack of genetically engineered fruit and vegetables, tended to by aerial drones and robotic arms which took routine readings, and periodically relocated tanks to the ground floor for processing into food.

"The hydroponics labs are entirely automated," Teller explained, leading the squad across the walkway towards a reinforced door at the opposite end, "each section can produce enough food to feed the entire facility for a decade."

"So no one needs to come down and monitor the labs at all?"

"Not at all," Teller replied, stopping in front of the door and turning to face the squad, "except when *catastrophe strikes!*"

Teller shouted those last two words at the top of his lungs. Without warning, the lights cut out and all the machinery stopped dead.

* * *

After the impromptu staff meeting had concluded, everyone filed out of the breakroom in a visibly sombre mood, dispersing back to their offices and workshops. Aster followed them, heading quietly back to her office, and locking the door behind her.

Then she sat down at her desk and held her head in her hands.

Everything was a mess. No one wanted to think about the fate of their Loki colleagues or what they had been working on. It was an open secret that many of J.E. Co.'s breakthroughs had come out of the Loki facility, and it didn't take a huge leap of the imagination to guess what they might have been based on. The less they knew, the safer their own necks were.

Gabriel was probably over there, too, risking his own life to investigate what had happened. Every time he deployed on some new mission he was gone for weeks or months at a time; she never knew where he was, or when – or if – he would return. But this time she was more or less directly involved. If he was only going to be gone for a few days, that meant he was staying in the Asgard star system. That couldn't be a coincidence.

Furthermore, as selfish as it seemed to even raise the subject, career prospects were also on everyone's minds. Once word got out about the scandal, clients and investors would flee like rats and new contracts would dry up, potentially forcing the firm to file for bankruptcy. J.E. Co. did offer decent severance pay, but the stigma of having worked for a company rumoured to have dabbled in xenotech would make it difficult to get hired again.

It had been over a decade since she'd left the frontier, leaving behind the prospect of a mediocre future as a mechanic's housewife with two children. Instead, she had an actual career…with four children and a taciturn supersoldier for a husband. Even so, it was a good life, and she wasn't about to let it fall apart. It just wasn't clear what she could do about it.

The buzzer sounded, bringing Aster's gloomy train of thought to a sudden halt. Felix Kessler's name was illuminated on the door's holographic display.

What did he want now of all times?

Aster hastily composed herself before buzzing him in. Felix entered the room, looking distracted and despondent. Without saying a word, he walked straight over to the lounge in Aster's office and slumped down on the couch.

Wondering why he had turned up, Aster got up and joined him on the couch.

Most days, Felix looked like a middle-class teenager dressed like a scientist. He was from the Clouds originally, and he retained a keen sense of fashion with his carefully styled hair, dyed black and gold, and a silver stud in one ear. It was hard to believe that he had advanced degrees in materials science.

Now, however, he looked more like a sleep-deprived corpse. His steel grey eyes looked heavy and his features were sullen, weighed down by the events of this morning. Even his ear-stud looked duller under the light.

"We did all the diagnostics this morning before you got here," Felix reported blandly.

"Good to know," Aster replied, equally blandly.

"We found 0.2367% corrosion on the primary lens of one of the initialiser lasers," Felix reported, "repairing the lens should be complete by the end of the day."

"That shouldn't delay the schedule too much," Aster answered, awkwardly aware that Felix was dancing around an entirely different issue, "how about the simulations?"

"The simulations have been done to death," Felix added with weary exasperation, "we really should be starting live-testing right now."

"I seriously doubt you came all the way to my office to tell me that."

Felix was silent for a moment.

"How well did you know Lawrence?" he asked suddenly.

"Not as well as I know you," Aster replied, "But then, I don't think anyone did."

"He did like to keep to himself..." Felix noted, hesitant to continue with the topic.

"You think he knew something about what was happening on Loki," Aster concluded, "Which would explain why the DNI had such an interest in him."

"Of course he would have known *something*," Felix pointed out, "or else he wouldn't be doing his job as liaison officer. So I was thinking maybe he kept backup logs–"

"No," Aster interrupted flatly.

"But I haven't asked you anything yet," Felix said.

"You came here to ask me if I would use my personal override code to open up his office and find out if he kept any backup logs there," Aster guessed, "and the answer is no."

"Well, you *are* project-lead," Felix continued hopefully, "And Lawrence's notes–"

"Would be incriminating material, if they exist," Aster pointed out, "and, if they contain anything of interest to the DNI, would also be grounds for arrest."

"So you really want to just bury the whole issue?"

"Yes, I do," Aster confirmed bluntly.

"Look, this isn't me being all emotional about what may or may not have happened on Loki," Felix tried to explain, "I just think it might be worth looking for any notes or logs he might have kept that could be useful to the DNI."

"The DNI searched all our offices, including Lawrence's," Aster reminded him, "if he kept any logs in his office, they would've found them already."

"But if he hid the logs well enough that the DNI didn't find them, they might still be there," Felix pressed, "And if *we* find them, we can make sure the DNI doesn't, and maybe even salvage some useful data out of this mess."

"…Are you serious?" Aster answered in disbelief.

"Of course I am," Felix stood his ground, "why wouldn't I be?"

"Does the phrase 'criminal complicity' mean anything to you?" Aster demanded, "Because that's the legal term for what you just suggested."

"Look, it's not like I want to get anyone else in trouble but–"

"Oh, that's good to know!" Aster shot back sarcastically, "if you mean that, why don't you drop the issue and never bring it up again?"

"Well, regardless of what we do with the data, would it really hurt to just look?"

"Yes, it would."

"Look, Aster, we were all involved," Felix persisted, "the fact that we all pretended not to know or care about Loki doesn't make us less complicit."

"So it's about moral absolution, is it?" Aster asked cynically.

"Partly, yes," Felix conceded, "we all benefitted from the research they did; and now, we're just washing our hands of them? It's horrible."

"I know it's horrible!" Aster shot back angrily, "This whole thing is horrible, I've been overseeing the whole project for over a year, remember?"

"So why in Terra's name shouldn't we look?" Felix asked in exasperation, "the worst case scenario is we don't find anything."

"No, the worst case scenario is we all get arrested for hiding data from the DNI – aka 'criminal complicity' – and spend the next few decades in a penitentiary facility."

"Do you really not want to find out what happened?"

"I'm afraid to find out," Aster admitted, "and of everyone getting arrested. Keeping our heads down is the best strategy for us."

"Well I'm afraid to find out too," Felix conceded with an earnest, almost pleading tone, "but if there's anything we can do—"

"I have four children, Felix, all of them under ten," Aster interrupted him, "I don't plan to watch them grow up through a weekly video link from a prison cell."

"So you won't even consider opening up Lawrence's office?" Felix asked desperately.

"I don't see what the point would be," Aster answered, "Especially since your plan involves potentially landing us in even more trouble with the authorities."

Felix looked away, sighing in resignation.

"Fine, then," he got up and left without another word.

Aster remained slumped on the couch long after Felix had gone, glumly processing the tense conversation that had just transpired.

'Trouble with the authorities'. That phrase had a completely different meaning out on the frontier. 'Trouble with the authorities' meant that the government suspected the colony of harbouring smugglers or trafficking their contraband. 'Trouble with the companies' meant the colony was behind on its payments, and the corporates' hired thugs had come to collect.

The reach of the government was infinitely long but seldom felt, and they allowed the corporates to roam more or less freely on the frontier. The former was distrusted but respected, the latter were despised. In spite of their dependence on both, the colonials valued their freedom, and successfully defying either was considered a badge of honour.

But here on Asgard, no such freedom was possible. 'Trouble with the authorities' meant far worse than a visit by the Marine patrols or the corporate loan sharks, and no one would congratulate you for it. If you ran afoul of the law here, everything could be taken away from you. Aster had built an entire life here within the hyper-urbanised milieu of this hub-world, and it could all just fall apart as a result of 'trouble with the authorities'.

So why was she already having second thoughts about Felix's suggestion?

* * *

As Teller shouted the key phrase, his verbal command caused the power to die, killing the lights with it. The squad was completely blinded as their helmet filters adjusted to the sudden darkness. Gabriel's helmet filters made the adjustment just in time to see their erstwhile guide charge at Ogilvy and body tackle him against the railings. They tumbled over the top of the railings together and went spinning down into the depths below.

"*Fuck!*" someone shouted.

"*Get that door open!*" Gabriel ordered, "*I'm going down there.*"

Without pausing to hear any objections, Gabriel mounted the railings and leapt down after Ogilvy and his attacker. He kicked back and forth between the glass tanks to slow his fall before landing cat-like on his feet, weapon ready.

Suddenly, the power returned, re-illuminating the hydroponics lab and briefly blinding the squad again as their helmet filters had to reset. When his visual filters had adjusted, Gabriel found himself in a maze of vertically arranged hydroponic tanks, the thick green trunks of genetically engineered food plants visible through the steamed glass. Neither Ogilvy nor Teller was anywhere to be seen.

"*Ogilvy!*" Gabriel called out through the comm., "*Status!*"

"*…Six…eight targets!*" Ogilvy shouted back, "*…maintenance area…Ah!*"

Gabriel heard struggling and more shouting; then a sound like electricity or surging static filled the comm. from Ogilvy's line before it suddenly went dead.

"*Ogilvy, come in!*" Gabriel tried to hail him, "*Lieutenant Ogilvy, respond immediately!*"

Silence.

Gabriel felt a small but treacherous fluttering of panic in his chest. A member of his squad had been captured, and with such speed and tactical competence that no one had managed to fire a shot in response. They had been blindsided. *He* had been blind-sided.

At least Ogilvy's bio-readings were still green. His comm. was dead, but he wasn't, and his tracking signal was still within detectable range. But now, Gabriel was confronted with the invidious choice of pressing on towards central operations – their primary objective – and rescuing Ogilvy, which was what the squad would demand.

"*Colonel,*" Bale hailed Gabriel, "*the door up here is sealed with a biometric lock. We can't get through without a staff member's DNA.*"

"*And it's based on a rotating encryption protocol,*" Doran added to the bad news, "*It'd take days to bypass the lock electronically.*"

"*Can you breach it?*" Gabriel asked.

"*Breach the fricking door?!*" Viker snapped in disbelief, "*Ogilvy's been captured—*"

"*Answer the question!*" Gabriel shot back, "*Can you breach the door?!*"

"*…Negative…sir,*" Viker replied through gritted teeth, "*not without damaging the lock, and it'd take about an hour to cut through with a torch.*"

"*Understood,*" Gabriel answered, "*Join me down here. We're going after Ogilvy.*"

"*Aye sir!*" they choroused.

Gabriel's decision had nothing to do with prioritising Ogilvy's life. If they couldn't get through the door to central operations, they would have to find an alternative route, and following the trail of Ogilvy's captors was the best way forward.

As the rest of the squad found their way down to the ground floor and fanned out to secure the processing area, Gabriel came across a small door on the far side of the room marked 'maintenance'. It was slightly ajar.

"*Found a service hatch, far end of the room,*" Gabriel informed the squad, "*Ogilvy must have been taken through there.*"

"*I'll rip that little snake Teller's throat out!*" Viker snarled over the comm.

"*Interrogation first, retribution later,*" Gabriel reminded him.

Viker's unprofessional anger irked Gabriel. The life of a fellow soldier was important, but if Gabriel were on this mission solo, he wouldn't let the desire for revenge distract him. Viker's attitude could be a problem.

The squad converged on Gabriel's position as he pulled open the hatch and ducked inside. On the other side of the threshold was a steep flight of steps leading down into the maintenance area. Not bothering with the steps, Gabriel jumped straight down, landing square on his feet and continuing on as the rest of the squad slid down the rails after him.

The ambient temperature was 35 Celsius, close to Human body temperature, rendering the thermal enhancement filters in their HUDs useless. It was also pitch black, requiring the squad's helmet filters to switch back to night vision.

"*This is clearly a trap,*" Cato muttered the obvious.

"*Doesn't matter,*" Viker shot back, "*we're not leaving Ogilvy behind.*"

Gabriel had to agree with Cato; this whole situation reeked of a trap in the making. Whatever the broader motivations were, the kidnapping of Ogilvy was tactically brilliant, and clearly intended as bait for a larger ambush. In which case, the service hatch had probably been left open deliberately in order to lure them further inside.

Out in the open, Teller would be dead meat; but down here, the squad was at a serious disadvantage. The maintenance area was a convoluted maze of narrow passageways barely wide enough for the fully armoured commandoes to walk down in single file. If it weren't for Ogilvy's tracking signal, they would have had no idea which way to go and would have been forced to split up to search for him.

And what was that surging noise over the comm.? It sounded like radio static, but the DNI didn't use radio technology. Was it some type of device for immobilising an exoskeleton? Technology like that existed, but DNI armour was supposed to be impervious to it. That someone might have found a way to defeat DNI safeguards was a disturbing thought.

More disturbing still, Ogilvy had shouted about at least eight hostiles attacking him; and yet the squad hadn't detected anyone or anything right up until the power died. Had they all been too distracted by Teller's guided tour to pay attention? Or had their ambushers found a way to defeat DNI sensor technology?

After a while, the path traced by Ogilvy's tracking signal brought the squad to another access hatch. They ducked through into a new area, a fully lit corridor wide enough for two people. Once again, the squad's helmets had to readjust to the light.

At the end of the corridor were two bodies slumped against the door, both dressed in maintenance overalls. One was clearly dead, his fingers still clutching his throat, having died while trying to staunch the blood dribbling from his neck. Moreover, he had clearly been left to die by his fellows as they rushed ahead with their prisoner.

The other was their treacherous guide. He was still alive, barely; clutching his stomach as blood trickled from a wound there. He looked up at the approaching commandoes and gave a wry smile in between catching his breath.

"Should've known…about those…damn claws," Teller wheezed.

There were cleaner and more professional ways of doing this, but there was no time to deal with Teller cleanly or professionally. Besides, Ogilvy's kidnapping had left the squad angry and unfocused; they might beat Teller to death before he could tell them anything.

With the rest of the squad holding the prisoner at gunpoint, Gabriel stowed his weapon and clenched his fists. The action caused three slightly curved blades on each hand to slide out from grooves on the back of his gauntlets. Gabriel used the eight-inch-long combat claws to impale Teller through his shoulders. Teller groaned and squirmed in pain as he was lifted bodily off the ground, hanging like a limp doll on a set of meat hooks.

"What is going on in this place?" Gabriel demanded through his helmet speakers.

"Things you can't begin to understand," Teller grinned defiantly.

Gabriel responded by twisting his claws inside Teller's shoulders, eliciting a howl of pain from the prisoner as little rivulets of blood trickled from his wounds.

"Answer the question," Gabriel said menacingly, "and we'll decide if we understand."

"Well, your earlier hunch was right," Teller admitted smugly, "there is xenotech here; the scientists have been studying it for years. But they found something new, something that enlightened them. And they made sure everyone else here was enlightened too."

"'Enlightened'?" Gabriel scowled suspiciously, "What in Terra's name does that mean?"

"It means the dissolution of a prior state of ignorance and the attainment of a state of knowledge," Teller replied sneeringly.

Gabriel didn't like being sneered at and made his displeasure clear by twisting his claws inside Teller's shoulders again. Teller let out another shriek of agony in response.

"What kind of xenotech did they find, and where did they get it?" Gabriel demanded.

"I don't know anything specific," Teller replied, "I'm just a junior tech."

Pleading ignorance wasn't an answer, and Gabriel twisted his claws again.

"I never attained that level of enlightenment!" Teller screamed, his prior smugness dissolving under torture, "I really don't know!"

"THEN WHO DOES KNOW?!" Gabriel bellowed.

"The scientists! Who else?!" Teller screamed back, "They studied it. They're the ones who required everyone to be enlightened by it."

"So where are they taking our squad member?"

"Enlightenment takes place in the heart of the Temple," Teller answered, "you can reach it by passing through the labs."

'Temple' was an odd choice of words, but at least he'd given them a clear answer.

"One last question," said Gabriel, "J.E. Co. sent one of its security teams to investigate this place, what happened to them?"

"You don't want to know," Teller replied with a madman's grin.

Gabriel made clear what he thought of that answer by giving his combat claws another vicious twist, turning the captive's grin into another agonised scream.

"If I didn't want to know, I wouldn't have asked you," Gabriel said menacingly.

"They were captured and taken to the Temple to be elevated," Teller replied, starting to lose breath, "they will serve far better… than they could…in life."

"Is 'elevation' different from 'enlightenment'?"

"…Very…" Teller replied, slurring his words, "…tell Dani… to go frick herself."

Gabriel want to ask him who 'Dani' was, but the prisoner had lost consciousness, so he let the dying man slide off his claws to the floor. Then he relaxed his fists, causing the claws to retract back into their grooves. It was safe to assume the J.E. Co. team was dead.

"*Priorities have changed,*" Gabriel said over the comm. as he readied his weapon, "*we're heading to the labs, since that's probably the epicentre of this.*"

"*Most of the doors on the way to the labs are biometrically sealed,*" Doran said.

"*No problem,*" Gabriel replied, pointing at Teller, "*Take off his hand.*"

The squad looked at him.

"*You heard me,*" Gabriel repeated, "*take a knife, cut off his hand, and bring it with us.*"

The squad hesitated at the bloody-minded order, but it was a direct order, and they could hardly disobey. Besides, there was no love lost for the treacherous Teller.

Doran crouched down and clasped one of Teller's hands, drawing a combat knife from his shoulder sheath. He flicked a switch with his thumb, and the edge of the dull-grey blade turned a soft orange colour as it was flash-heated and wreathed in a thin cloud of energised plasma. Teller had already passed out, so he didn't feel the knife touch his skin, severing his hand in one clean slice and instantly cauterising the wound.

Doran deactivated the flash-heated blade and replaced the knife in its sheath, rising to his feet before waving the severed hand in front of the door's biometric sensor. The door light flashed green and the door unlocked, sliding open in response.

"*One more thing: the rules of engagement have changed. If you see anyone other than Ogilvy,*" Gabriel fired a single round into Teller's skull, followed by a second shot through the skull of the other technician, "*Shoot to kill.*"

THE LABORATORY

Yanking open the biometric scanner beside Lawrence Kane's office door, Aster uncovered a hidden keypad and punched in her personal override code to bypass the biometric lock. The red light flashed green, and she slipped inside like a thief in the night before anyone noticed. Once the door was sealed behind her, she leaned against the wall and hyperventilated to dispel the panic over what she had just done.

As project-lead, Aster could use her personal override code to access almost any place in the labs, including other people's offices if necessary. That meant it was a privilege of her position meant only for emergencies, not for snooping around a co-worker's office. Even though it wasn't technically a violation of her employment contract, she certainly didn't have a legitimate reason for doing it.

Felix's insistence on digging up whatever Lawrence might have found had stoked a dangerous curiosity in her. Part of her *did* want to know what had happened to their colleagues on Loki if only to provide some sort of closure. Not to mention, anything she found might help the authorities and thereby clear the cloud of suspicion hanging over everyone else. Of course, Aster had adamantly rejected versions of those arguments only an hour ago; but they had slowly eaten away at her resolve until she could stand it no longer.

Most companies in the high tech sector used the same highly compartmentalised research and development chain. The researchers carried out the basic research with no immediate commercial value in one facility, then passed on their findings to the engineers to develop into a usable product in another facility.

In theory, this was supposed to leave each section free to focus on their respective areas. In practice, it was just legal cover, and everybody knew it. Hardly a year went by without a major corporate scandal being uncovered involving experiments of a legally questionable nature, either due to an industrial accident, or the revelation that corporate espionage was involved. In the event of legal trouble, the research end of the chain was the most likely to be cut loose to save the rest of the company.

Of course, the process couldn't be completely stovepiped. Lawrence's job as 'liaison' was to observe the research process and ensure at least one point of contact between the two ends of the chain. It also meant that if anyone knew for certain whether the Loki staff had been breaking the law, it had to be Lawrence. He must have had a set of notes about what he saw at the Loki facility, and his office was as good a place to look as any.

The office itself was cramped and austere and looked like it hadn't been used in weeks, which it hadn't, of course. At the back of the office was a stack of crates, and at the front was a simple desk welded to the wall like in any standard office. An automated cleaning drone buzzed back and forth across the floor, silently vacuuming up the dust collecting in the corners. Other than that, there wasn't much to see.

Aster sat down at the desk, and the holographic computer screen lit up in response to her presence, displaying the computer's main menu. Everyone had their own locked office, so nobody bothered to password-lock their computers. Besides, if it were code-locked, Aster could use her personal override code to access any project-related files she wanted – another way of abusing her authority as project-lead.

Cycling through the main menu, Aster came across a folder labelled 'Loki Observation Notes'. That was a little too easy to find. She opened the folder and scrolled through the notes. All of them were second-hand observations of experiments conducted by the Loki team along with Lawrence's comments. None of it was recent.

Aster kept glancing at the office door, fearing that someone might walk in and catch her looking through someone else's files. She knew of course that no one would; she was the only one on this floor with a personal override code. But the wrongness of what she was doing and the paranoia of being caught made it hard to concentrate.

Eventually, she stopped scrolling and threw her head back in silent frustration. Of course they were just second-hand observations; that was Lawrence's whole job. What exactly was she looking for, a written confession of guilt? If he had been kept in the dark, he wouldn't have known anything worth writing down in the first place; and if he had known, why would he leave behind evidence indicating his own complicity?

Aster got up to look at the collection of boxes stacked at the back. Would he have hidden anything in them? They were standard storage crates with a simple turn lock, not meant for storing anything valuable. She popped open one of the crates without much effort, finding old components and circuit boards inside. There was nothing immediately relevant to the project, let alone anything nefarious.

There were more boxes piled up at the back of the office, and Aster spent the next half hour rummaging through each of them. She found an assortment of worn-out parts, burnt out circuits, spare tools, an extra set of dirty engineer's overalls, and nothing else.

Aster slumped against the wall. Again, she had to ask herself: what exactly was she hoping to find? Lawrence hadn't been to this office in weeks, why would he have left anything incriminating behind? Every entry-level engineer and technician had their own office, but Lawrence's office was just a glorified storage closet.

The cleaning drone zipped along the edge of the wall, meticulously scrubbing the corners before vacuuming up the dust around Aster's shoes. Moving on, the drone found its path blocked by the pile of boxes. It paused its routines and hummed patiently, waiting for someone to clear the obstruction.

Aster looked at the drone curiously. Since Lawrence was hardly ever here, why would he bother having a cleaning drone in his office? She bent down and plucked the drone off the floor, flipping it over and examining the underside.

It was a simple, commercial model, though the counter-espionage techs would have scrubbed it for malicious components and software before allowing it into the building. It was an older model, too, moving about on six motorised wheels instead of an antigravity cushion. Wheels? Really? In an age when Humanity could make a 100,000-tonne spacecraft hover above the ground, why not a simple cleaning bot? However, that also meant the drone had a simple, pop-open panel on its underside.

Aster dug her nail into the groove and prised open the panel, exposing the components. There, hidden in the guts of the machine, was a red memory chip secured to the inside of the drone's casing by adhesive. This wasn't the kind of chip that a simple cleaning drone would need, in fact, it wasn't even connected to the drone's circuitry. The manufacturing code indicated that the chip could store at least a zettabyte of data.

Aster felt a leaden weight drop in her stomach. This kind of data chip was used to store and transport sensitive company information between locations rather than transmitting it through potentially insecure data links. The data chip, and whatever was on it, were proprietary material, and it clearly wasn't meant to be found.

Worming a finger into the circuitry, Aster peeled the chip cleanly away from the adhesive and held it up to the light. The weight in her stomach only grew heavier as she stared at the blood red data chip; but having come this far, she couldn't just leave it where she'd found it. Aster slipped the fingernail-sized chip into her pocket and hastily reassembled the drone, before placing it back on the floor where it resumed its mindless cleaning routine.

Then she fled the office.

* * *

After navigating the maze of service tunnels, the squad finally re-emerged into the main facility, itself a maze of pristine corridors and corporate offices. Ogilvy's increasingly faint tracking signal was heading towards the laboratories at the opposite end of the enormous facility; at least that's what their onboard maps were telling them.

Losing a comrade in the field was bad enough; having a comrade be taken prisoner was almost worse. You could make your peace with the death of a brother-in-arms and resolve to avenge him later, but if he was captured there was no telling what might be done to him in captivity. The bizarre ravings of the treacherous maintenance technician didn't give them any peace of mind, either; but that wasn't even the strangest thing.

The whole place was deserted.

The facility was supposed to be big enough for a staff of a thousand or more, and yet apart from Marcus Teller and his dead accomplice, they had yet to encounter another staff member. There was no way only two men could carry a fully armoured operator on their own, let alone whilst he was struggling and thrashing, so there had to be a lot more than just a dozen people in on the conspiracy.

So where was everyone?

To Gabriel, it was just as well that Ogilvy was being taken in the direction of their primary objective. Otherwise, this rescue mission was pure foolishness. As a soldier, he could certainly feel the need to rescue a brother-in-arms – or avenge him if he were killed, particularly one under his command. But if he had to choose between saving a soldier and completing the mission, he would have left Ogilvy to his fate. That wouldn't make him popular with the squad, but events seemed to be conspiring to unite the two priorities.

Ogilvy's weakening signal meant that his captors were widening the distance between them. That, or the signal was being jammed, a difficult thing to do. Eventually, the signal disappeared from the squad's sensors altogether.

"*Fuck!*" Doran cursed, "*Now all we have is his last known location.*"

"*It's better than nothing,*" Bale pointed out.

As they were speaking, Gabriel used his wrist-top computer and his command authority to deauthorise Ogilvy's ID and remove him from the squad's local network.

"*Woah! What the frick are you doing, Colonel?*" Viker demanded.

"*Using my command module to follow protocol,*" Gabriel replied, minding Viker's tone.

"*But you've cut him off from the squad's comm. system!*" Viker shot back, "*what if he gets free and tries to contact us?*"

"*He can still use his comm. to let us know that he's free again,*" Doran explained, "*but unless Colonel Thorn reinstates his ID, he won't be able to hear anything we say in reply.*"

"*And more importantly, neither will his captors,*" Gabriel added firmly, "*Once a squad member is MIA, their gear is to be considered compromised until proven otherwise.*"

Viker was silent.

"*Unless you would prefer to allow the enemy to listen in on us?*" Gabriel added.

"*No, sir,*" Viker acknowledged grudgingly.

"*Good,*" Gabriel answered, "*then let's go rescue Ogilvy.*"

The squad continued through the deserted facility until, at length, they reached the entrance to the laboratory complex. Ogilvy's tracking signal had vanished beyond the door, but he had definitely passed through this way.

The entrance was an atmospherically sealed door with a viewing window and another biometric lock, leading into a decontamination chamber. While the squad covered him, Doran planted Teller's severed hand on the biometric reader. The reader rejected the hand with a red light and an angry beep.

"*Figures,*" said Doran, tossing the now-useless hand aside, "*either they've de-authorised his biometric signature or he was never allowed in here in the first place.*"

"*It's another breach resistant door,*" noted Viker, running his hand around the edges of the door, "*Blast resistant too. Hard work even for a plasma torch.*"

"*So you can't cut through it?*" Gabriel asked.

"*I probably could,*" Viker replied doubtfully, "*but we'd be here all week.*"

"*I could try cracking the encryption, instead,*" Doran suggested.

"*Do it,*" Gabriel ordered.

The squad's motion trackers flashed red.

"*Contacts! Behind us!*" Bale shouted as the squad spun round to face the threat.

A silver object bounced off the wall at the far end of the corridor and slid to a halt in front of the laboratory door. Before the squad had time to take cover, the object detonated, releasing a wave of concussive force that sent them flying against the walls, temporarily scrambling their suits' sensors.

At the far end of the corridor, several creatures appeared from around the corner, bounding on all fours towards the squad with vicious, hungry snarls. Still climbing to their feet, the squad managed to raise their weapons fast enough to open fire, spraying flash-moulded pellets into the faces of the oncoming creatures.

Two of the creatures dropped dead before they could close the distance, their flesh and wiry sinews torn to shreds by the gunfire. But one of the creatures managed to evade most of the bullets – ignoring the few that grazed its body – and got close enough to leap into the air towards Gabriel, knocking him to the ground.

Gabriel found himself pinned down by a snarling mass of teeth and claws. His shields could protect him from extremes of pressure as well as block or deflect high-velocity objects like bullets or shrapnel, but they were no good against the beast's comparatively slow-moving teeth and claws. However, his armour still made him virtually invulnerable, and the creature's teeth fractured as it clamped its jaws around his gorget armour.

Someone managed to wrap an arm around the creature's belly and yank it away from Gabriel, tossing it back down the corridor. As the creature rolled across the floor and tried to scramble to its feet, someone else shot it with a single round. The bullet penetrated at the base of the creature's neck, punching straight through the vertebrae, and almost severing its head in one go. Death was instantaneous.

"*Thanks for the assist,*" Gabriel said.

He picked up his weapon and jumped back to his feet. With the immediate threat apparently neutralised, Doran returned to work on the door lock's encryption while Cato covered the corridor in case of other threats. The rest of the squad turned to examine the vicious animals that had attacked them.

The three creatures were vaguely canine in appearance, but bioengineered beyond recognition as normal dogs. They had grotesquely enhanced musculature and elongated snouts lined with razor-sharp teeth. Upon closer inspection, their teeth and claws had a dull grey sheen to them. They had been coated with nanopolymer, strong enough to make the enamel and keratin that made up the teeth and claws much sharper and more durable.

There was something else visible in the mutant creatures' ruined flesh. Gabriel stuck his gauntlet into the mangled meat of the mutant canine, and plucked out a single sinew of muscle, holding it up to the light. It was a dull grey colour and was strongly elastic. Holding both ends, he tugged sharply on the strand, but no matter how hard he pulled on it, the strand of muscle wouldn't snap.

"*Synthetic muscle tissue?*" Bale asked, crouching down beside Gabriel for a look.

"*Looks like it,*" Gabriel concurred.

"*Who the frick would do this sort of thing to animals?*" Viker said in disgust.

As if to answer Viker's question, the squad's motion trackers flashed red again.

"*Another contact!*" Cato shouted a little redundantly.

The squad snapped back to attention and trained their weapons on the newest threat, closing ranks to cover Doran as he worked on the door lock.

A lone figure stood motionless at the far end of the corridor, clad in a jet-black suit. The silhouette looked vaguely female, but it was difficult to tell. The squad's networked sensor suite couldn't make heads or tails of her, but all she did was stand there, watching them intently whilst making no effort to take cover or attack them. Gabriel altered a setting on his weapon, switching from full-automatic to a single, high-powered shot.

"*One shot from me,*" Gabriel said, crouching down on one knee, "*kill burst from you.*"

The squad understood exactly what he meant, and readied their weapons accordingly. Gabriel's helmet optics were synced with his weapon's electronic sights, so there was no need for an old-fashioned targeting scope. His HUD marked the target with a red outline and zoomed in for greater detail, projecting a virtual targeting reticle on the mysterious figure.

With a clear image of the target now filling his HUD, Gabriel could see that the figure was indeed female, and the jet-black suit she was wearing was combat armour, albeit not a kind he had ever seen before, lacking any visible protective plating. Her helmet was bulbous looking, like a classical drawing of an alien without any features drawn on, and she wasn't carrying any sort of weapon, not even a simple sidearm.

Gabriel took dead aim at the eerily calm target's head, his helmet labelling the range as 38.913 metres, a reasonably close range.

Just as he was about to squeeze the trigger, the figure slowly raised a hand and traced a finger across the back of its other hand.

The biometric lock chimed approvingly and the reinforced door slid open, breaking the squad's focus as they reacted to the unexpected sound behind them.

"*We're in!*" Bale said, relieved, "*Good job, Doran!*"

"*I didn't do anything,*" Doran replied, mystified.

Gabriel snapped his attention back to the mysterious target. She was gone.

"*What do you mean you 'didn't do anything'?*" Viker demanded of Doran.

"*I mean the decryption program needed another few minutes,*" Doran answered, "*something or someone opened the door for us.*"

"*Who wants to bet our mystery target opened it?*" Gabriel asked rhetorically.

"*Codename 'black widow' for later?*" Cato suggested.

"*Sounds good to me,*" Gabriel replied.

The squad filed into the decontamination chamber and the door sealed behind them, the chamber filling with anti-hazard gas. The three mutant canine corpses were still visible through the now-clouded glass, bleeding out in the corridor like piles of discarded meat.

But the 'black widow' was nowhere to be seen.

* * *

Slipping out of Lawrence's office like a thief – which now, she technically was – Aster powerwalked down the deserted corridor back to her office, hoping to reach the safety and privacy of her own office before someone saw her.

"Dr Thorn!" a voice called out from behind her.

Aster froze up. Had she been caught already?

She turned around slowly as someone approached; a young woman with a ponytail and a tablet computer in hand. One of the newer hires.

"I just wanted to update you on the reactor core simulations we've been running," she said, sounding slightly out of breath as she showed Aster a table of results on her tablet, "all the metrics look green."

Aster inclined her head to examine the graph of results; her muscles were rigid and her heart was pounding with the guilty fear of being caught.

"Looks good to me," Aster assured the woman woodenly, "email me the results directly and I'll take a look at them later."

"We won't know for sure until we do live-testing–" the junior engineer began.

"I know, I know," Aster answered, anxious to end the conversation, "but without authorisation from the board, we can't do any live-testing. Good work though."

"Thanks…Dr Thorn," the junior engineer answered, puzzled by her boss's less than enthusiastic attitude, "I'll send you the results in a minute."

"Good. See you later, then."

Aster abruptly turned on her heel and headed back to her office. She didn't stop walking until she had sealed and locked the door behind her.

Though safe from prying eyes, she couldn't bring herself to heave a sigh of relief. There was no relief to be had now. Unless she handed over the data chip to the authorities, she was now officially complicit in whatever Lawrence had been involved in.

Aster fished the little red memory chip out of her pocket and stared at it. Logically speaking, Lawrence wouldn't have gone to the trouble of hiding the chip if it didn't contain important information, particularly information that he'd wanted to hide from his colleagues, or even from the company itself.

Aster gulped at that thought. Normally, the stovepiped nature of the R&D process meant that the company board would be willfully ignorant of the actual research activities, the better to reap high returns from questionable sources, and the better to sweep any incidents under the rug. But if Lawrence had evidence that the company board had direct knowledge of the incident; that would have made him a loose end…

Still staring at the blood red chip, Aster's head was swimming with unmade decisions. Should she look at the data at all or leave well enough alone? Should she access the data here in the labs or somewhere offsite? Should she hand over the data chip to her employers and risk a criminal complicity charge from the DNI, or give it to the DNI and risk getting permanently blacklisted from the private sector?

The first decision was easy enough. Having taken the data chip, she may as well find out what was on it; but that still left the question of where to access the data from. The board of directors would be scrambling to contain news of the incident and rumours of malfeasance on their part. They would also be vigilant for employees seeking to jump ship by using stolen corporate secrets as leverage.

All computer workstations had spyware installed to guard against corporate espionage from a turncoat employee, so accessing the data here in the lab would necessarily alert her superiors. However, taking the data chip offsite was also out of the question. Even if she could get it past the security scanners undetected, the data was corporate property and she would be stealing from her employers by taking it out of the building.

Finally, whether or not she looked at the data herself, there remained the question of what to do with it. Accessing the data on a computer with company spyware on it would make running to the DNI afterwards a problem, whereas simply giving back what already belonged to the company might make the problem go away.

But there was also Gabriel's position to consider. There were any number of ways in which she could be caught, all of which could burn Gabriel if his own wife was found to be involved in criminal activity, especially if it involved xenotechnology.

Whereas if she went to *his* bosses instead of her own, it might earn them both points. As much as nepotism disgusted her, surely their marriage had to count for something.

Aster clenched her fist around the data chip to hide it from her sight. People were dead because of the data she was holding, and the blood red colour was a far too literal reminder of that fact. Just looking at it made her stomach churn as much as her mind.

It was also proving difficult to shake the unnerving thought that the company might simply cut her and the others loose once it knew for certain that anything incriminating had been safely locked away. The board of directors had already effectively sacrificed hundreds of their own employees to protect themselves, why wouldn't they do the same to the rest of their workforce? In that case, there was no reason for Aster to alert them to the fact that she had the data. She would have to hide the chip first, then go to the DNI.

Aster cast a fresh eye around her office. Where could she hide the data chip in case her office was searched again? The workstation was no good since that was the first place anyone would think to look. What about the furniture? No. A decent scanner would detect anything electronic stuffed under the cushions. She couldn't dismantle her computer and try to hide the data chip inside, and making a hidey-hole in the wall or floor also wasn't possible.

There were no good hiding spots in her office. Come to think of it, why hide it in her office at all? If she came under suspicion, her office would be the most obvious place to search. She would have to hide the memory chip somewhere else in the building.

Aster stuffed the chip back into her pocket and took a deep breath to calm herself. No one was any the wiser, and Felix had been convinced to drop the issue. She was still in charge of this research section, and in the absence of instructions from the board of directors, everyone was looking to her for direction. That ought to make it easier.

She left her office and took the elevator down to the primary testing floor where the actual 'project' was being built. It was a concert hall-sized space, with a dozen little workshops scattered all over, all revolving around the project itself: an experimental fusion reactor the size of a sky-car. The reactor frame was double the size, however, covered as it was in a jungle of wires, cables, and supporting equipment.

It was the work of several years' research and another year's worth of construction and was almost ready for activation, and yet the incident on Loki could sink J.E. Co. and render the whole project redundant. It was a shame to think it might be moth-balled before they had gotten a chance to see if it worked. Then again, it was potentially based on xenotechnology research; how many lives had been lost to build it?

Acting as casually as possible, Aster made her way to the side office at the far end of the testing floor. The side office stored a variety of things, mostly spare tools and computers, but in pride of place was the activation key safe. The safe had a biometric lock, preventing anyone except the project-lead or one of the company directors from accessing it.

Aster allowed the scanner to flash-scan her eyes and the safe door popped open in response. Then she plucked the red data chip from her pocket and stuffed it in the far corner of the safe, shutting the door before anyone could walk in on her. The chip was safe for now. Unless, of course, someone with more authority than her decided to look inside.

Aster left the side office and headed back the way she had come across the testing floor, only to freeze up when she saw who was coming the other way. It was Felix – of all people. Had he seen her leave the side-office? Would he try and get her to change her mind about something she had just done?

Felix was still walking in her direction but apparently hadn't noticed her. She started walking again, trying to keep her pace slow and steady. As they walked past each other, their eyes met for a split second before quickly averting again.

The awkwardness was cringe-inducing, but at least she was safe from suspicion.

* * *

The main conference room in J.E. Co.'s corporate offices was swanky and spacious, with an oval conference table carved from bioengineered wood, and lined with comfortable, high-backed chairs. An entire wall of the conference room was a single pane of glass, providing a sweeping, panoramic view of Asgard City.

No one dared stop to enjoy the view, however, because the boss was furious.

"Who does that bitch think she is?!" Chairman Darius raged at nobody in particular, pounding his fists furiously against the table, "first she shorts my stock, then she brings over some military prick to threaten me, then she rats me out to the fleeking spooks?!"

One of the intimidated spectators opened his mouth to point out that there was no proof Jezebel Thorn had tipped off the DNI, then thought better of it.

"This could sink the entire company," Darius continued, growing short of breath from the effort of venting his anger, "The Loki rumours alone made the stock price tumble 15%. When the media finds about the DNI raid...or worse still, if they find out about the missing security team we sent in..."

The chairman was silent for a moment as his anger ran out of steam. The assembled staff waited with baited breath, wanting to be sure that their boss's temper really had died down.

"We've...finished screening all the staff," someone announced nervously.

Darius looked up with interest, a signal that it was safe to continue talking.

"Based on an analysis of staff members' personalities, behavioural patterns, and personal circumstances, we were able to cross—"

"I don't know what any of that means," Darius said impatiently, his hardened tone warning the man to get to the point.

"…No one we looked at has done anything to warrant suspicion," the security officer said, knowing full well that the chairman wouldn't be happy with that answer.

"In other words, you're telling me that you didn't find the mole," Darius answered. It wasn't a question, it was a statement tinged with anger.

"Sir, we don't know for certain that there is a mole," someone else in the security team spoke up, not wanting to leave his colleague to face the storm alone.

"Of course there's a mole!" Darius bellowed, his temper reigniting, "How else would Jezebel Thorn have known that the Loki facility had gone dark before the rumours came out?"

Again, no one dared to contradict the chairman, especially since his logic actually made some sense this time. Instead, a security technician stepped forward with a flexi-computer and laid it out on the table for the chairman to see.

"We did flag these individuals as warranting extra attention," he said.

Chairman Darius looked over with interest. Then his interest turned to puzzlement.

"What the fleek is all this supposed to be?" he demanded.

"Bribery and blackmail are the two most common ways to recruit a double agent," the security technician explained, "so by compiling and cross-referencing information on the personal circumstances and private lives of the staff, we can determine who is most vulnerable to being recruited as a mole."

"And thereby find out who the mole is," Darius concluded, sounding encouraged.

The security technician wasn't actually going to say that but kept his mouth shut.

The names on the list included, among others, an applied mathematician who liked to frequent strip clubs, a married junior accountant who was having a lesbian affair, and a metallurgist with medical bills.

"What about this person?" Darius tapped one of the names.

"Dr Lawrence Kane," the security technician said, "He was the liaison officer for the Loki facility. He's a loner, likes to drink at bars alone, and occasionally brings home a prostitute. He was also diagnosed with some kind of blood disorder five years ago."

"Pitiful loser," Darius sneered, "He'd be an easy target."

"However, he's been up at the Loki facility for the past few weeks," the technician continued sceptically, "which means he's probably dead by now."

"That doesn't mean he wasn't a mole when he was alive," Darius pointed out, "look into him, just in case. Who else is there?"

"There's also the lead scientist for the reactor project," the technician said, highlighting her name from the list, "Dr Aster Thorn."

"'Thorn'?" Darius growled, his fingers curling into fists at the mention of the name.

"By marriage," the technician clarified, "it's not her maiden name."

"Even so, there's no fleeking way that's a coincidence!" the chairman exclaimed with absolute certainty, "Does she tick any other boxes of suspicion?"

"No, she doesn't," the technician replied, warily but truthfully, "She's originally from the colonies, happily married, four kids, no criminal record or history of questionable behaviour, and an excellent credit score. Other than the coincidence of names and her colonial background, her profile gives her the weakest probability of being a mole."

"Check her again," Darius ordered, "Do a deep probe of her if you have to. There's no way that slippery snake Jezebel wouldn't consider recruiting a family member or an in-law."

"We can check her workplace activity," the technician suggested, "See if she's tried to requisition any equipment or use her personal override code."

"Do it," Darius ordered, snapping his fingers commandingly at the other technicians. They nodded and hastily departed the conference room. The technician waited until he was alone with the chairman before continuing.

"We also did a search for this 'Gabriel' person," the technician said.

"What did you find?" Darius demanded.

"This," the technician answered, opening up a separate file.

It was marked: '*Access Denied: Tier 2 classification*'.

"I see," Darius said simply, his eagerness for revenge evaporating in an instant, "forget about him. Focus on Kane and Thorn."

* * *

The squad exited the decontamination chamber and fanned out to secure the area. They found themselves in another atrium, more spacious and high class than the first waiting lounge, and with holographic screens displaying soothing images and sounds from nature.

"Welcome to the Research Labs," the android receptionist said congenially, "please check in at the front desk before–"

Viker silenced the android with a single headshot. The round punched a hole clean through the robot's forehead, blowing out the back of its head in the process and spraying shattered electronics against the back wall.

No one questioned Viker's decision. Any amateur techie could reprogram an android to be hostile. Furthermore, the squad no longer had the element of surprise, and there was no telling what kind of booby-traps might have been rigged in anticipation of their arrival.

There was one detail, however, that arrested the squad's attention, one which looked decidedly out of place in this otherwise generic corporate lounge. It was a message scrawled on the wall above the front desk in dark red capital letters:

'KNOWLEDGE SETS YOU FREE'.

Cato climbed up onto the desk and swiped his hand across the bottom part of the right-hand '*E*'. The sensors in his gauntlet confirmed what they suspected.

"*Blood. Human,*" Cato confirmed grimly, "*But not Ogilvy's, thankfully.*"

The letters were enormous, too large for one person to have provided all the blood. That still left open the question of what kind of psychopaths would kill people just to daub giant slogans on the walls in their blood.

"*Colonel,*" Bale asked, "*what exactly are we looking for here?*"

"*No one goes to this amount of trouble just to kill a prisoner,*" Gabriel reasoned, "*Whatever they want with Ogilvy, they'll need to get his armour off first.*"

"*The medical bay, then?*" Cato suggested.

"*That's as good a place to start as any,*" Gabriel resolved.

Gabriel took point as the squad proceeded down the eerily deserted corridors, following the signs on the walls towards the medical bay. The whole place resembled a deserted hospital from a classical horror film with perfectly perpendicular walls and floors, and the eerie absence of people; even the lights were flickering to complete the effect.

Perhaps 'mental asylum' was a more appropriate metaphor. The walls, ceilings, and floors were covered with disturbing writing; bizarre slogans and phrases crudely daubed in block capitals, and in what was almost certainly also Human blood.

'TO KNOW GOD IS TO BE GOD'.

'SUBMISSION MEANS PEACE'.

The sinister invocations of the divine became creepier and creepier as they proceeded through the eerily deserted corridors. Warnings about monsters and demons in the dark, awe-filled references to the 'Temple' and the 'Voice', and many other pseudo-religious babblings covered virtually every surface.

There was also more esoteric graffiti: long passages of text written in an indecipherable script that the squad's suit computers didn't recognise. Alongside these were complicated mathematical and chemical equations scrawled on the walls like devotional art.

The squad turned yet another corner into one last corridor leading towards the medical bay. Painted on the floor, next to the fundamental theorem of calculus, was one piece of writing that was refreshingly straightforward: 'FUCK THE CORPORATES!'

"*At least we agree on something,*" Cato remarked.

"*Just how many people worked here?*" Viker wondered aloud, changing the subject.

"*Officially, around 1000,*" Doran reminded him.

"*Yeah, the 'official' number is clearly bollocks,*" Viker retorted, "*We've encountered a grand total of three people so far, and two of them are corpses.*"

"*Leave it to Viker to complain about a LACK of things to kill,*" Cato joked.

"*Hey, I just want to know where everybody is,*" Viker answered, "*Also, how in Terra's name did J.E. Co. manage to build a facility this big right under our noses in a major star system? Is the DNI's intel really that bad?*"

"*Any insights, Colonel?*" Doran asked.

"*I agree,*" Gabriel responded, "*normally illegal labs like this are small and hidden out on the frontier. But this place must have taken years and cost tens billions of credits to construct, and probably a lot more to keep it secret.*"

"*What are you saying, sir?*" Bale asked.

"*I'm saying that either there was an awful lot of corporate – and possibly political – buy-in to this project,*" Gabriel clarified ominously, "*or something about this location meant that the base couldn't have been built anywhere else. Maybe both.*"

Without warning, the lights died. The squad closed ranks as their visors readjusted, then two office doors slid open on either side of them simultaneously and the squad opened fire.

Bale shot one target through the wrist, who screamed in agony as his hand was severed clean off, his fingers still wrapped around a grenade. The other target opened fire with an auto-pistol, hitting Viker in the back. His shielding deflected the shots, and Doran returned fire, three controlled bursts eviscerating the target's organs.

Cato and Gabriel covered the corridor while Doran and Bale secured the two rooms.

"*Clear!*" each of them shouted in turn.

The attacker who'd lost his hand was still alive. He lay on the floor, groaning in pain and struggling to breathe, clutching the mangled remains of his wrist.

Bale stowed his weapon and picked the captive up by the throat.

"Where's the prisoner?" Bale questioned him through his helmet speakers.

"Go to hell!" the prisoner spat back defiantly.

Bale paused for a moment.

"You first," he replied, snapping the man's neck with an audible crack and discarding him on the ground like a limp doll.

"*If killing the lights is their only plan for slowing us down,*" Cato remarked, "*this'll be an awful lot easier than I thought.*"

"*Found something,*" Doran announced.

Still covering the corridor, the squad filed into the room Doran had secured, stepping over the bleeding corpse on the floor. They found themselves in a small security room with banks of computers and security monitors. The monitors were dead, the computers had been powered down, and the equipment lockers had been emptied of their contents.

Doran held up a datapad that had been discarded on the table.

"*Looks like they were worried about an infiltrator,*" Doran said, scrolling through its contents, "*listen to this: 'the walls have eyes and the floors have ears. Dani is watching and listening, an agent of the fricking corporates and government spooks. The Voice has whispered to me that only the Temple can be deemed safe; fall back there and leave her to watch over nothing and listen to silence'."*

"*What the fuck does all that mean?*" Cato asked rhetorically, "*Apart from the fact that they have a leader who receives instructions from voices in his head.*"

"*'The walls have eyes and the floors have ears',*" Gabriel said pensively, "*could there be spyware in the system?*"

"*That's what I think,*" Doran replied, "*It would explain why the computers were shut down; and if it had root access, it could hijack all the security camera feeds.*"

"*That doesn't mean there wasn't an infiltrator,*" Bale replied sceptically, "*Assuming those aren't just paranoid rantings, if there really is spyware in the system, someone would have had to plant it in the system. Perhaps someone called 'Dani'.*"

"*That doesn't make sense,*" Viker objected, "*if 'Dani' is a Human mole, then retreating to some stronghold further back wouldn't root him out.*"

"*Well, what else would 'Dani' refer to?*" Bale asked.

"*I don't know,*" Viker admitted defensively, "*a codename, a metaphor, a figment of the facility's staff's imagination, it could be anything—*"

"*It doesn't matter who or what Dani is,*" Gabriel interjected, cutting short the discussion, "*We can find out more on the way to the objective.*"

"*The medical bay is on the other side of the 'live-testing hall', whatever that is,*" Doran said as he consulted the map, "*it should be at the other end of this corridor.*"

Practically on cue, the door at the far end of the corridor opened, letting in a beam of light from the other side that forced the squad's visors to readjust yet again.

"*New contact!*" Gabriel shouted.

The squad exited the room and took aim at the source of light.

A figure appeared, standing on the other side of the doorway, partially obscured by the light behind him. Though difficult to make out, the figure was dressed in a technician's overalls with the J.E. Co. logo instead of body armour and was apparently unarmed. Of course, this wasn't the first time they'd encountered a supposedly harmless techie.

Gabriel primed a single high-powered shot and crouched down on one knee, taking dead aim at the silhouette's head. His helmet's optical suite was equipped with a variety of visual filters, and the software darkened the otherwise blinding halo of light around the target whilst highlighting the target itself in enough detail to line up a clear shot.

Then the doors shut again, plunging the corridor back into darkness.

Somewhere, deep down beneath the layers of training and psychological conditioning that had made him a voidstalker, Gabriel was starting to feel a rankling hatred for this deranged enemy. They had brazenly kidnapped a member of his squad and were using his life to lure them deeper into this Mastermind-forsaken deathtrap.

Gabriel didn't mind deathtraps. He did mind being mocked on his way through one.

"*Everyone,*" Gabriel growled over the comm., "*On me.*"

The squad followed Gabriel's lead as they walked towards the door, weapons raised and ready to shoot. 'Walk to your death, don't run', the drill instructors always said.

The door light was green; it was open and didn't need to be breached. Doran and Viker leaned against the door on either side whilst Cato, Bale, and Gabriel crouched down with weapons ready. Doran stretched out his free hand above the electronic lock, indicating a countdown with his fingers. Four…three…two…one…

On zero, Doran tapped the green button and the doors slid open.

With weapons raised, the squad emerged into the 'live-testing hall': a cavernous chamber with a domed roof illuminated by floodlighting high up on the ceiling. The walls were lined with supplies and mechanical gear, but the centre of the chamber had been cleared to create a big open area that looked like an arena. Exactly like an arena.

In the centre of the chamber was a giant metal frame equipped with restraint clamps and a set of robotic arms. Housed in the frame was a mobility-platform: a piloted mechanical walker twice the height of a Human, consisting of an armoured cockpit with mechanical legs and arms. Mobility-platforms were typically used for heavy lifting.

This one was equipped with military-grade weaponry.

The squad froze. They kept their weapons trained on the threat, but it wasn't clear they could win this fight; at least not without heavy weapons or explosives. They had been lured out into the open against a threat they weren't equipped to fight, with limited cover and nowhere to which they could fall back.

A klaxon sounded and yellow lights flashed around the mobility-platform's support frame as the restraint clamps were retracted. The walker took a slow, heavy step forward and stomped its foot down loud enough to echo throughout the chamber.

"*Cover, now!*" Gabriel shouted.

He took aim and fired.

THE MOLE

ETERNITY passed before the work day finally ended. Doing the same checks and diagnostics again and again while waiting for instructions from above was mind-numbingly tedious, and the cloud of scandal and uncertainty that hung over the place didn't help either. The project was pretty much ready, but with the company's future in doubt, there was no point in the board of directors authorising a final test.

That was the least of Aster's worries as she passed through the security checkpoint with everyone else. Except for a smartphone – which had to be checked in and out of storage – nothing electronic was allowed in or out of the building. Barring a power failure, smuggling the data chip out of the building would be next to impossible. Still, it was safely tucked away inside the activation key safe, so she could figure out what do with it later.

Aster joined a group of other people in the elevator back up to the station. Awkwardly, Felix was part of that group, and she tried to stand as far away from him as possible. The two spent an incredibly uncomfortable minute trying not to exchange glances; Felix started typing out a message on his smartphone whilst Aster stared intently at the wall. The hypocrisy of doing exactly what she had refused to allow him to do was almost too much to bear.

When the elevator doors finally opened, Aster all but fled the awkward space, racing to the platform and joining the tussle to get aboard the first mag-train that turned up. Only when the doors had closed and the mag-train had started moving did she start to breathe normally. After a ten minute ride to the medical centre, she could pick up the children, hail a sky-car, and they'd all be home before sundown.

Aster looked out the carriage window and took in the breath-taking scene before her. The first time she had seen it was almost a decade ago, and the shimmering forest of skyscrapers still looked like a heavenly citadel to her; a far cry from the tiny mining colony where she had grown up. But as she looked out on the man-made vista below, Aster's sense of awe was tinged by a familiar emotion, like a bad aftertaste: resentment.

Like hundreds of other frontier colonies – not to mention the intermediate hub-worlds – her own home planet had supplied some of the ore that had gone into building this city. The pay-per-tonne offered by the corporates was usually paltry, the better to sell it on at a profit to the manufacturers.

The whole arrangement was a racket in which the frontier worlds were bled dry to sustain the core worlds. As a consequence, most of the frontier worlds were desperately poor. Few could afford to go it alone, and many survived on financing from the same corporate parasites who fleeced them. Parasites like Jezebel Thorn.

Aster's smartphone buzzed, informing her of a new message. She fished it out of her pocket, and her face darkened when she saw who it was from.

'*I need to speak with you, urgently*,' said the message from Jezebel Thorn.

As Aster glared at the screen, a follow-up message arrived.

'*Ignoring this message would be inadvisable.*'

Was that a warning or a threat? Knowing her, it was probably both.

'*I'm picking up my children from their check-up*,' Aster messaged back, then put her smartphone back in her pocket.

It buzzed again almost immediately.

'*Already done. Come here first.*'

Aster's heart leapt into her mouth. Had Jezebel picked up the children from the medical centre without her permission? That seemed to be what she was saying.

'*Where?*' she messaged back.

* * *

"*Cover, now!*" Gabriel shouted.

He took aim and fired, squeezing off a single, high-powered shot at the titanic mobility-platform. A flash of blue energy covered its armoured skin as its shields activated. Unfazed by the shot, the mobility-platform extended one of its arms and Gabriel dived into cover with the rest of the squad as it opened fire.

Literally opened fire. From the mouth of the nozzle mounted on its right arm spewed a stream of bright orange flames at high speed. The squad barely made it into cover as the infernal jet doused the floor and wall, leaving black scorch patterns wherever it touched.

But the flames didn't persist, they dissipated almost as soon as the jet of flame had ceased, and the jet itself didn't drop with gravity whilst travelling through the air. It must be a pressurised gas mixture, maybe even plasma based. If that was the case, then the fire would burn at a much higher temperature than a liquid fuel.

The mobility-platform stomped towards them like a heavy-weight wrestler, bringing its railgun-equipped left arm to bear, and taking aim at the cargo crates. A single, supersonic round tore through the boxes, eviscerating their contents, and leaving Bale and Doran exposed. Bale managed to scramble to cover, but Doran was thrown to one side by the blast.

The whole squad opened fire as the mobility-platform advanced on Doran, who rolled onto his back and sprayed bullets on full auto at the advancing mechanical enemy. It didn't do any good; the mobility-platform's shielding rippled and flashed with sapphire-coloured light as the hypersonic rounds were deflected to either side.

Doran was a sitting duck as the mobility-platform focused on him exclusively. He tried too late to scramble to his feet, and the mechanical walker took a swing with one of its arms, knocking him back down to the ground. He was helpless as the mobility-platform raised its mechanical foot and stomped down on him.

"*Doran!*" one or more squad members screamed as their squad-mate bore the full weight of a multi-tonne metal foot crushing him.

Doran's life-signs turned red, and so did Gabriel's vision.

Violating every possible rule of combat training, Gabriel broke cover and ran straight towards the mobility-platform. Taking a running jump, Gabriel removed an explosive from his belt and leapt into the air, the exoskeletal motors in his combat armour boosting him by several feet. He primed the explosive in mid-jump and landed on the mobility-platform's back, shoving the explosive into the mechanical enemy's shoulder joint.

A flurry of crackling energy erupted between himself and the mobility-platform as their shielding interacted in a dramatic feedback loop. The resulting interaction produced mutual repulsion, sending Gabriel flying backwards in a spectacular storm of energy and light. As he hit the ground, he rolled back onto his feet in one movement.

The explosive Gabriel had used was a special anti-armour limpet mine equipped with a shield dampener. When it detonated, the shaped charge directed all of the explosive force down into the mechanical joint of the mobility-platform's right arm.

The heat and power of the detonation ate straight through the arm joint like acid through plastic, and the mobility-platform's flamethrower-equipped arm was blown clean off. It clattered to the floor like a chunk of scrap metal, leaving only a glowing orange stump and damaged, spark-spitting circuitry.

Both Gabriel's and the mobility-platform's shields had been frazzled out by the feedback interaction and would need a minute to recover. But even though the mobility-platform had lost its shields, its armour was still virtually impervious to small arms fire. Even having lost an arm, it was only marginally less dangerous.

After regaining its balance and focus, the mobility-platform's torso swivelled all the way around on its waist to face Gabriel and walked backwards in his direction. Its targeting optics singled him out, painting him with an infrared targeting laser as it lined up a shot with its railgun. In the half-second before the mobility-platform opened fire, Gabriel noticed something about the glass canopy protecting the pilot: it was cracked.

Gabriel dived to one side as the railgun fired, the shot just missing him as he vaulted over a set of storage crates and into cover. The railgun was a single-shot cannon with a slow rate of fire; a weapon that large could only carry a limited amount of ammunition. All Gabriel had to do was keep the mobility-platform wasting its ammo until it ran out. But then the doors on the other side of the testing hall opened and a new group of enemies appeared.

Four lithe figures dressed in beige-coloured flight suits entered, using special jump-packs to soar through the air towards the squad. Gabriel paused for a brief moment to wonder just where this bizarre cult had gotten their hands on so much military hardware before being plunged straight back into the fight.

Two of the jumpers came sailing over Gabriel's head, landing catlike on their feet and opening fire with sawn-off shotguns. The double spray of pellets battered his unshielded armour to no effect, and he quickly returned fire. To his surprise, all of his rounds hit their mark, punching straight through the faceplate and blowing apart the target's skull. Dispensing with armour and shielding? In favour of what, being quick on their feet?

As Gabriel dispatched one of the jumpers, the other dropped its weapon and activated a device on its wrist: a portable shield generator that projected a shimmering barrier of energy in an oval shape. Even at point-blank range, it was powerful enough to deflect Gabriel's bullets, sending them swerving off to each side.

With its personal barrier still raised, the jumper reached over its shoulder with its free hand and drew a sword from its back. A sword? An actual sword? Gabriel wanted to laugh. Instead, he charged at his skinny foe, clenching his fist to unleash his combat claws and finish off his attacker up close.

The jumper bolted forwards at the same time to meet Gabriel head-on; in the same motion it activated a switch on the handle of the sword and brought the blade swinging round in an arc to meet Gabriel's combat claws. There was a high-pitched whining sound as they connected, and the sword's blade kept on slicing through the air.

Gabriel was stopped dead in his tracks. His combat claws were made of reinforced carbon nanotubing, the same material as his armour. But the sword had cut clean through them, leaving behind three polished stumps. What kind of weapon could do that?

The jumper didn't miss a beat, completing the motion by spinning on its heel and trying to follow through with a stab to Gabriel's gut. Gabriel kept enough of his wits about him to dodge the thrust and grab his attacker by the wrist. In the same motion, he kicked the jumper's legs out from under it and snapped its wrist, catching the sword as it fell from the jumper's grasp and severing its arm in one stroke.

Another railgun shot narrowly missed Gabriel's head and punched a scorching hole in the wall beside him. He rolled into cover, dropping the sword, and picking his gun up off the floor. Keeping low and rushing back around towards the main entrance, he pulled another explosive from his belt.

Gabriel's earlier shot must have gotten through before the mobility-platform's shielding had activated. Normally for a vehicle that size, the pilot could simply look out through the glass canopy to see, but the enormous spider web-like crack left by Gabriel's lucky shot made that impossible, forcing the pilot to rely exclusively on the optical sensor suite.

Priming the grenade, Gabriel tossed it at the mobility-platform. The grenade's arc took it straight over the target before detonating. The damage to the mobility-platform's armoured skin was minimal, but the explosive spray of shards hit the optical sensor suite, blinding the mobility-platform's pilot. While the wounded mech was still reeling from the damage, Gabriel primed another high-powered shot, took aim, and fired.

A high-powered shot was a single round, flash-forged in such a way as to pierce armour, and accelerated to near-escape velocity. The mobility-platform's shielding was too weakened to block or deflect the shot as it punched straight through the damaged glass canopy, shattering it into thousands of pieces.

The mobility-platform froze up completely, the death of its pilot causing it to shut down. As its systems died, the mobility-platform's mechanical legs locked their joints to prevent it from toppling over, freezing the fearsome mech into an awkward-looking pose like a half-finished sculpture missing an arm and a face.

Keeping his weapon raised, Gabriel approached the mobility-platform to make sure it really had been neutralised. Through the smoke, he could see the pilot, now a piece of mangled meat with an entry wound through the chest. The rest of his flesh, including his respirator-covered face, had been sliced up beyond recognition by the storm of glass fragments.

But the evisceration of the pilot's body was nothing compared to his state when he had been alive. Not only was the respirator mask surgically attached to his face, but his entire body was filled with wires and tubes connecting him directly to the systems he controlled. The connections were so extensive that he was literally a part of the machine he piloted.

It was grotesque.

"*Colonel!*" Bale's voice came over the comm., "*Doran's alive! Barely.*"

Gabriel flinched. It hadn't even occurred to him to check on his squad.

"*Ok, I'm coming over*," he replied.

Gabriel rushed over to join the rest of his squad. He saw the other two jumpers lying dead on the floor. One had been shot through the guts with gunfire, the other had a cauterised neck stump instead of a head. Viker was standing over the headless jumper, replacing his combat knife in its sheath and confiscating the dead jumper's wrist-mounted personal barrier, whilst Cato and Bale tended to Doran.

Doran lay motionless on the floor where he had fallen as Cato ran his gauntlet over Doran's body, the sensor suite in his palm interacting with Doran's own armour to evaluate his condition. As he did, the results were uploaded to each squad member's suit computers.

The results looked dire.

Doran's armour had held against the multi-tonne weight and pressure of the giant mechanical foot, and his suit's shielding had negated much of the crushing pressure applied. But the sheer amount of force brought to bear had still been enough to break his ribcage in numerous places. In spite of his suit's pain suppressants, the agony of simply breathing would have caused him to pass out. Were it not for his shielding, armour, and physical enhancements, he would have been flattened like a pancake.

"*He's out cold, and his suit's systems have been badly damaged as well*," Cato explained gravely, "*if we don't get him to a proper medical facility quickly, we'll lose him.*"

"*The medical bay is on the other side of this chamber*," said Gabriel, "*move!*"

No one needed to be ordered twice. Cato and Bale took Doran by the arms and legs and hoisted him carefully into the air while Gabriel and Viker provided cover.

Gabriel spotted the surviving jumper take off and soar through the air towards the door through which it had come. He took a quick aim and squeezed off a shot, hitting the jumper in the back, and causing it to tumble from the air, rolling head over heels across the floor.

In spite of a broken wrist and a missing arm, the jumper had still had the presence of mind to pick up its sword and stow it on its back before trying to make a break for the exit. Gabriel's shot had damaged its jump-pack, rendering it useless; but the jumper continued to crawl with impressive determination across the floor towards safety.

Gabriel marched over to the wounded enemy and took aim, preparing to put it out of its misery, but then thought better of it. Stowing his weapon, Gabriel picked the scrawny enemy off the ground and took it prisoner, twisting its remaining arm behind its back.

"*Aren't you gonna kill that thing?*" Viker asked, bewildered by the apparent mercy.

"*Not yet,*" Gabriel replied.

* * *

The elevator doors opened on the 201st floor and Aster stepped out into the hallway of an opulent penthouse. The floor of the main hall had a blood red carpet – probably made from bio-engineered fur – and was lined with exquisitely carved statuettes in various poses; there was even a water feature depicting two aquatic monsters intertwined in a vicious embrace. The statuettes seemed to stare at Aster as she passed them; perhaps they were, it would be easy enough to install micro-cameras in the eyeholes.

Aster hurried past the creepy statuettes and turned a corner into a palatial living room. The arched ceiling was covered in a single giant fresco decorated with winged Humans dancing in the clouds, seeming to move ever so slightly. Completing the setting was a replica fireplace with flickering holographic flames, and a set of plush furniture arranged around the skin of some giant animal laid out on the floor as a trophy carpet.

Madam Jezebel Thorn sat on one of the couches, waited upon by two servant androids and an antigravity platter floating next to her. The hostess herself was dressed in a snow white business suit, her black hair with blonde streaks tied into her trademark corn-braid.

Aster gasped when she saw who else was there.

"Mommy!" her four children chorused in welcome.

They dropped what they were doing and came running to greet their mother. Aster squatted down and pulled her children into a protective embrace, squeezing them close, then gave her mother-in-law a murderous glare.

"I picked them up after their medical appointment was finished," Grandma Jezebel explained, "The poor things were exhausted, and bored."

"We're leaving," Aster said with a scowl.

"I haven't told you why you're here, yet," Jezebel said.

"I'm here to pick up my children," Aster shot back, "and then to find out how you managed to convince the medical centre staff to let you pick up my children."

"Lawrence Kane," the mention of the name made Aster freeze up.

"As a blood relative, I'm not recognised as a threat by the medical centre androids," Jezebel answered, "so why don't you have a seat and we can discuss this like grown-ups."

With profound reluctance, Aster took a seat opposite her hostess, and the children returned to their distractions. Orion, the oldest, picked up a tablet computer he had been playing with and sat down beside his grandmother while Rose and Violet returned to entertaining their younger brother Leo on the animal skin carpet.

"Would you like a drink?" Madam Jezebel asked.

"Tell me what you know about Lawrence Kane and why."

"I've heard he was a colleague of yours," Madam Jezebel replied, then added, "I've also heard that he wasn't entirely loyal to his employers."

Aster felt a wave of self-conscious dread wash over her. Was this Jezebel Thorn's way of telling her she'd been found out?

"Although, you surely suspected as much," Madam Jezebel added coolly.

As she spoke, she pulled out a tablet computer of her own and opened up a video file, then she placed it on the antigravity platter and gave it a tap. The platter floated silently over to Aster and landed on her lap. With trepidation, Aster picked up the tablet and pressed play, seeing an image of an office door secured with a biometric lock.

The colour drained from Aster's face when she saw herself appear on screen, open up the biometric sensor's panel and type in her personal override code to bypass the lock before slipping inside the office. The video then cut to a shot of her exiting Lawrence's office.

"Water," Madam Jezebel ordered the servant android with a snap of her fingers.

Aster was definitely thirsty. The service android returned with an ornate glass filled with water and offered it to Aster who took it and drained it to the dregs.

"What the fuck is this supposed to be?" Aster demanded.

"Do you usually talk that way around the children?" Madam Jezebel asked snidely.

The children were too engrossed in their activities to notice or care.

"Answer the question!" Aster snapped back, "What is this?"

"Something to secure your cooperation," Madam Jezebel replied.

"With what?" Aster asked, her eyes narrowing with suspicion.

"Retrieving something," Madam Jezebel replied, "and I think you know what it is."

"By asking me here, you're guilty of conspiracy to commit corporate espionage," Aster pointed out, hoping to turn the tables.

"And by coming, you're officially complicit," Madam Jezebel retorted breezily, "unless, of course, the real reason – the one you'd like me to corroborate if the investigators ask – is that you simply came to pick up your children from their grandmother's home."

Jezebel was right. This whole setup made her look bad, even without the incriminating video. Not to mention her head was swirling with the implications of what she had just been shown: someone in her staff was on Jezebel's payroll.

There were no surveillance cameras in the research labs, lest an outside hacker hijack the video feeds. That meant someone had to have either smuggled the camera in or built it from scratch using materials in the lab.

"…The data chip," Aster said hesitantly, "the blue one, that's what you're after."

"Your employer, Darius Avaritio, came to me some years ago to help finance a new facility on Loki," Madam Jezebel explained, "in return, I would get favourable stock options. Later, I found out he was deliberately undervaluing the company's stock and thereby cheating investors, including me."

"So you planted someone inside J.E. Co. to steal 'your' share of its intellectual property for your own business ventures," Aster concluded.

"Life is so much sweeter when someone else picks up the tab," Madam Jezebel said philosophically, "and the returns are so much higher when someone else does the hard work of research and development."

"Do you even care that hundreds of people are probably dead?"

"No, I do not," Madam Jezebel replied with sociopathic honesty, "Toying around with xenotech in the hopes of inventing the next trendy widget is like dismantling a fusion bomb to make a drum set. I want no part of that, and those who do are welcome to the consequences. But I *do* want my share of that ill-conceived investment back."

Oblivious to the tense exchange, seven-year-old Orion shuffled over to his grandmother and tugged on her sleeve. Grandma Jezebel looked at the tablet computer he was holding.

"No, sweetheart," she said helpfully, pointing to the exercises he was doing on screen, "that's meant to be the future-continuative conjugation. You 'will be doing' the verb."

"Thank you, grandma," Orion said with a smile, his father's luminescent green eyes shimmering under the light. Then he returned to playing with his tablet.

"It's so nice to have intelligent grandchildren," Grandma Jezebel beamed, making it sound as though she were taking credit for how smart they had turned out.

"I'm sure their grandfather would be proud," Aster quipped.

Madam Jezebel's implacably superior composure cracked. It was difficult to describe the expression she now wore on her face, but it was definitely not a calm one.

"On their mother's side, of course," Aster added, satisfied that her barb had worked.

"Bring me the data-chip," Madam Jezebel instructed her daughter-in-law imperiously, "and there won't be any problems."

"Understood," Aster replied as she got up to leave, "time to go, sweethearts."

Obediently, the children gathered up their things and lined up to say goodbye to their grandmother. Grandma Jezebel's composure returned as she kissed her grandchildren goodbye, then she snapped her fingers at one of the servant androids.

"Summon a taxi for five," she ordered the android.

"Thank you," Aster said with a courteous smile.

It was the least her fleekster mother-in-law owed her.

Without getting up from her seat, Madam Jezebel waved goodbye to her grandchildren. When the door had shut behind them, her smile disappeared.

"Frontier bitch," she muttered.

* * *

Gabriel forced the captured jumper's hand against the biometric scanner, and the door to the medical bay opened. Viker secured the room whilst Gabriel strapped his captive down to an examination bed using the patient safety restraints. Meanwhile, with immense care, Cato and Bale laid the unconscious and badly wounded Doran down on a surgical table, and a suite of robotic medical arms descended automatically from the ceiling to assess him.

He was barely alive.

"*The room's sealed*," Viker told everyone, "*We're secure in here.*"

Having tied down the prisoner, Gabriel came over to join the rest of the squad.

"*Doran's suit's taken too much damage*," Cato explained gravely, "*his shields and armour saved his internal organs from being crushed, but he's out of this fight.*"

"*Will he live?*" Bale asked.

"*The nanobots in his bloodstream should stave off the worst of the damage,*" Cato explained, "*but the best we can do right now is stabilise him.*"

The robotic medical arms paused in their work. The holographic patient monitoring screen displayed an error message: "*obstruction detected*".

"*It's his armour,*" Cato explained, "*We need to remove it.*"

"*Well, let's do it, then!*" Viker demanded.

"*Only the commanding officer can do that,*" Cato elaborated, looking to Gabriel.

"*Well, fricking hurry up and open it–*" Viker began to shout frantically.

"*STAND THE FLEEK DOWN!*" Gabriel barked, the volume of his voice making the rest of the squad flinch with surprise.

The squad, including Viker, stepped back as Gabriel approached the surgical table and placed the palm of his gauntlet against the cheek-plate of Doran's helmet, establishing a peer-to-peer connection between his own suit and Doran's.

"*Override. Lieutenant Doran, disassemble suit,*" Gabriel instructed Doran's suit computer, "*Victory. Sovereign. One. Seven. Zero. Seven.*"

The voice command was accepted and Doran's suit began to unlock and disassemble, the pieces unfolding and retracting like a sentient jigsaw puzzle. Only his respirator remained secured to his face. Doran's skin, visible through the under-suit, was a mess of fresh red bruising. His head looked unharmed, but lack of consciousness and a brush with death had turned his skin ghostly pale.

The error message disappeared and the robotic medical arms resumed their work, cutting open Doran's under-suit with an incredibly fine circular blade, and subjecting his torso to a series of microinjections, targeting the areas of most serious injury with cocktails of drugs mixed into a solution of nanobots.

"*It'll take a while to stabilise him,*" Cato explained, "*But we can't be certain if he'll make it, we need to get him back to a proper DNI facility.*"

"*We still have a mission to fulfil,*" Gabriel reminded everyone.

"*Frick the mission!*" Viker exclaimed, "*Ogilvy's missing and Doran's close to dead. The mission parameters have changed!*"

"*The mission parameters change when I say they change,*" Gabriel shot back, shutting Viker down without raising his voice.

"*Respectfully sir, they HAVE changed,*" Captain Bale pointed out, attempting to defuse the building tension, "*We can't rescue Ogilvy AND look after Doran without splitting up.*"

"*Then splitting up is exactly what we'll do,*" Gabriel replied with steel in his voice, "*This is still an IRS op., which means we still have to investigate the nature of the xenotech being studied here and find out how J.E. Co. acquired it in the first place. If you would prefer to abandon the mission, so be it.*"

"*You want to go alone, sir?*" Cato asked, his tone reflecting the squad's incredulity.

"*Going alone is the whole point of a voidstalker,*" Gabriel replied coldly.

The squad was silent.

"*Are we that much of a burden to you?*" Viker asked, a note of anger creeping into his voice, "*or did the DNI assign us to you as cannon fodder for this suicide mission?*"

"*If you were mere cannon fodder to me, I would have left Doran to die and Ogilvy to his fate,*" Gabriel replied truthfully.

The squad was silent again.

"*Tell me when Doran's condition improves, and see what you can find in the computer systems,*" Gabriel instructed the squad, "*I need to have a word with our prisoner.*"

"*Computers are Doran's field,*" Bale said doubtfully.

"*Then learn fast,*" Gabriel ordered him, "*we need as much intelligence as we can get, and right now the best place to find it is the computers.*"

Gabriel turned away and headed over to the captive. Besides the skin-tight flight suit, the jumper's entire head was contained inside a bulbous helmet with a reflective black visor. Its right arm had been cleanly severed at the elbow joint, and yet it made no attempt to struggle or break free. It didn't even show any signs of being in pain.

Gabriel reached under the jumper's helmet, feeling under the rim for a release switch. There was no switch that he could find or any other means of removing the helmet, but he still needed to take it off or cut through the jumper's helmet to speak to him.

Before making a run for it, the jumper had retrieved his sword, giving Gabriel an idea. The sword's sheath was actually a magnetic plate on a strap slung over the back of the jumper's suit, strong enough to hold the sword in place, but weak enough to allow the wielder to draw the sword by simply pulling.

Drawing the sword and placing the tip on the ground, Gabriel found that it came up to his hip, with the handle alone accounting for a quarter of the length. At the base of the handle was a little switch, and Gabriel flicked it with his thumb, causing the blade to shimmer.

With immense care, Gabriel placed the blade under the jumper's helmet and pressed against the chin. The blade sliced cleanly through the material, giving off only a faint whining sound with no smoke and no signs of heat or plasma scouring. The sword was almost certainly based on xenotechnology; in fact, it might even be an actual piece of xenotech. Once Gabriel had sliced clean through the jumper's helmet, he discarded the faceplate on the ground.

What he saw underneath disgusted him.

The jumper's androgynous face bore the marks of extensive cybernetic modification to the point that 'he' was barely recognisable as Human. His skin was a normal colour, but there were glowing signs of circuitry just visible underneath. His cybernetic eyes turned to regard Gabriel, and the corners of his lips curled into a grotesque smile.

"You took off my arm," the jumper rasped in an electronically enhanced voice.

"You took off my combat claws," Gabriel replied through his helmet speakers.

"And now you want to know the truth about this place," the jumper surmised with a leering grin, "Otherwise you would have killed me on the spot."

"How long has this facility been experimenting with xenotechnology?" Gabriel asked, deactivating the sword and laying it to one side.

"Five years," the prisoner replied.

"How long has J.E. Co. been smuggling xenotech and from where?" Gabriel asked.

"They didn't smuggle anything in," the prisoner answered, "it was already here."

"What does that mean?" Gabriel asked with narrowed eyes.

"It means exactly that," the prisoner explained, "the Temple was already here. This facility was built specifically to learn its secrets."

"What is the Temple?"

The prisoner's eyes lit up, literally. A blue glow from inside his pupils illuminated the circuitry inside his bionic eyes.

"You have to see it for yourselves."

"I asked you a question," Gabriel warned, drawing his knife, "What is the Temple?"

"No amount of pain will cause me to give you a different answer," the prisoner replied, "Besides, I am volunteering all of this information to you."

"I'll ask you one last time," said Gabriel menacingly, flicking the hilt-switch to flash-heat the blade of his knife, "what is the nature of the Temple?"

"It is far beyond the ability of mere Humans to comprehend, even I am not worthy to be enlightened with most of its secrets," the prisoner replied, unmoved by Gabriel's threats, "but it is alien in origin. You have to see it for yourselves to appreciate its glory."

The prisoner's words and expression were filled with sincere awe. This was not a rational POW resisting interrogation, this was a fanatic who did not care to save himself and practically dared Gabriel to venture into the 'Temple'.

"Why has there been so little resistance?" Gabriel continued his interrogation.

"Has the challenge been insufficient to satiate your lust for battle?" the prisoner asked.

Gabriel's already thin patience wore out, and he decided to test just how indifferent to physical agony the captive really was.

He took the prisoner's remaining hand – pausing briefly to note how baby-sized it was – then pressed the flash-heated blade of his knife against the wrist, slicing clean through the flesh and cauterising the wound in one go. The prisoner inhaled calmly then exhaled with relief, as though he were relaxing in a hot-tub instead of having his hand amputated.

"Pain sensation has been dulled to the point of triviality," the prisoner explained with a grotesque smile on his face, "the flesh's loss is the spirit's gain. It is of no consequence to those of us who have been enlightened."

Gabriel had performed countless field interrogations on subjects who resisted the pain as best they could before finally breaking. But he had never encountered a subject who seemed to actually enjoy it, let alone someone who calmly spouted pseudo-spiritualist nonsense to explain why they didn't mind the pain.

"You've been trying to lure us deeper into this place ever since we arrived," Gabriel pressed, deactivating his combat knife and returning it to its sheath, "I want to know why."

"I have already given you the answer to your question, DNI," the prisoner responded, "We want you to see the glory of the Temple for yourselves."

"Where is the entrance to the Temple?" Gabriel asked.

"At the far end of the laboratories you will find an elevator that will take you down to the Temple entrance," the prisoner replied obligingly, "the access code is 52133. No need to take my hand for biometric clearance."

The prisoner's imperviousness to torture meant that he didn't have to give away anything. He was volunteering this information – whether freely or as part of a larger plan – to goad Gabriel into leading his squad into an obvious trap. Worst of all, Gabriel had no choice but to take the bait being offered because the mission objective was inside the trap.

Furthermore, given what they now knew about this enemy, Ogilvy was almost certainly dead or worse. The squad had been banking on his armour to keep him alive and safe, but their crazed enemy had technology that could cut through even the toughest materials. Judging by the enhancements given to the mobility-platform pilot and the jumpers, it was almost certain that something similar had been done to Ogilvy.

In any case, the prisoner was of no further use.

"Now that you have no further use for me," the prisoner said, pre-empting Gabriel's thoughts, "you probably plan to kill me."

"Do you fear death?" Gabriel asked with an undertone of menace.

"No," the prisoner answered confidently, "at worst, I will be brought back with steel to replace the flesh you cut away, and at best, I will leave this material world completely."

Gabriel drew his gun.

"No need for that," the prisoner said.

Suddenly, his head snapped back violently and the cybernetic light in his eyes faded to black as he passed away. The prisoner lay limp and lifeless in his restraints, like a partially amputated crash dummy.

Gabriel didn't trust this enemy to stay dead; he set his weapon to a low-powered single shot and fired, aiming between the chin and the Adam's apple. The bullet travelled through the roof of the mouth and into the deceased target's brain, spattering the back wall with blood, brain matter, and bits of neurocircuitry.

Gabriel returned to the squad.

"*We have good news and strange news,*" Bale told Gabriel as he approached.

"*Same here,*" Gabriel replied, "*you first.*"

"*The good news is that there's a way to get Doran out of here without backtracking all the way back to the loading bay,*" Cato said, tapping a few keys on an interface panel.

An entire section of the wall opened up, revealing an entry point into an automated cargo conveyor system, complete with empty storage boxes for transporting medical samples and equipment. There was even an unused casket for transporting corpses.

"*This entire facility is serviced by an automated logistical transport system,*" Cato explained, "*supplies are brought in, and packages are sent out. That automated freight truck we encountered earlier is part of the same system.*"

"*So if we put Doran in one of these caskets, we can send him to safety?*" Gabriel asked.

"*Exactly,*" Cato answered, "*I can adjust the life support systems in his suit for the trip. His transponder should also make sure the DNI picks him up.*"

"*Good, get ready to move him,*" Gabriel ordered.

Cato nodded and started preparing Doran for medical transport.

"*What about the strange news?*" Gabriel asked.

"*I searched the computers and...*" Bale ventured to explain, "*...found spyware; sophisticated spyware, too, embedded in a hidden boot file called 'Dani'.*"

"*I guess Doran was right,*" Gabriel replied, "*Still, it's not that surprising; corporate espionage in the tech sector is common enough.*"

"*That's not all,*" Bale continued, "*the timestamps date back nearly five years.*"

"*A mole in deep cover for five years?*" Gabriel said, "*Now that is impressive.*"

"*I thought we'd just ruled out the presence of a mole?*" Viker asked.

"*The research labs run on an airtight computer system,*" Bale explained, "*Like I said earlier, someone with access to the labs had to have personally installed the spyware.*"

"*That doesn't mean there was an agent here for five whole years,*" Viker responded sceptically, "*Someone could have planted the spyware and left it to transmit on its own.*"

"*An airtight computer network, by definition, is totally disconnected from any other network,*" Gabriel pointed out, "*it couldn't have transmitted anything.*"

"*In which case,*" Bale continued, "*the mole would have had to periodically download the spyware's latest observations, then smuggle the data out somehow.*"

"*The automated logistics system can take cargo to and from the landing pad without anyone having to physically inspect it,*" Cato suggested, still preparing Doran for transport.

"*Which means that the mole must have known how to use the logistics network*," Gabriel concluded, "*Any clues on who the mole was?*"

"*The spyware would never reveal the identity of the person who planted it*," Bale replied.

"*Anybody on the staff roster who looks suspicious?*" Gabriel suggested, "*Someone with a name that includes 'Dani' in it, maybe?*"

"*There's three Daniels, one Danielle, and a Dr Penelope Daniels*," Bale answered as he searched through the records, "*Other than that, nobody.*"

"*What about 'Lawrence Kane'?*" Viker asked.

The squad turned around to see Viker examining a set of hatches on the wall. They were mortuary alcoves for storing corpses; only one of them had a name.

"'*Dr Lawrence Kane*'," Bale read from the staff roster, "'*Project Liaison Officer from Jupiter Engineering Co.'s headquarters in Asgard City*'. *Every time he visited this facility, he made at least one trip to the medical bay for some kind of blood disorder. The records say he had to send regular blood samples back to some lab on Asgard.*"

"*And probably slipped a data chip full of stolen research into the blood samples*," Cato speculated, "*Then used the facility's own system to smuggle the samples out.*"

"*Do we know what happened to Dr Kane?*" Gabriel asked.

"*It just says 'status: deceased'*," Bale answered inconclusively, "*No information on how or when. Is he even in there?*"

Viker pulled open the mortuary hatch and the tray extended automatically, releasing a cloud of refrigerated vapour.

Sure enough, there was a body inside. It was a man's corpse, with skin that was a pale shade of blue. He was still wearing clothes, and he had a holographic ID tag still attached to his chest. Viker tapped the ID tag and it lit up with a name: 'Dr Lawrence Kane'.

"*Mystery solved*," said Viker, pushing the tray back in and shutting the hatch, "*Partly.*"

"*So, what did you get out of the prisoner?*" Bale asked, changing the subject.

"*The elevator down to the 'Temple' is at the other end of the facility, and the access code is 52133,*" Gabriel replied, "*no biometric lock, apparently.*"

"*He gave it up just like that?*" Viker asked incredulously.

"*I sliced his hand clean off and he practically orgasmed as a result,*" Gabriel answered, "*He wanted us to go down there.*"

"*Doran's ready,*" Cato announced, "*and his suit has a week's worth of oxygen.*"

The empty casket was brought out by the conveyor system and elevated to the right position, and Doran – his suit now reassembled – was carefully placed inside. Once the casket was sealed, internal padding filled with special memory gel expanded to fill the leftover space to minimise shocks to the valuable cargo.

Cato then used the system to file an off-world transport request for the package. Once approved by the system, the sealed casket was plucked from its stand by a set of robotic arms and taken inside where it disappeared into the guts of the logistics network.

"*Which would look worse on our reports,*" Cato wondered as the wall panel resealed itself, "*putting Doran in a coffin to save his life, or losing him in the mail?*"

Bale and Viker chuckled, and even Gabriel couldn't help but crack a smile until he remembered to deauthorise Doran's ID from the squad's comm. system.

"*We still have a mission to complete,*" Gabriel reminded the squad, "*let's move out!*"

"*The 'Dani' spyware copied and stored virtually every single file on the system,*" said Bale, "*including a map of this 'Temple'. So we won't get lost in the lion's den.*"

"*Do we even know what this 'Temple' is?*" Cato asked.

"*We'll find out once we get there,*" Gabriel replied.

"*You might want to take that thing's sword, just in case,*" Viker recommended, "*Masterminds know what other fricking monsters they have waiting for us.*"

Gabriel nodded and walked back over to the semi-Human corpse he had been interrogating. He took the magnetic plate that stored the jumper's sword and slung it over his own shoulder, the strap tightening of its own accord. Then he retrieved the jumper's sword, checked that the cutting field was switched off, and returned it to the magnetic sheath.

Perhaps Viker's earlier outburst was right, and Red-eye really had assigned him a squad of operators for cannon fodder. With no backup and no way of contacting the DNI for support, their odds of survival weren't exceptional.

And Viker's use of the phrase 'suicide mission' was more accurate than he knew.

THE TEMPLE

KINGPINS of industry and finance like Jezebel Thorn dominated much of the interstellar economy; and Aster, like everyone else she had known growing up, regarded them and the other fleeksters with a mixture of envy and contempt. Being roped into one of their schemes was galling.

The children entertained themselves and each other in the back of the sky-taxi, oblivious to the turmoil that occupied their mother's thoughts all the way back to the apartment. Madam Jezebel would never harm her own grandchildren, but taking them from the medical centre was clearly intended as a message to Aster personally.

Above all, Aster regretted her impulsive decision to go snooping around Lawrence's office after explicitly telling Felix not to. And now, thanks to that incriminating video, she had no choice but to go along with Jezebel's blackmail, or risk being framed as the mole.

Given what Jezebel Thorn had insinuated, her mole had to have been Lawrence himself. Who else would have thought to plant a camera outside his office? Why else had he hidden an industrial-grade data chip in his office in a place where most people wouldn't think to look? And how else would Madam Jezebel have gotten her hands on the video?

Still, the makings of a counter-plan were starting to form in Aster's mind. She had blurted out how the data chip she had taken was blue in colour, and Jezebel seemed to accept that as fact. If she gave Jezebel a blue data chip and convinced her that it was genuine, then handed over the red data chip – the real one – to the DNI, she could get official protection by the time Jezebel discovered she had been duped.

The sky-taxi alighted on the nearest public landing pad, and the Thorn family walked the short distance back to the apartment. Aster ushered the children through the front door and locked the door behind her, heaving a sigh of relief once she had done so. The children were glad to be home, too, and raced to the living room. After piling onto the couch, they began fighting over the wireless data-glove that controlled the holo-TV.

"Holo-TV, on," Aster enunciated as she walked into the room.

Responding to her voice command, the holoscreen activated, covering the opposite wall with the projection. The channel happened to be the news.

"...*stock price collapsed by an eye-watering 27% after unconfirmed reports that its labs were raided by the DNI. Chairman Darius Avaritio hasn't been seen in public for...*"

Aster plucked the data-glove out of Orion's hands and slipped it over her own hand, dismissing the news report with a swipe of her fingers and flicking rapidly through the hundreds of channels in search of something other than the evening news.

She found a decent family movie to watch and snapped her fingers with the data-glove to select it. The children moved over to give their mother some room on the couch and she sat down with them, removing the data-glove and tossing it onto the coffee table.

As the movie began to play, Aster was too distracted to pay attention. It was nice to be home, but the first night without him was always hardest, even without the day's events weighing on her thoughts. She was also bothered by how her mother-in-law had so easily picked up her children from the medical centre. Just how many connections did she have? The paranoia was starting to get to her, and she stood up abruptly.

"What's wrong, mommy?" Rose asked.

"Nothing, sweetheart," Aster replied with a reassuring smile, "just keep watching the movie. Mommy has some work to do."

Leaving the children in the living room, Aster went to the master bedroom and shut the door behind her. She approached what looked like an armoured closet on Gabriel's side of the room and slid her thumb across the sensor panel. The light on the biometric sensor panel went from red to green and the twin doors slid open.

Inside was a humanoid figure with a matte-black finish standing still as a statue, its faceless and featureless head drooped in programmed slumber. On its right breast in white letters was emblazoned the model name 'Maganiel'.

Aster reached up and rapped her knuckles against the android's forehead. The android's eyes lit up electric blue as it activated. It inclined its head towards Aster, looking her straight in the eyes before flash-scanning them.

"*Good evening, Aster Thorn,*" the android greeted her in a digitised voice without any Human inflexions, "*Maganiel Mark V online. How may I be of service?*"

"Personal protection for the family," Aster enunciated.

"*Understood. The DNA signatures of Aster Thorn…Orion Thorn …Rose Thorn…Violet Thorn…Leonidas Thorn…Gabriel Thorn… are already stored in my database. Please confirm that these are the individuals who require personal protection.*"

"Confirmed," Aster replied.

"*Understood,*" the maganiel acknowledged, "*Please be aware that the use of lethal force is strictly regulated, and in most cases is prohibited, by Asgard Municipal Codes. Do you wish to authorise lethal force?*"

"Yes."

"*Understood,*" the maganiel replied, "*Please be aware that the use of lethal weaponry, including firearms, is strictly regulated, and in most cases is prohibited, by Asgard Municipal Codes. Do you wish to authorise the use of firearms?*"

"Yes."

"*Understood*," the maganiel replied, "*Mission directive and parameters confirmed.*"

The maganiel reached back into the closet and pulled out a military-issue sidearm, checking the settings before stowing the weapon on a magnetic plate attached to its thigh. Aster stepped aside as the armed android exited the closet and waited quietly in the corner. Mentally exhausted, Aster flopped down on Gabriel's side of the bed.

After staring at the ceiling for a while, her gaze drifted sideways until she was looking at Gabriel's bedside table. There, in pride of place, was a framed holo-photo from their wedding day. It was one of the few times Aster had seen him smile, and it stood in remarkable contrast to the stern expression he usually wore around the house.

Madam Jezebel had attended the ceremony and paid for the venue. She had even put on an award-winning performance pretending to be thrilled that her son was marrying a colonial girl – even one with multiple engineering degrees. Most of the other guests had been former classmates of hers at engineering school as well as some sinister-looking DNI types that Gabriel presumably knew from work.

At least, they had looked sinister to Aster. She couldn't help but wonder if the DNI did something to its operatives to make them that way. Was Gabriel always so dour, or had he been put through the same personality-dulling process?

Even so, it was a nice photo, and Aster smiled back.

* * *

Latched onto the underside of a nearby mag-rail track was a small pod, its presence concealed by a variety of cloaking systems. Inside the cramped surveillance pod, two men watched on a holographic screen as the Thorn family stepped out of the sky-taxi and headed inside, following them through the camera network all the way to their front door.

One of the men touched the holographic screen with his finger and thumb and zoomed in on Aster Thorn as she walked away from the camera.

"Damn, that is one fine piece of ass," he said with a grin.

"We're on assignment, Blake," the other man reminded him.

"Hey, I'm just saying," Blake replied unapologetically, "good on the lucky guy who gets to bang that every night. Don't you think?"

"She's not really my type," the other man casually slid his hand across Blake's thigh.

"Ugh! What the fleek are you doing, Gibson?" Blake wriggled away in alarm.

"Serves you right for perving out on the mark," Gibson replied with a satisfied smile.

"What do you mean 'the mark'?" Blake said, confused, as he settled back into his seat, "we're on a surveillance op., not a hit."

"Of course it's not a hit, moron," Gibson replied, "you surveil a *mark* for intelligence, and you mark a *target* for death. Who let you out of the academy early?"

"Ok, whatever," Blake said dismissively.

"So, are you gonna call it in, or would you rather ogle the *mark* some more?"

"Fine, fine," Blake said as he activated a secure link, "Big Brother, Big Brother, this is Watchdog-two-zero, Agents Blake and Gibson checking in."

"*Roger, Watchdog-two-zero, Big Brother reads you,*" a gruff voice replied.

"Big Brother, the...mark arrived by sky-taxi just now with her four kids," Blake reported, "but she took a detour on her way back from work."

"*Affirmative, Watchdog-two-zero,*" their handler replied, "*The kids were scheduled for a series of medical tests today.*"

"Understood, Big Brother, but the mark never went to the medical centre," Agent Blake explained, "she went to a residential address on the 201st floor of the Elysium Tower, stayed there for a few minutes, then picked up the kids from there."

There was a pause on the other end of the line.

"Big Brother, come in?"

"*Watchdog-two-zero, that address is registered to a certain Jezebel Thorn,*" the handler explained, "*she is also an active surveillance mark. Please immediately forward all signals intelligence collected from the exchange.*"

"Uh, that's a negative, Big Brother," Agent Blake answered, "the entire 201st floor was equipped with garblers; no usable SIGINT data could be gathered."

"*Understood, Watchdog-two-zero,*" the handler replied.

"Big Brother, Jezebel Thorn is the kids' grandmother, confirm?" Agent Blake asked.

"*Affirmative, Watchdog-two-zero,*" Big Brother answered, "*But your hunch about it being just a family visit is unlikely.*"

"Big Brother, please clarify."

"*The Thorn children were being examined by Directorate medical staff,*" the handler explained, "*only two people are authorised to drop them off and collect them afterwards. Even though she's a blood relative, Jezebel Thorn isn't one of them.*"

"Understood, Big Brother," said Blake, then he turned to Gibson and wondered aloud, "why the hell would DNI docs be examining these kids?"

"*Irrelevant and above your pay-grade,*" their handler replied brusquely, "*mine as well.*"

"Uh, understood, Big Brother," Blake hastily recomposed himself as Gibson smirked quietly, "Big Brother, the Thorn family is home for the night. We're recommending a snatch op. to question the mother."

"*Acknowledged, Watchdog-two-zero,*" their handler replied, "*standby.*"

The green comm. light turned yellow as the connection was put on hold.

"Somebody's scalp's gonna get nailed to Red-eye's office wall," Gibson remarked.

"What the fleek for?" Blake asked.

"The only reason they'd have DNI doctors examining those kids is if they have a parent in the DNI," Gibson explained, "and pretty high up too."

"Which means that anyone other than the parents picking them up from the medical centre is a major security failure," concluded Blake.

"Not as dumb as you pretend to be," Gibson replied as he pulled up Aster Thorn's personnel file and tapped on her spouse's name.

"Gabriel Thorn...oh, look," Gibson noted, "'Access Denied: Tier 2 classification'."

"So, that's pretty high up?" Blake asked.

"Tier 1 classification would mean only the director-general and the Masterminds can look at the file," Gibson explained, "And, by the way, the mere fact that I just tried to look up his information will have been logged by the DNI techs."

"Doesn't Red-eye trust her own spies?" Blake asked, miffed.

"Of course not," Gibson answered, "we spy on people for a living."

The yellow standby light turned green as their handler re-established the connection.

"*Watchdog-two-zero, Watchdog-two-zero, come in,*" their handler hailed them.

"Big Brother, this is Watchdog-two-zero," Blake responded, "We read you."

"*Watchdog-two-zero, that is a negative on your recommendation for a snatch op.,*" their handler informed them, "*repeat, negative on a snatch op. The mark herself hasn't done anything overtly suspicious yet. Until she does, continue observation.*"

"Understood, Big Brother," Blake acknowledged, "over and out."

* * *

Five…two…one…three…three. Sure enough, the elevator doors slid open, and the squad filed in. There were only two levels: laboratories and excavation site. Gabriel pressed the button for the excavation site and the doors sealed shut.

There was total silence all the way down. No one knew what they would find or if they would live to report back; not to mention one of their own was now probably a guinea pig for the insane staff. Critically injured though he was, Doran might be the lucky one.

Gabriel felt nothing in particular. That was normal. Voidstalkers weren't supposed to feel anything in particular. He had made his peace with Ogilvy's probable demise and Doran's incapacitation, but he could sense that his remaining squad members were wary about continuing any further. Not that they were cowards – far from it – but they had more of a sense of self-preservation than he did. That was Human.

The elevator finally reached the bottom. The doors slid open and the squad emerged into a cave hewn from the rock. Floodlights were bolted to the ceiling and storage crates were stacked around the walls. High up on the rock wall opposite, painted in Human blood, were the words: 'TEMPLE OF KNOWLEDGE'.

Directly below the message was a dark tunnel entrance, like a breach in the cave wall leading into a black abyss. Shining a light into the hole revealed a passageway whose walls and surfaces resembled pitch-black basalt with a smooth finish and precise angles.

"*This cave is not a natural formation*," Cato remarked.

"*I would never have guessed*," Gabriel replied sarcastically, eliciting chuckles.

Their levity was tempered by the ominous nature of the path ahead. The light-eating tunnel before them resembled the entrance to an alien tomb or a gateway to the underworld. Natural or not, it looked like a trap, especially given the hideous showpiece on display.

There were four corpses, two on each side of the tunnel entrance, mounted on pikes with their arms tied to crossbeams like crucified scarecrows. They had been savagely mutilated, either through sadistic torture or ineptly performed surgery – or both – with bloody maws in their torsos and dried blood caking their cheeks beneath their closed eyelids.

All four of the crucified corpses sported the remains of J.E. Co. security uniforms.

"*At least now we know what 'elevation' means,*" Bale remarked grimly.

"*What the fuck kind of savages do this to people?*" Cato wondered rhetorically.

No one cared to guess, especially since they were probably going to find out soon.

"*Look at this,*" Viker called out, holding up a heavy belt with a large activation button in the buckle. There was a whole crate full of them sitting largely untouched in the corner.

"*Gravity belts?*" Bale asked in bewilderment, "*underground?*"

"*Gravitational anomalies inside the structure, perhaps?*" Viker surmised, "*This is definitely the weirdest op. I've ever been on.*"

"*If the research staff felt they needed these to go any further, we probably do too,*" Gabriel concluded, "*Everybody grab a belt.*"

The squad complied and Viker passed out a gravity belt to each person before wrapping one around his own waist and tightening the buckle.

"*Do we have a plan beyond 'kill anything that moves', sir?*" Cato asked apprehensively.

"*Not really, but we are going to finish this quickly,*" Gabriel answered resolutely, "*the schematics for the 'Temple' feature a central chamber of some kind. We find the chamber, destroy whatever's causing the insanity, and kill everything that gets in our way.*"

"*It can't possibly be that simple,*" Cato said with reservations.

"*It never is*," Gabriel replied, knowing from experience how right Cato was.

With Gabriel taking point, the squad approached the tunnel entrance step by cautious step, walking past the macabre display. Gabriel stepped over the threshold and planted his foot on the smooth floor. As his armoured boot connected with the floor, he felt a tiny tremor reverberate in his sole, like a wave of vibrations rippling outwards from his foot.

Of course it was a trap.

A chorus of mechanical shrieking erupted from the crucified 'corpses'. The scarecrow-like monstrosities began to thrash in their restraints, shaking the pikes from side to side as they struggled to be free. Their eyelids were open, revealing that their eyes had been replaced with cybernetic implants which glowed electric blue. The squad backed away from the passageway and grouped together with their backs to the elevator.

"*Weapons free!*" Gabriel shouted.

The squad opened fire on the mutilated monstrosities; but to their surprise, their bullets were deflected to the sides in flashes of energy. The research staff had surgically implanted shield generators inside the scarecrows' bodies – an innovation both twisted and ingenious – protecting the creatures from small arms fire.

The scarecrows broke free of their restraints and dropped down to the ground, landing deftly on their feet. One of them picked up the giant pike on which it had been crucified and hurled it like a javelin at the squad. The 12-foot long scaffolding rod travelled slowly enough to pass through Viker's shields whilst connecting with his stomach with enough force to knock him backwards. But it rebounded from his armour and fell harmlessly to the ground, the sharpened tip blunted to a stub without leaving a scratch.

Bale and Cato covered Viker as he got back on his feet, overwhelming the scarecrow's shields at point-blank range with concentrated fire to the head. The second scarecrow took a running jump at Gabriel, arms spread out as if it could fly. Gabriel readied a concussive shot and fell onto his back as the semi-machine monstrosity pounced on him, lining the barrel up with the incoming creature's mouth and pulling the trigger.

The concussive shot was a shower of ball-bearings sprayed at the target for maximum impact force rather than penetration – no good at range, but lethal up-close. The shot entered through the scarecrow's howling maw, blasting out the back of its head. Gabriel tossed the half-headed corpse to one side and returned to his feet.

The third and fourth cybernetic scarecrows had attempted the same airborne pounce. One landed on top of Viker, grabbing him by the shoulders. Viker deftly planted his foot on his incoming opponent and performed a reverse roll, using the cybernetic zombie's own momentum to flip it head over heels onto its own back. Viker then leapt back to his feet and executed the scarecrow with a single shot to the head.

Bale was slower to react as the fourth scarecrow tackled him to the ground and began pummelling and clawing at his helmet like a rabid beast. Cato grabbed the scarecrow by the ankles and yanked it backwards onto its stomach, then knelt down on its back, grabbed it by the head and chin, and snapped its neck 180 degrees around.

With its head facing backwards, the surgically enhanced scarecrow screamed at Cato, treating him to the revolting view of a face that was both half-rotted and mechanically enhanced. The scarecrow smacked Cato in the head, knocking him down before trying to climb on top of him. Bale charged forwards and struck the creature under the chin with the butt of his gun, sending it flying backwards before following up with a kill shot through the skull.

More shots rang out, this time from the passage entrance. Flashes of gunfire illuminated the darkened passageway as more enemies joined the fight. Several stray shots hit the squad's shields as they took cover on either side of the entrance, returning fire into the passageway.

The squad switched their HUD filters to false-colour thermal enhancement, turning the walls of the pitch-black passageway to a cool shade of blue with computer-generated contouring superimposed over the edges and angles. Highlighted in red were several hostile silhouettes, shooting at them from the cover of the passageway.

Viker removed a frag grenade from his belt, primed it, and tossed it down the corridor. It bounced off the walls and exploded in mid-air, spraying hypersonic shards in all directions and shredding the targets' comparatively light body armour. The squad followed up with kill bursts before the survivors could recover.

"*Forward!*" Gabriel ordered, "*If we keep moving, they can't pin us down!*"

The squad followed Gabriel into the passageway as more defenders appeared. Viker raised his hand and activated the wrist-shield he had taken earlier. The oval-shaped energy shield appeared as distortion in the false colour enhancement filters; but it easily deflected the incoming gunfire as the squad returned fire, dispatching the defenders with ease.

Viker took point and led the squad down the right-hand fork of the corridor with Gabriel beside him, while Cato and Bale covered the rear. The squad followed the spyware's map through an otherwise bewildering maze of corridors and cube-shaped chambers, all of which looked identical and engineered to mathematical precision.

More familiar was the blood-red graffiti on the walls and floors – and even some on the ceilings. In addition to scientific equations and passages of alien script, there were more of the same pseudo-religious scribblings they had seen earlier.

'PEACE THROUGH SUBMISSION.'
'THE VOICE SPEAKS TRUTH.'

There was no time to wonder at the distinctly alien architecture, or messages painted on almost every surface, as the squad entered yet another chamber and were promptly fired upon by entrenched defenders.

The squad rolled into cover behind a set of equipment crates as a hailstorm of bullets greeted them, punching shallow holes in the crates or glancing off the metal edges with audible pings. Many of the bullets struck the opposite wall – not one of them leaving a discernible mark on the alien material – before clattering to the floor.

High-speed motion capture software in Gabriel's HUD allowed him to see the bullets' trajectories as thin red streaks in his visor, some of which were coming down at them at an angle. Gabriel returned fire, aiming for the square-shaped spaces at the top of the opposite wall; the spray of bullets he fired ricocheted off the roof and silenced the intended targets.

The suppressing fire continued from behind makeshift barricades on the other side. Viker stepped out from behind the crates to confront them with wrist-shield raised. The gunfire was redirected towards Viker, bursts of bullets zeroing in on him before swerving abruptly sideways as they came into contact with the wrist-shield.

Cato returned fire from the cover of Viker's wrist-shield to distract the defenders while Gabriel and Bale snuck around the side. Bale removed an explosive from his belt, primed it, and tossed it at the enemy with a flick of his wrist. The device travelled through the air in an arc, spinning at high speed like a gyro-ball before detonating behind the defenders.

The explosive core flash-heated an outer layer of gas into an ionised state, discharging it in the form of an arc of plasma which overwhelmed the defenders' shielding and ate straight through their armour and flesh. The squad could imagine – even though they couldn't hear – the dying screams of the defenders as they were scorched to death by the superhot plasma.

The squad didn't pause for a moment. They continued through the alien labyrinth and were ambushed repeatedly by waves of lightly armed, by highly determined defenders. Of course, the fighters were no match for commandoes, and they were steadily beaten back.

"*Just how big is this place?*" Viker wondered in exasperation as the squad walked down yet another perpendicular passageway.

"*One central chamber, eighty sub-chambers, and 264 connecting corridors,*" Bale answered, "*according to the map, at least.*"

"*Speaking of which, what kind of fricking place is this?*" Viker continued.

"*Your guess is as good as any of ours,*" Bale replied.

Cato pressed his hand against the wall so that his suit sensors could scan the material.

"*It's a metallic substance of some kind. Composition, unknown. Faint but uniform traces of energy beneath the surface,*" Cato announced mysteriously, "*Definitely alien.*"

"*We're here,*" Gabriel announced, leading the way to the end of the corridor.

Unlike the maze of identical, cube-shaped sub-chambers they had passed through, the central chamber was a perfect sphere the size of a small stadium, with a disorienting lack of visible angles. Extensive scaffolding encircled the rim of the chamber, extending down several levels, resembling an archaeological site at a geometrician's tomb.

At the centre of the enormous chamber was a single glowing light, floating in mid-air in the centre, and illuminating the enormous chamber with an unearthly glow. Bale, Cato, and Viker stared at the light like moths entranced by a flame.

"*Keep an eye out for hostiles,*" Gabriel ordered, snapping them out of their awe.

Cautiously, the squad ventured into the chamber, descending a ramp onto the topmost level of the scaffolding. On the other side of the scaffolding, a short distance from the light, was a raised dais, like a jumping board from which to leap towards the light… or perhaps an altar from which to worship it. As they approached, the squad could see that the light was actually a faintly glowing sphere of translucent energy with a silver orb suspended at its heart.

Atop the platform, a lone figure stood with his back turned to the squad. He was wearing what looked like snow white hazmat overalls, but which had been covered entirely in dark red symbols, like the macabre scribblings in the main facility.

"Finally, you have come," the figure proclaimed, turning around to face them.

He had the look of a mad scientist who had spent years in the wilderness, complete with a full beard and untamed, greying hair; and his skin was covered in what looked like microdots which glowed faintly under the dim light. The squad saw another figure on his knees with the speaker's hand on his shoulder.

It was Ogilvy.

"Ogilvy, status!" Gabriel shouted through his helmet speakers.

"He cannot hear you," the figure spoke with a mocking grin, "the Voice instructed us on how to cut through his armour and disable its systems."

Ogilvy's helmet had been carefully removed, revealing closed eyes and features that looked weighed down by exhaustion, and a gravity belt had been strapped around his waist. Although he didn't look injured, he was clearly out of the fight.

"Who are you?" Gabriel demanded.

"I am the Leader of the Faithful," the figure replied grandiosely, "the Slave of the Voice. The Prophet to whom the Voice's knowledge was first revealed."

"Is the Voice that thing in the containment shield?" Gabriel asked.

"It is the physical vessel of the Voice," the prophet replied, looking back at the silver orb, "We thought it to be merely a xenotech artefact, albeit one ancient beyond compare; even more ancient than the place in which it has been imprisoned. But none dared approach to study it. None, that is, save for me."

"So, you're responsible for this madness?"

"Madness?" the prophet said with a grin, "I was mad before the Voice spoke unto me. Now, I have been cured of the madness and ignorance that plagued my mind, just as I have cured all those who now follow me."

The squad's motion trackers flashed red.

"*Contacts!*" Bale yelled, "*And lots of them!*"

All around the enormous central chamber, figures began to appear. More disorienting were the figures who appeared directly above, spilling out onto the ceiling as if defying gravity. The squad spread out to cover as many angles as they could, but it was impossible. The enemy was all around, oozing out of every entrance and blocking every avenue of escape.

"The Faithful are numerous," the prophet gloated, "you cannot hope to kill them all."

He was right. They were exposed, outnumbered, outgunned, and surrounded on all sides. Not only that, but the enemy had cannibalised xenotechnology for much of its weaponry, making it vastly superior to what they had.

"We have attained peace through submission," the prophet declared, "and so shall you."

With those words, he shoved Ogilvy over the edge of the platform. Instead of falling, the unconscious Ogilvy was borne aloft by some kind of gravity field and drawn, spread-eagled, up towards the spherical containment field.

Gabriel opened fire on the prophet, but the microdots all over his skin lit up in response. Gabriel's bullets rebounded in a series of sapphire-coloured energy flashes, leaving the target unharmed and grinning triumphantly at his invulnerability.

"Subdermal shield emitters," the prophet explained, "the knowledge required for their manufacture is one of innumerable gifts bestowed upon us by the Voice. You cannot hope to slay me, for I am its messenger."

Ogilvy was pulled inside the containment shield. The prophet and his followers watched in awe – and the squad in horror – as the silver orb disintegrated into a cloud of particles which swarmed in through Ogilvy's mouth. As the cloud of particles took over Ogilvy's body, the containment shield suddenly dissipated, repelling Ogilvy back towards the platform.

The squad trained their weapons on their squad-mate as an invisible force carried him back towards the platform, where he landed on one knee. Gabriel primed a high-powered shot; whatever had happened to Ogilvy, he was better off dead. The colour had drained completely from his skin, and his eyes were shut as he rose slowly to his feet.

When they opened again, it was clear that Ogilvy was gone.

His eyes were now jet black as he focused his gaze on the squad. He opened his mouth, and from it poured forth the multitude of silver particles that had taken over his body. They swarmed around him, enveloping him entirely like a shimmering cloud of miniature locusts. Gabriel took aim at the possessed Ogilvy's exposed head and fired.

The high-powered shot was fired at high-hypersonic velocity, giving it enough power to punch through vehicle armour. But the swarm of particles around Ogilvy's body generated their own shield around him, and the bullet was violently slapped aside. The possessed Ogilvy began to walk towards them, each footstep punctuated by an ominous, echoing thump.

"*Colonel, I seriously fricking hope you're not out of ideas, yet,*" Viker spoke for the remainder of the squad, a note of panic creeping into his voice.

"*Steady,*" Gabriel replied calmly, removing a grenade from his belt and priming it.

He felt anything but calm.

The possessed Ogilvy and this so-called prophet were impervious to their weapons and intended to kill them or worse. The chances that they would all die in this xenoarchaeological madhouse were growing by the second. If they stood and fought, their possessed former squadmate would make short work of them. But if they retreated the way they had come, they would be caught between the possessed Ogilvy and the 'Faithful', and be finished off anyway.

Gabriel glanced up and saw that even the 'ceiling' of the chamber was swarming with the Faithful – standing upside down relative to where he stood. If every wall and surface had artificial gravity which varied in different parts of the complex, that would explain why the researchers had brought along gravity belts.

An idea formed in Gabriel's mind.

"*Sir?*" Cato's barely suppressed panic was evident in his voice.

"*Follow my lead and jump on my mark,*" Gabriel ordered.

He angled his arm to throw the grenade as the possessed Ogilvy got closer and closer.

"*Sir!*"

"*Go!*" Gabriel shouted, bolting to the right as he tossed the grenade at Ogilvy's feet, who walked unheedingly forward just as it detonated.

The explosive wave of flash-heated plasma melted straight through the floor at Ogilvy's feet. It wasn't powerful enough to shake the structure of the scaffolding, but it did generate enough force to knock Ogilvy backwards. The possessed commando let out a bloodcurdling scream as he fell down, even as the swarm of alien particles protected him from harm.

The squad followed Gabriel's lead and sprinted right.

"*Grav-belts!*" Gabriel shouted as he leapt off the far edge of the scaffolding, hitting the activation button on his gravity belt as he jumped.

Gabriel felt his innards being pulled straight down as the gravitational pull suddenly changed direction. Without the gravity belts, the squad could have run along the entire circumference of the spherical chamber without falling off; but although the chamber's artificial gravity was cancelled out by the gravity belts, the effect wasn't powerful enough to counteract the moon's own gravity.

That was the idea.

Instead of falling flat against the wall, Gabriel and the squad hit the side and kept on falling, sliding towards the bottom at high speed like water circling a drain, towards a quartet of square openings at the bottom. The Faithful below opened fire, and Gabriel and the squad fired back. Hitting moving targets was hard, especially when you were the one moving, but several shots still hit their marks, and the Faithful scattered as they took casualties.

"*That's our way out!*" Gabriel yelled, pointing to the square openings, "*Go!*"

Given the topsy-turvy geometry of this place, each opening was probably another corridor leading to a sub-chamber below; and so plunging back into the labyrinth was the squad's best way out. As they slid towards the bottom of the chamber, the squad used their momentum to slide back to their feet.

Several jumpers drew their deadly, armour-cutting swords, and tried to close the gap before the squad could make their escape. Viker dropped one with a concussive shot to the chest, sending it flying backwards and 'up' the side. Bale performed a forward roll, evading the otherwise decapitating swipe of another sword, and rolled straight into the hole, followed by Cato, Viker, and Gabriel.

As they fell, the squad kept enough of their wits about them to hit the buttons on their gravity belts, deactivating the gravity-cancelling effect. Gravity's direction shifted abruptly by 90 degrees, pulling the squad members down towards the 'floor' of the corridor instead of continuing to fall straight down into the next chamber.

As the squad recovered their orientation, the remaining fighters leaned over the edge and kept shooting down at them. From the squad's perspective, the shots were travelling horizontally, even though the sub-chamber 'behind' them was actually below them. When they returned fire and kill one of the attackers, the body fell down only to hit the 'floor' – or the wall – of the corridor.

The multi-directional gravity would certainly make the fight more interesting.

"*Straight down!*" Gabriel ordered, activating his gravity belt again.

Gravity abruptly reoriented by 90 degrees again, and Gabriel fell off the 'floor' and straight down, kicking back and forth against the walls of the vertical corridor to slow his descent. The rest of the squad followed his lead, reactivating their belts and dropping like stones down into the chamber below, where they landed more or less on their feet.

"*New plan, sir?*" Bale asked.

"*We keep moving,*" Gabriel replied, "*or we die.*"

THE OBSERVER

Night came and went quickly on Asgard, thanks to its unusually fast rotation as it orbited Odin. Before long, it was time to get up and start another day at work. Aster was up before the sun was, the better to prepare for the day ahead. The children needed some convincing to trust the imposing maganiel android – especially since it lacked a Human face – but ultimately they climbed into their learning pods without complaint.

Aster didn't like leaving them alone with an armed escort robot, but the conventional household android couldn't fight, and she would sooner entrust a mindlessly loyal machine with childcare duties than her scheming mother-in-law. Besides, if everything went according to plan, she could be rid of Jezebel Thorn for good.

It was the same route to work as always: a twenty-minute mag-train ride straight to J.E. Co.'s head offices. But the journey felt more tense than usual, perhaps because she was about to violate her employment contract in multiple ways. She kept her eyes glued to her smartphone for the entire journey, wondering if she was being followed or watched.

As the mag-train stopped and the doors slid open, Aster joined the shoal of people who poured out onto the platform. She was trying hard not to look suspicious as she walked to the elevators, a little too hard as she barged into someone by accident. Aster ignored the man and kept on walking, marching straight through the elevator doors.

Aster and her colleagues all proceeded in silence down fifty or so levels to the research labs and queued up at the security checkpoint. There, everyone was required to check their personal electronics into storage before passing through the scanner gate. Aster passed through the checkpoint without incident and headed straight for her office, giving only perfunctory greetings to her colleagues as she passed them.

Once she was safely in her office, she began rummaging through the storage cabinet in her desk. Her drawers were filled with all sorts of junk that she needed to clear out, but she eventually found what she was looking for: a spare blue data chip.

The data chips were actually colour-coded: blue was generic company information, yellow was confidential, red was highly sensitive, hence the red chip hidden in Lawrence's office. Lawrence would have known about the colour-coding system; come to think of it, so would Jezebel if Lawrence had been her mole. But a blue data chip would arouse less suspicion, and Aster could pass off the colour difference as a necessary deceit to smuggle it out.

Plugging the chip into her computer, Aster deleted the generic reports and other data, and instead installed a simple tracking program and keylogger from the company's in-house security software box. That way, whoever tried to access the chip's contents would reveal their location to the company's security techs.

Aster removed the chip and slipped it into her pocket. Coming up with a decoy chip was easy, getting the data chip past the security checkpoint and out of the building was the real challenge. The same would go for the red chip.

Aster left her office and headed to the main laboratory floor. It was almost reassuring to see everyone starting the day like nothing had happened, flitting back and forth with datapads and other equipment, even though the company's future was still in doubt. Thanks to her, its fate would probably be sealed.

Avoiding eye contact with everyone as she passed, Aster slipped into the side office where the activation key safe was and stood in front of the biometric scanner. The scanner flash-scanned her eyes and the door popped open. Aster snatched the chip out of the safe and stuffed it into her pocket, with the blue decoy chip in her other pocket.

She hastily turned to leave and barged straight into someone.

"Oh! Sorry, Aster," said Felix as he appeared to stumble past her.

"Sorry," Aster mumbled nervously.

There was an awkward silence between them as they avoided eye contact for a moment.

"Aster, I…" Felix began, his left hand clenched into a fist, "about yesterday…I guess it's better to just let old ghosts rest, huh?"

"Yeah," Aster replied, unsure of what to say to that, "…listen, I hate this too. But the best thing we can do to honour their memory is to keep working on the project."

"Sure, that's something to work for," Felix said with a nod.

He didn't really seem to believe it, and neither did Aster.

They hastily parted ways as Aster hurried back across the main lab floor to her office. Now all she had to do was leave the building, give the blue decoy chip to Jezebel and the red chip with the real data to the DNI, and everything should be fine.

Aster had to pass through the breakroom on her way back. But as she stepped through the doors, she found several of her staff gathered there being questioned by a team of security guards. Their uniforms were those of J.E. Co.'s in-house security team, and the staff looked anxious. One of them pointed a shaking finger at Aster as she walked in.

"There she is, sir," the technician said nervously.

The security guards turned to her, then stood to one side as someone stepped forwards. He was instantly recognisable to everyone who worked for the company.

He was a stout man with a bushy black moustache and carefully combed, dark hair styled with white streaks. He was dressed in a smart blue suit but had ditched the frilled collar he usually wore with it, and he had a scowl on his face even nastier than his usual frown.

"Dr Aster Thorn?" He asked gloweringly.

"Good morning, Chairman Darius," Aster said respectfully.

"Come with me," Darius ordered.

"Is there something–?" Aster tried to ask.

"Now," Darius barked like a drill instructor.

Being spoken to in such an imperious tone by some pompous fleekster made Aster twitch involuntarily in anger. But this particular 'pompous fleekster' was her boss, so she swallowed her pride and did as she was instructed.

Then the power died.

The entire facility was plunged into pitch blackness amid scattered yelps of panic in the corridors before dull-red floor lighting activated automatically, guiding people to the exits. Aster was left disoriented by the sudden darkness, even as the backup generators kicked in after a brief delay, restoring power and light to the building.

"What the fleek!?" Darius bellowed.

The emergency floor lighting remained on, and staff members followed them as they hastily made their way to the exits. Aster was carried along with the crowds as she followed the floor lighting along with everyone else to the main entrance hall, pushing and shoving her way through to get enough space.

Blackouts were virtually unheard of. This was, after all, a modern city with a modern power infrastructure. It had to be a localised blackout, and since there was no emergency alarm or automated voice advising people to head for the exits, it couldn't be an emergency shutdown. Someone had to have manually shut off the power.

Darius didn't have to push or shove his way through the crowds, his security escort did that for him as they cleared the way for their boss.

"Everyone, shut up!" Darius bellowed, silencing the hubbub of panicked chatter, "It's just a temporary power failure. Someone go and look at the systems to see what happened. Everybody else, get back to work. All work schedules will continue as normal today."

The crowd murmured their acknowledgement and began to file back out of the entrance hall in a more or less orderly fashion. Darius wasn't the most pleasant boss to work for, but at least he was back and giving some sort of leadership.

"You," Darius pointed a pudgy finger at Aster, "You're coming with me."

"You think *I* had something to do with this?" Aster demanded incredulously.

"I don't know what the fleek is going on," Darius shot back, red-faced, "but I'm pretty damned sure Jezebel is responsible for it."

Aster's heart leapt into her mouth. Had she been found out already?

Two burly security guards tried to grab Aster, but she yanked her arms free and scowled at them, making clear that she wouldn't be dragged away like some convict. Without another word, they escorted her to the elevator – in full view of her colleagues – following close behind Chairman Darius.

Apprehension built in Aster's stomach as she was led into the elevator and escorted up to the top floors of J.E. Co.'s head offices. She put her hands in her pockets, holding the blue decoy chip in her right hand nervously.

Her left hand closed around air.

Aster's stomach tightened into a horrified knot as she groped around frantically in her pocket for the red data chip. But she couldn't feel anything in her pocket.

The red chip was gone.

* * *

'You can't kill your way to victory', or so a great general whose name had been lost to obscurity is said to have remarked. In theory, that meant the key to victory was to break the enemy's will to fight rather than to kill him outright. Or perhaps it was just a piece of strategic folk wisdom passed down through the centuries. In any case, Gabriel and what remained of his squad were testing that theory to destruction.

The Faithful hunted them through the endless, three-dimensional labyrinth of the Temple, showing no sign of wanting to give up the chase. Time and again, the squad escaped from, or beat back, one hunting party only to be ambushed by another as they pushed through the maze of identical corridors and sub-chambers. The only 'progress' they could measure was in the number of kills they made.

They weren't heading in any particular direction, either. There was no place to which they could fall back, and the mind-bending inconsistency of the gravity made it impossible to get their bearings one way or another. They would leave through the side of one sub-chamber only to emerge on the ceiling of another.

The Faithful, on the other hand, were accustomed to navigating through their Temple and made effective use of jump-packs and gravity belts as they bounced from surface to surface. But what the squad lacked in numbers and firepower, they made up for in tenacity and determination to survive; and they managed to fight their way through wave after wave of fanatical pursuers to the bottom-most chamber of the Temple.

Cato fired several bursts at the enemy behind them. But the attackers had formed a shield wall with their wrist-mounted personal barriers, and the bullets swerved sharply up into the ceiling or sideways with a series of clattering noises.

"*Spare frag, anybody?*" Cato called out.

"*Nope!*" Viker replied.

"*None here!*" Gabriel said.

"*I'm out as well!*" Bale answered.

This was bad. Each of their weapons fired tiny pellets of metal shaved off from a single block inside the gun's frame, which meant they could expend tens of thousands of rounds without running out of shots. But their bullets were next to useless against those wrist-shields, and the squad had run out of explosives to overcome them.

Gabriel glanced around at the chamber, noticing that it was much larger than the cube-shaped sub-chambers they had passed through. The chamber was shaped like a hemisphere and was full of lab machinery arranged around some kind of basalt column in the centre stretching from floor to ceiling. But there was nothing that could help them fight back.

"*Viker, cover me!*" Gabriel ordered as he stowed his weapon and drew the xenotech sword he had taken earlier.

Viker understood his plan and raised his wrist-shield to cover him, advancing on the phalanx of enemies with Gabriel huddled behind. Gabriel wasn't sure what effect the alien sword would have against energy shielding, but if the blade could cut clean through carbon nanotubing, it was worth a try.

Gabriel clicked the switch at the base of the sword's handle, activating the energy field and causing the blade to shimmer ever so slightly. Cato and Bale provided covering fire as the two sides closed in on one another. Once they were close enough, Gabriel rolled forwards and swung his sword in a massive arc.

The xenotech blade scythed through the wrist-barriers as if they weren't even there, creating a flash and a discordant whirring noise as it interacted violently with the shielding. The sword continued on through the bodies of all three shield wielders, cutting cleanly through their armour and flesh. As they crumpled to the ground, the squad of attackers behind them were quickly gunned down by Cato and Bale, eliminating the immediate threat.

Or so they thought.

Their motion trackers and other sensors became scrambled with junk data as something approached. At the other end of the corridor appeared a vaguely female figure clad in a black suit with a bulbous helmet and a featureless black visor who tossed an object their way. It bounced off the walls and rolled to halt on the floor in front of the squad; they dived into cover right before it detonated.

Bale and Cato managed to duck behind the corner and avoid getting hit, whilst Viker crouched down behind his wrist-barrier, the energy shield absorbing most of the force that came his way. But Gabriel was closest to the device when it detonated, and the shockwave sent him flying across the chamber like a ragdoll. He hit a robotic arm set up next to the central column, the impact of his body pushing the machine forward into the column.

The robotic arm was equipped with an electric arc projector, and when the projector's prongs touched the column, close to a million volts were transferred to its surface. The column lit up like a carnival showpiece, illuminating an intricate pattern of circuitry that covered its surface and spreading across the ceiling, walls, and floor like a fast-moving rash all the way to chamber's entrance.

The edges around the corridor entrance began to glow and a translucent wall appeared, sealing off the corridor from the chamber and trapping the black widow outside. It also meant that the squad was trapped inside the chamber. Gabriel picked himself up off the ground and looked up at the mysteriously reactivated column.

"*About time for a deus ex machina stroke of luck,*" Gabriel remarked as he deactivated his sword and stowed it on his back.

"*What was that, sir?*" Bale asked, the classical metaphor passing straight over his head.

"*Nothing,*" Gabriel replied, "*We've got some breathing room. Look around the chamber for supplies or anything we can use.*"

Mindful of the shimmering barrier, the squad fanned out to explore the chamber.

In addition to the suite of ceiling-height robotic arms meant to probe the glowing column, several thick cables had been attached to it using special clamps, forming crude connections between the alien machine and the banks of computers and scanner equipment that lined the walls of the chamber. There were no guns or explosives anywhere to be found; although being a field laboratory, that wasn't terribly surprising.

In one corner was a spectroscopic analysis chamber with an oblong shaped block suspended in the middle. The analysis had been left to run in a continuous loop, bathing the basalt-coloured block in a sensory light while the computers mindlessly churned out the results onto the unattended holographic screens.

"*Does anyone see any square-shaped holes in that column?*" Gabriel asked as he examined the oblong block.

"*Yeah, there's one right near the bottom,*" Viker replied, "*Why?*"

"*I've found a piece that might fit,*" Gabriel answered, reaching in and plucking the block out of the chamber, the sensors deactivating automatically as it was removed.

"*I'm not sure it's a good idea to switch this thing on, sir,*" Cato said hesitantly.

"*But it's already been switched on,*" Viker pointed out.

"*And you want to activate it even more?*" Cato shot back.

Gabriel's instincts landed him solidly on Cato's side. He had dealt with xenotechnology before, and you never just switched on an alien device without first knowing exactly what it was, what it would do when switched on, and how to switch it off again.

"*Colonel, what do you want us to do with this thing?*" Bale asked.

The squad didn't have the experience that Gabriel did, but they understood the dilemma all the same. They were safe – or trapped – inside the chamber thanks to the machine they had inadvertently revived. That didn't mean it was a good idea to switch it on all the way.

One of the computer screens began to flash, brightly enough to illuminate the chamber, arresting the attention of the squad.

As they turned to look at it, the flashing stopped and a pair of shapes appeared on the screen: a rectangle with a gap in the side, and a smaller block moving across the screen until it filled the gap.

"*Spooky coincidence, or a message?*" Viker wondered aloud.

"*I vote we ignore the machine telling us to switch it back on,*" Cato said.

"*For what it's worth, I second Cato,*" Bale added.

A banging sound coming from the corridor snapped their attention back. Someone or something on the other side of the energy barrier was striking it in an effort to break through. Just as they were wondering how hitting an energy field could make a noise like that, the lights in the column began to flicker and grow pale.

"*That electric jolt must be wearing off,*" Gabriel said, kneeling down in front of the socket in the column with the block in hand, "*and once it does, the barrier will probably fail.*"

"*Are you sure we can hold them off once they break through the barrier, Cato?*" Viker asked, tightening his grip on his gun, "*because I'm fricking not.*"

The brightly lit alien circuitry continued to flicker, and the glowing energy forming the barrier around the threshold grew fainter and weaker. Seeing that the energy barrier was weakening, the enemies on the other side began to bang even harder, causing the translucent barrier to light up each time it was struck.

"*Nothing ventured, nothing gained,*" Gabriel said as he inserted the block into the slot.

The tepid and flickering lighting in the column re-illuminated and became bright green, re-energising the circuitry and restoring the barrier to full power.

"RESTORED," a booming voice reverberated throughout the chamber.

The squad instinctively raised their weapons, fanning out in search of the source of the voice. They were so focused on the apparent threat that it took them a moment to realise that the voice had spoken to them in Standard Human Speech.

"Identify yourself!" Gabriel demanded using his helmet speakers.

"YOU FIRST," said the voice, seeming to emanate from everywhere at once.

"Voidstalker," Gabriel answered, declining to give his actual name or rank.

"A stalker of the void," the voice said, lowering its volume, "one who hunts by means of stealth through the emptiness of space. A curious choice of self-identifier."

"That's what you can call me," Gabriel shot back, "now what do we call you!"

The voice was silent for a moment.

"No appropriate self-identifier exists," the voice answered, "but if you desire to ascribe a designation, you may use the term 'observer'."

"Ok, 'observer'," said Gabriel, "have you been watching us this whole time?"

"Correct," the observer confirmed, "the observer has been observing your kind ever since you first gained entrance to the observatory."

"Observatory? You mean this place?"

"Correct."

"What were you 'observing'?" Cato asked.

"Permitting one's subordinates to speak out of turn is a behaviour the observer has not observed amongst your kind before," the observer noted condescendingly.

"Answer the question!" Gabriel snapped back impatiently.

"The observatory's purpose is beyond your ability to comprehend," was the imperious response, "but it has traversed the void between countless stars to fulfil it."

"'Void between stars'?" Gabriel asked, "This is a ship?"

"Correct," the observer replied, "However, it is no longer capable of interstellar travel. The observer's own systems were reduced to minimal functionality. Only sensory capacity has remained fully functional."

"How long has this ship been here?"

"The observatory's landing occurred approximately 605,936 local solar years ago," the observer replied, "Your kind gained entrance to the observatory through a breach in the hull approximately five local solar years ago."

"*That's just over a million Terran years*," Viker said over the comm. in amazement, "*that means it's been lying here since before Humanity invented fire…*"

"The observer can detect your transmissions, but is unable to decode their content."

"The thing we found in the central chamber, what was it?" Bale asked.

"The Swarm," the observer replied, "It was contained safely in the central chamber of the observatory until your kind disturbed it approximately one local solar year ago in an effort to study it. One after another, it corrupted their minds and instead of studying it, they began to display behaviour towards it indicative of extreme, superstitious awe."

"Is that why they began doing all those sick experiments on each other?" Cato asked.

"The observer observed that the earliest test subjects were those who refused to be 'enlightened'," the observer explained, "Later subjects were volunteers. It was then that those of your kind who have settled within this ship began to self-identify as the 'Faithful'. However, the observer prefers the term 'Enthralled'."

"The thing you called the 'Swarm'," Gabriel said, "the Faithful's leader referred to it as the 'Voice'. What did he mean by that?"

"When the Swarm enters the body of an organic host," the observer explained, "it initiates temporary neural fusion, resulting in neurological data transfer directly into the host's mind. The Enthralled refer to this process as 'enlightenment', since it imparts technical knowledge otherwise beyond the host's grasp.

After the Swarm leaves the host, the effects of the neural fusion remain long afterwards in the form of a 'voice' or 'whispering'."

"*That explains the tech advantage they have*," said Viker.

"Furthermore," the observer continued, "the data transfer appears to be bi-directional, permanently imparting a portion of the host's own memories and knowledge to the Swarm."

"So they know what it knows, and it knows what they know," Gabriel said.

"Correct," the observer confirmed.

Gabriel's stomach tightened when he realised what that meant.

"*Colonel...*" Viker said over the comm., having had the same thought, "*Ogilvy...*"

"*The Swarm knows what he knows*," Gabriel's blood ran uncharacteristically cold.

"Before they became enthralled to the Swarm, your kind deemed it unacceptable to exclude an individual from a conversation by means of secrecy," the observer noted.

"You said you still had sensor functionality," said Gabriel, "Can you track the Swarm?"

"The observer has full sensory capacity throughout all chambers and passageways of the observatory," the observer replied, "The observer detects 732 distinct life signs, excluding your own, including one possessed by the Swarm."

"Where is the Swarm right now?"

"On the other side of the barrier," the observer responded.

The squad snapped to attention and trained their weapons on the barrier.

"Can it get through?" Gabriel demanded, having run out of ideas on how they were supposed to fight an enemy like this.

"Unknown," the observer replied, sounding unconcerned.

The translucent barrier began to glow, releasing a bizarre whining sound as an armoured foot, then a knee, and finally a body stepped through as if the barrier weren't there. Ogilvy looked like a supernatural plague made manifest with his jet-black eyes, his mouth twisted into a demonic snarl, and the cloud of alien particles that orbited his body like a dark storm.

"Correction," the observer observed wryly, "Yes, it can."

The squad opened fire but to no avail. Ogilvy didn't even flinch as the bullets struck his Swarm-generated shielding and were violently slapped away in all directions.

"Observer! We need an exit, now!" Gabriel shouted.

A section of the basalt-black wall flashed green, repelling a quarter tonne bank of computers away from it and across the room straight into the possessed operator's torso, pinning him against the wall. He screamed in rage, the Swarm buzzing violently in a reflection of his fury as he pounded at the bank of computers that trapped him.

There was a whirring sound and the glowing circuitry on the central column suddenly died. Then the column itself began to move, retracting smoothly and noiselessly into a slot in the domed ceiling, and opening up a manhole-sized escape route in the floor.

"Here is your exit," the observer informed them congenially, "It will take you directly to the…*untranslatable*…at the opposite end of the observatory."

"Why do we need to go there?" Viker demanded.

"The observer requires your assistance in containing this threat," the observer informed them, "By restoring the…*untranslatable*…in this location, all local systems have been restored to full functionality. Once you have repeated the action in the other five chambers, the observer will be able to do more than merely observe."

"*Down the hatch, boys!*" Gabriel ordered.

Anywhere was better than here, and the squad members hopped into the hole one after another without complaint, each one vanishing suddenly as a powerful gravity field sucked them downwards at high speed.

The Swarm-possessed Ogilvy finally tossed the bank of computers to one side, freeing itself from the imprisoning weight.

Then it turned and fixed its evil, alien gaze on Gabriel who stared back through his visor.

"You must go now, voidstalker," said the observer.

Gabriel snapped out of the staring match and took the plunge.

* * *

Aster's blood ran cold in her veins for the entire elevator ride up.

The red data chip was gone. Had someone snatched it out of her pocket during the blackout, or had it simply fallen out amid all the jostling? It really didn't matter how the data chip had vanished; the important thing was it was gone, along with whatever leverage she might have had over Jezebel Thorn.

On second thought, it was probably an incredible stroke of luck. Chairman Darius must have gotten wind that Jezebel had a mole in his company, and the shared surname made her the obvious suspect. If a data chip full of J.E. Co.'s secrets were found in her possession that would be clear proof of guilt; whereas the only thing on the blue decoy chip was company spyware which *she* had installed.

The elevator arrived near the top of the tower, and the guards led Aster past a series of swanky offices and conference rooms, with Darius pacing ahead of them. She'd never been up to this part of the building before; this was where the actual business operations of the company took place: accounting, sales, client relations, and so on. Presumably, this was also where they took suspicious employees to be questioned.

The closer they got to their destination, the faster Aster's heart raced. In fact, her apprehension was turning to palpable fear. But why should she feel afraid? After all, she was innocent – mostly. She hadn't stolen or sabotaged anything, and she hadn't passed on any sensitive information to J.E. Co.'s competitors or to anyone else. She hadn't actually done anything to violate her employment contract, let alone the law; so this ought to be a breeze.

Finally, after passing through a security door, they arrived at an interrogation room. It was a windowless chamber with a single chair in the centre, a neuroimaging scanner on a robotic arm suspended overhead. It was oddly spacious for an interrogation room, with one whole corner given over to a monitoring booth with a bank of holographic screens where her neural activity could be monitored.

"Have a seat, Dr Thorn," Chairman Darius ordered her, and she did as instructed.

The chair was more comfortable than it looked – probably to make the subject lower their guard – but as soon as Aster settled into the chair and gripped the armrests, the restraints closed around her wrists and ankles, securing her to the seat. Aster breathed and relaxed; she had things to hide, but nothing illegal. As long as she stayed calm, she would be fine.

The neuroimaging scanner descended from the ceiling and settled into place around her head, illuminating her head with a soft blue light as it activated. Over at the monitoring booth, Aster could see a mirror-image of her neural activity on the holographic screens; that was probably a design oversight on the part of the engineers since the subject wasn't supposed to be able to monitor their own progress.

The two guards left the room, leaving Aster alone with the chairman and a technician.

"Let's begin, shall we?" said the chairman, stepping into the booth with the technician.

Aster gulped but kept a straight face. Normally, a trained interrogator was required to conduct a neuroimaging-assisted questioning. So why was the chairman going to do it himself? Was he really that paranoid?

"Is your name Aster Thorn?" the chairman asked.

"Yes," Aster replied calmly.

"Are you a licensed pilot?"

"No."

"Are you married?"

"Yes."

"Have you ever met the Masterminds?"

"No."

"Do you have children?"

"Yes."

"Are you hiding anything?"

"No."

The serene blue readout displaying Aster's neural activity flashed a tepid yellow as her brain caught up with her mouth. Darius exchanged a glance with the technician while Aster pursed her lips and tried to stay calm.

She had blurted out 'no' without thinking, then remembered the decoy data chip still in her coat pocket. The readout would show various shades of four colours depending on how truthful her statements were based on her brain activity. Blue was truthful, yellow was mildly untruthful or evasive, orange was substantially untruthful, and red was a blatant lie. A numerical score would be more accurate, but the colour coding was more visually intuitive.

"How do you know Jezebel Thorn?" Darius demanded.

"Uh…sir?" the technician said haltingly.

"What?" Darius snapped irritably.

"In order to provide unambiguous results, the system requires unambiguous yes/no questions," the technician was visibly nervous about interrupting him but managed to hold her composure under the chairman's withering stare.

Darius nodded and turned back to Aster.

"*Do* you know Jezebel Thorn?" he asked, this time in a calmer voice.

"Yes," Aster replied.

"Have you ever met Jezebel Thorn?"

"Yes, I have."

"Have you met Jezebel Thorn recently?"

"Yes," Aster said honestly.

"Are you on friendly terms with Jezebel Thorn?"

Aster looked her employer dead in the eye.

"Yes."

The holographic readout flashed bright red. Darius exchanged another look with the technician before looking back at Aster with a suspicious scowl.

"She's my mother-in-law," Aster explained innocently; the readout stayed blue.

Darius's scowl softened ever so slightly, almost sympathetically.

"Let's continue then. Have you ever handed over sensitive company information to an unauthorised person or entity, or facilitated the disclosure of sensitive company information to an unauthorised person or entity?"

"No," Aster said truthfully.

If the chairman were a trained interrogator, he would have known to ask the two questions separately, but no matter.

"Have you ever attempted to sabotage this company's products or research?"

"No."

"Have you ever conspired to smuggle data or components out of this building?"

"No," Aster replied more or less truthfully.

The readout registered a faint yellow blip.

"Have you ever smuggled data or components out of this building?" Darius asked, his suspicion rekindled by the yellow blip.

"No," Aster answered.

"Have you ever used your personal override code to access re-stricted areas?"

"Yes."

"Did you use your personal override code yesterday?"

"Yes," Aster replied.

No point in lying about that.

"Have you used it more than once since yesterday morning?"

"No," Aster answered, registering blue on the readout.

Darius didn't follow up with another question. Instead, he exchanged yet another look of suspicion with the supervising technician, making Aster nervous. Had she slipped up? Were they testing her in some other way? Or did they know something she didn't?

"Have you used your personal override code more than once since yesterday morning?" Darius repeated more aggressively.

"No, I have not," Aster replied again, her own suspicions now piqued.

"Have you ever disclosed your personal override code to anyone?"

"Never."

The readout remained blue, and there was another exchange of suspicious glances.

"Have you ever used your personal override code to access another employee's office?" Darius asked, his eyes narrowed to leery pinpricks.

"Yes," Aster confessed, nervous about how much trouble she might already be in.

"Was it Dr Lawrence Kane's office?"

"Yes."

Aster's pulse was starting to race faster than it should. Her personal override code was a prerogative of her position and seniority and using it didn't violate any company rules. So why this line of questioning?

"Did you have an accomplice?"

"What?" Aster asked, nonplussed by the question.

"Don't pretend to be stupid!" Darius snapped, "Did you have an accomplice?"

"An accomplice to what?!" Aster snapped back.

"ANSWER THE FLEEKING QUESTION!" Darius bellowed, red-faced.

"No! No, I did not, and do not, have an accomplice!" Aster shouted back.

The readout fizzled to grey before returning to its normal blue colour.

"That was inconclusive, sir," the technician said nervously.

"What the fleek do you mean 'inconclusive'?" Darius demanded.

"Subjecting her to undue stress or anger muddles the readings and makes it difficult to determine whether she's telling the truth or not," the technician explained.

Perhaps they should have swapped roles.

"I did not, and do not have an accomplice," Aster intoned.

The readout remained a cerulean shade of calm.

"Your personal override code was used to access Dr Lawrence Kane's office twice yesterday," Darius asserted, "and yet you're telling me that you only used it once."

"I accessed Lawrence Kane's office using my personal override code *once*," Aster replied, registering blue on the readout.

"Are you hiding anything?" Darius asked.

"There's a data chip in my pocket that I was planning to use later," Aster responded truthfully, "then suddenly the blackout occurred and you brought me up here."

On its own terms, that statement was entirely truthful, whilst leaving out details and context that would have made it sound suspicious. The blue readout bore out her thinking.

Darius pointed to Aster and snapped his fingers. The technician nodded and stepped out of the booth to approach Aster, who felt suddenly vulnerable as the technician rifled through her pockets, digging out the blue decoy chip and returning to the booth with it. Darius took the chip from her and glared at it under the light.

The door burst open and one of the guards barged in looking panicked.

"Sir! There's a…" the guard began to speak before trailing off.

"There's a what?" Darius demanded, annoyed at the interruption.

"It's about the power loss just now," the guard replied.

Darius followed the guard outside, the door sealing behind him with an ominous clang. Aster gulped nervously and tried to sit still as she avoided eye contact with the technician.

After a minute or so the door was opened again, more violently than necessary, and Darius re-entered with a furious look on his face. Instead of returning to the booth, he stormed over to Aster and grabbed her by the scruff of her shirt.

"Did you disable the power generator?!" he demanded angrily.

"No!" Aster answered, taken aback by the chairman's outburst.

The readout fizzled into an inconclusive shade of grey before turning blue again. Darius looked back at the technician who nervously shook her head. Turning back to Aster, he reluctantly released her and took a step back.

"Did you cause the blackout?" Darius demanded, his tone only slightly calmer.

"No," Aster replied, keeping the readout blue.

"Do you know who caused the blackout?" Darius demanded.

"No."

"Have you ever used your personal override code to gain access to restricted areas other than another employee's office?"

"No, I have not."

"Then why was your personal override code used less than ten minutes ago to gain access to the primary power conduit for this building?"

"Sir, the questions need to be–" the technician tried in vain to explain.

"I know they need to be yes/no questions!" Darius snapped.

"I have no idea who caused the blackout or what you're talking about," Aster replied calmly, trying to keep her breathing level.

The readout stayed blue.

Darius stood over Aster like an angry drill instructor overseeing the punishment of a cadet, visibly fuming with frustration. Evidently, the blackout had been sabotage, and he was convinced that Aster had had something to do with it. But even though people lied, the neuroimaging scanner didn't.

After a full minute of silent fuming, Darius turned away and snapped his fingers at the technician who nodded and deactivated the machine. The neuroimaging scanner was lifted back up to the ceiling and Aster's restraints unlocked, releasing her from the chair. Aster stood up, rubbing her wrists to soothe the welts, then looked up at Darius.

"Dr Aster Thorn," Darius said in a more formal and level tone, "you mostly passed the lie detection session, but the fact remains that your personal override code was used to access Dr Lawrence Kane's office twice – not in itself a violation of company rules, but curious given that the Directorate of Naval Intelligence was so interested in him."

"I went into his office exactly once," Aster said truthfully, "I don't know who could have gotten my personal override code."

"Probably the same person who used it to enter the power conduit chamber and cause the blackout," Darius answered with calm authority, "thereby disabling security long enough to sneak out during the confusion."

Aster felt her stomach tighten as she realised that someone had tried to frame her.

"In any case," Chairman Darius continued, "the secrecy of your personal override code is your responsibility, and you are therefore responsible for any security breaches resulting from its use or abuse. I am hereby suspending you as project-lead pending an internal investigation; your security clearance and other associated privileges are also suspended. Go home and don't return until further notice."

Aster's spirit crumbled.

"…Yes sir," she replied, feeling utterly crushed.

* * *

Between the wealthy Clouds and the Undercity far below, the middle levels of Asgard City were a patchwork of homes, shopping centres, industrial complexes, and other assorted pieces of real estate. Buried in the maze of back alleys was an entertainment club, the sort of place in which Jezebel Thorn normally wouldn't be caught dead.

She had occupied a private room, flanked by two android servants, and was passing the time by wrinkling her nose at this foul place. The lighting was dim, her chair was uncomfortable, the surfaces were less than spotless, and the decor was a crime against good taste.

And then there was the nature of the establishment itself. It was an 'entertainment' club where the main feature was a stage and a set of vertical poles which female entertainers used to flaunt themselves in front of a pack of drooling male patrons, all set to faintly gyrating dance music. Jezebel had come in through a side entrance, partly for discretion's sake and partly to avoid having to witness the lurid spectacle.

There was a knock at the door and a person entered without asking to be allowed in, slamming the door shut behind him and laying back against the door. Jezebel sat and waited patiently whilst he caught his breath. He was late, but as long as he'd acquired what she wanted, she could wait another minute.

"I got it," he said breathlessly.

"The blue data chip?"

"Blue data chips are for non-essential data only," he replied, reaching into his left pocket and pulling out the prize, "red data chips are for sensitive data. This is what you want."

Jezebel motioned for him to approach and give her the chip, not deigning to get out of her seat to collect it. She took it from him and held it up to the dim light with her finger and thumb, smiling like a shark smelling blood.

"Well done," she replied, getting up to leave.

"I'm sick of doing this," the informant exclaimed, "everyone on Loki is dead, and now the company could well go under because of the scandal. I'm sick of being your rat."

"'Mole'," Jezebel corrected him, "a 'rat' would be an informant for the authorities. Plus, I prefer to think of you as an unofficial observer of sorts."

"Whatever, I'm sick of being your mole or observer."

"Not as sick as your partner, I bet," Jezebel quipped cruelly.

"We'll manage without your financial help," he said defiantly, "so are we done?"

"We are," Jezebel confirmed.

She snapped her fingers and the two androids grabbed the man by his arms and kicked him behind both knees, forcing him to the dirty ground. He struggled in vain against the superhuman strength of the androids as they gripped his arms and each kept a foot planted on the back of his knees to hold him there.

"What the fleek are you doing?!" the informant shouted, struggling frantically.

No one could hear him. The thick walls dampened most of the noise he made and the thumping dance music beyond drowned out the rest.

"You've been incredibly useful to me over the years," Jezebel replied coldly, "but as you pointed out, J.E. Co. is about to go under, so I no longer require your services."

"You bitch! You bitch!" he screamed, struggling like a wild animal.

One android forced the informant's left arm down to his side and held him by his black-and-gold hair while the other placed a gun in his right hand, forcing his fingers to close around the gun's handle. The android then used its other hand to push down on the inside of his elbow, forcing the gun to his temple.

Jezebel turned away from the staged suicide and looked at the blood-red data chip in her hand, smiling in quiet satisfaction as her erstwhile informant's screams and struggles were silenced with a single gunshot.

THE WIDOW

Out of the frying pan and into the firefight. That was the last thought that passed through Gabriel's mind as he leapt into the escape hole. As soon as he jumped, he felt a powerful force yank his body straight downwards. The instantaneous acceleration was disorienting but not nearly as disorienting as the insane journey that followed.

The walls of the tunnel dissolved into an imperceptible blur as the gravity field carried Gabriel along at incredible speeds, like one of those theme park rides that carried revellers along a winding tunnel before depositing them into a pool of water. Except that he was hurtling along ten times as fast, and whatever was waiting at the other end wanted to kill him.

The tunnel didn't travel in a straight line either; it twisted, turned, and corkscrewed seemingly at random as it carried Gabriel along at breakneck speeds, making him feel that he might be dashed against the side of the tunnel. The most he could do was hug his weapon close, keep his feet together, and hope that didn't happen.

Strangest of all was the sound, or lack thereof. The air resistance in the gravity tunnel ought to be a deafening roar; but to prevent hearing damage, the auditory software in Gabriel's helmet artificially reduced the volume of loud noises or filtered them out altogether.

It was eerily silent all the way down – or up, rather.

A faint light appeared at the end of the tunnel before rushing up to meet Gabriel. As he shot out of the tunnel at high speed, he felt his innards decelerate dramatically as the sudden change in gravity slowed his descent to a safe speed. The rest of the squad was already there, recovering as best they could from the trip.

"*That was…not bad!*" Viker hyperventilated.

"*Sit-rep!*" Gabriel replied, deadly serious.

"*No threats detected,*" Bale replied, "*but that'll probably change soon.*"

They were standing on the ceiling of a hemispherical hall identical to the chamber from which they had just escaped. Unlike the previous chamber, however, this one was totally bare, with no storage crates, weapons caches or research equipment to be seen.

Without warning, the chamber's column began to extend from its slot in the ceiling directly beneath Gabriel's feet. He stepped off the moving column just in time to avoid falling back into the tunnel as the column slid inside, sealing off the entrance to the gravity tunnel; but he was removed from the artificial gravity field keeping him on the ceiling and tumbled down to the floor, landing on one foot and falling awkwardly onto his side.

"*You alright, sir?*" Cato asked.

"*I'm fine,*" Gabriel replied, climbing back to his feet, "*it seems the observer is trying to help us. Join me down here and we can get this over with.*"

Rather than activating their gravity belts, the squad jumped 'up' towards the floor, leaving the gravity field keeping them on the ceiling and landing more or less on their feet.

"*Cato, check the column for the number of slots we need to fill,*" Gabriel ordered, "*Everybody else, fan out and look for the blocks.*"

"*Found one!*" Viker announced, holding up a block discarded on the floor.

"*Found a slot too!*" Cato announced.

"*Two slots?*" Viker asked.

"*No, I mean I found a slot as well*," Cato clarified.

"*Whatever*," Viker said dismissively, "*just catch.*"

Viker tossed the jet-black block to Cato who caught it deftly and inserted it into the corresponding aperture at the base of the column.

As the block slid home, the intricate network of circuitry on the plain black column was illuminated as the machine was restored to power – or to life, they didn't know anything about the technology they were bringing back online.

"RESTORED," boomed the observer's voice.

"Are your systems back online?" Viker asked.

"Correct," the observer replied, "That is what the word 'restored' means."

"*Fricking smug xeno-computer*," Viker muttered in annoyance.

"*I'm sure it didn't mean to hurt your feelings, Viker*," Bale joked.

"The observer finds your propensity for private communication amongst yourselves most curious," the observer observed without actually sounding curious at all.

"We need you to put up those barriers before the Faithful can get in!" Gabriel shouted.

"Unnecessary," the observer replied, "The Enthralled's pursuit attempts have left them concentrated around the chamber from which you arrived, at the exact opposite end of the observatory from your current location. Even if they knew your location, it would require a considerable amount of time to reach you."

"What about the Swarm," Cato asked, "can it reach us via the same path?"

"No," the observer reassured them, "the observer sealed the entrance to the gravitic transport network as soon as the voidstalker embarked. It cannot follow."

"Good, so the sooner we get to the other four chambers, the better."

"Correct," the observer confirmed, "It would be most efficient for the four of you to split up, one individual per chamber."

The squad collectively flinched.

"*No fricking way we're splitting up,*" Viker said over the comm.

"If you harbour reservations, voice them aloud," the observer demanded.

"We're not splitting up," Gabriel replied.

"Clarify your reasoning," the observer commanded.

"Four guns are better than one in a firefight," Gabriel explained, "We're not dividing our strength just to save time on the task."

"The voidstalker wishes to prioritise the concentration of meagre firepower over time-efficient completion of the task at hand?" the observer enquired.

"Correct," Gabriel answered emphatically, "I don't care if it takes us four times as long to get you back online; we're not splitting up."

There was a moment of silence.

"Understood," the observer noted.

The glowing circuitry on the newly restored central column went black, and the column receded back into the ceiling, reopening the entrance to the gravitic transport network.

"Please enter the gravitic tunnel," the observer requested, "the observer will transport you to one of the remaining four chambers."

"*You know the drill!*" Gabriel said.

* * *

It was a relatively brief ride on the train back home, but it felt like forever. Aster spent the entire journey feeling totally crushed. There were no goodbyes or reassuring explanations for why she was being suspended – her colleagues and subordinates would be informed of her 'period of leave' by email – just the deauthorisation of her security clearance, the collection of her smartphone from storage, and an elevator ride down to the station.

If she hadn't broken into Lawrence's office and snooped around in the first place, none of this would have happened. No red chip. No blackmail. No cloak-and-dagger scheming. No cloud of suspicion hanging over her head. No potentially career-ending suspension. The events of the past day or so were ultimately her fault.

By the time she got to the apartment door, she was fighting back tears.

The biometric sensor flash-scanned her teary eyes and Aster hurried inside, slamming the door shut behind her. She ignored the maganiel android standing guard in the hallway and headed straight for the master bedroom, closing the door behind her more gently this time before flopping down on the bed in despair.

It felt useless to cry about what had happened, let alone wallow in self-pity over a partly self-inflicted predicament. She'd only been suspended from work, after all; and unlike the poor souls at the Loki facility, she was still alive.

Rolling over to stare at the ceiling, Aster felt the tears roll down past her ears. She couldn't help but wallow in self-pity; self-pity was all she could manage right now. Having unearthed more questions than answers, her stupid hunt for the truth was now effectively over. That ought to be a huge relief, but it wasn't.

There was a little knock on the door.

"...Yes?" Aster called, hastily composing herself.

The door opened a crack and Orion peeked in, his younger siblings visible behind him.

"Hey, sweethearts," Aster smiled at them, hoping her eyes didn't look too red.

"Hi, mommy," Orion replied with a weak smile, he could see his mother's teary eyes.

"Come in, sit down," Aster beckoned them to come inside.

Orion opened the door a little wider and walked in clutching his tablet computer, followed by Rose and Violet. Together they climbed onto the bed and sat down.

"Leo's still sleeping," Violet said.

"That's ok, let him sleep," Aster replied, "So what did you learn today?"

"Ionic and covalent bonds in chemistry, algebraic long division, and how to construct 'while loops' in a program," Orion replied, playing with his tablet computer.

"Are you understanding it ok?" Aster asked her oldest child.

"Mostly," he replied.

"We also had an essay on the history of space exploration," Rose added.

"I'm sure you did great," Aster reassured them with a hug.

"How was your day, mommy?" Violet asked.

"Tough," she replied, a gross understatement, but truthful enough.

"Are we going to see Grandma again?" Orion asked.

"Not anytime soon," Aster replied, "Why?"

"You don't seem to like her very much," he noted astutely.

"What makes you think that?" Aster asked, embarrassed that her children had noticed.

Orion went silent and started staring at his feet.

"Nothing," he said sheepishly.

"Ori recorded you," Rose blurted out.

Orion flinched in embarrassment and jabbed his sister's shoulder in retaliation.

"Hey! Don't do that your sister," Aster remonstrated.

"But she told on me!" Orion protested.

"But it's true!" Rose counter-protested.

"Apologise to your sister, now!" Aster snapped.

"…Sorry," Orion mumbled half-heartedly.

"Now what's this about a recording?" Aster asked, her curiosity piqued.

Orion frowned self-consciously; then with great reluctance, he pulled up an audio file on his tablet and pressed the play button.

"…*By asking me here, you're guilty of conspiracy to commit corporate espionage*," Aster's own voice played over the speaker.

"And by coming, you're officially complicit," Grandma Jezebel's voice played in response, *"unless, of course, the real reason – the one you'd like me to corroborate if the investigators ask – is that you simply came to—"*

Orion paused the recording, embarrassed that his snooping had been found out. Aster was stunned. Not by the recording itself, but by what a stroke of luck this was.

"How much of my conversation with Grandma did you record?" she asked Orion.

"All of it," Orion replied sheepishly, "from when you walked in, all the way to when we got in the taxi. If you want, I can delete it—"

"No! Don't do that. Actually, could mommy borrow your tablet for just a minute?"

Orion nodded and handed over his tablet. Aster went over to the armoured closet where the maganiel was usually kept, and the children quietly left to give her some privacy.

Aster slid her thumb across the access pad. The light went from red to green and the doors of the maganiel's armoured closet opened. The maganiel was still standing guard in the hallway, but there was a little side compartment next to its alcove containing an electronic screen and a communications box. It was labelled: "EMERGENCY USE ONLY".

"Pretty sure this qualifies," Aster muttered as she activated the device.

"Please state your emergency," the box demanded.

"Someone attempted to blackmail me into committing corporate espionage, potentially involving xenotechnology," Aster replied to the box.

"Do you have evidence for that?"

Aster placed Orion's tablet on top of the comm. box's interface pad to establish a wireless connection, then uploaded the audio file.

"File received," the box replied, *"standby."*

Aster heaved a sigh, though not of relief. She had now ratted on Jezebel Thorn and indirectly ratted on her bosses, thereby officially violating her employment contract. She would never have dared to do so without proof, which had been the whole point of trying to pull that bait-and-switch with the data chips in the first place. Now that it was done, she had to trust that the DNI would believe what they heard on the file.

Still, there was something tremendously satisfying about sticking it to her sleazy bitch of a mother-in-law. The kind of woman who would use members of her own family, including her own grandchildren, to further her own goals. Perhaps that shouldn't be surprising for a vulture capitalist who'd gone into business after being mysteriously widowed.

* * *

The sudden change in gravity and the sensation of having one's guts yanked downwards were no less disorienting the second time around. The walls became a high-speed blur and the roaring of the air in the gravitic tunnel was reduced to an imperceptible din as the auditory sensors filtered out the otherwise deafening noise.

Gabriel hugged his weapon close and kept his feet together as he hurtled along the tunnel at breakneck speeds before veering suddenly to one side. The tunnel was uncomfortably narrow, wide enough for two or three people to stand shoulder to shoulder, but narrow enough to worry about hitting the side at such speeds.

A light appeared at the end of the tunnel and in a split second it rushed up to meet Gabriel. He re-emerged, just like before, on the ceiling of another hemispherical chamber. The sudden deceleration yanking his innards upwards as the gravity field dramatically slowed his descent, landing him squarely on his feet.

Standing upside down on the ceiling, the retracted column beneath Gabriel's feet protruded from its slot again to reseal the tunnel entrance. Gabriel jumped to one side to avoid being pushed back into the tunnel, and the change in gravity carried him down to the floor. This time, he was able to twist his body in mid-air and land squarely on his feet again.

Gabriel looked around the chamber with his weapon at the ready, scanning for threats. But there were no targets to be seen; in fact, he was the only person present. Viker, Cato, and Bale had all jumped into the gravitic tunnel before him and should be here already. So why weren't they here?

"*Squad, sound off!*" Gabriel ordered them.

There was no response. In fact, his squad members' comm. signals weren't showing up in his HUD at all, and neither were their tracking signals or bio-readings. It was as if the three of them had completely vanished.

"*Viker! Bale! Cato!*" Gabriel shouted, "*Someone, respond!*"

Silence.

Gabriel felt a surge of anger in his chest. They had been tricked; he wanted to shout and rage at the observer for its duplicity in splitting them up and still expecting them to help restore the columns. And for what? It wasn't even clear why the observer needed them restored.

As logic began to encroach on his anger, Gabriel acknowledged that whatever the truth of the matter, the observer couldn't – or wouldn't – respond until the blocks were restored to their appropriate sockets. Once they were, he could demand answers.

Gabriel looked around the chamber and found that he was in a makeshift armoury. Racks of armour and weapons lined the walls as well as jump-packs, spare gravity belts, and all manner of other military-grade equipment, most of it non-standard.

More interestingly, the chamber was dominated by a 3D fabrication module that towered over everything else. 3D fabricators were very difficult to design or build from scratch, and those capable of manufacturing weapons were illegal. For all their insanity and barbaric experimentation, Gabriel couldn't help but be impressed by this enemy's resourcefulness, even if that 'resourcefulness' had come from knowledge imparted by the Swarm.

There was also a large, semi-automated workbench with a half-assembled submachine gun and its components lying discarded on top. Stacked to one side were a pair of black oblong blocks, the very items for which he was searching. Gabriel stowed his weapon and picked up the two blocks, one in each hand.

His motion tracker flashed red.

Without thinking, Gabriel dropped the blocks and drew his weapon again as he spun around to face the threat, just in time to squeeze off a few rounds. The target's shielding rippled and flashed as it slapped aside the few bullets that he managed to fire; then she extended a hand in a 'stop' gesture, causing a circular pattern on her palm to light up.

Gabriel felt an invisible force grab him and hoist him into the air, yanking his limbs out into an X shape. He was helpless. His shielding was still active, but the force holding him in mid-air felt far more intense than the gravitic tunnel, like being restrained by a dozen invisible hands. He still had his gun, but it felt far too heavy to move.

Gabriel had seen this kind of technology before, but it was often too large for a single user to carry. That the Faithful had managed to shrink the technology down to the size of a glove was genuinely impressive. Not that being impressed helped him much.

His captor was a lithe female figure in a jet-black suit of combat armour with a bulbous black helmet and a featureless visor. She looked like the mysterious figure who had opened up the door to the labs for them earlier; the one the squad had decided to designate as the 'black widow' – it might even be the same person.

She curled her fingers, and Gabriel felt the gravitic force pull him in until he was face to face with his captor. Holding him in place directly above her with one hand, she slid her free hand across the side of her helmet, causing the visor to retract and reveal her face.

Her face was Human, devoid of androgynising cybernetics or other modifications. Her skin had a living hue without the corpselike complexion of the monsters in the Faithful's ranks. Her eyes were icy blue and her hair was raven black. She was disarmingly attractive, a strange observation to make about a lethal foe. Black widow was the right designation.

"Why are you trying to restore the Temple?" the black widow asked.

"It's not a temple," Gabriel pointed out dryly, talking through his helmet speakers.

The black widow smiled – or was it a snarl?

"The only way of knowing about the totems and the keys is through enlightenment by the Voice," the black widow looked at him with an icy stare, "But you haven't been enlightened, so why are you attempting to restore the Swarm's prison?"

"I like puzzle games," Gabriel answered sarcastically.

The black widow used her gravity glove to pull Gabriel in even closer until they were almost close enough to kiss. Those piercing blue eyes seemed to stare straight through his visor and into his own, and part of him couldn't help but stare back.

Gabriel felt a strange ripple of emotion run through his chest.

"I'll kill you if you don't answer," the black widow said in a gentle tone.

"I wouldn't do that if I were you," Gabriel replied.

The black widow thrust her hand back out again, and the action threw Gabriel violently upwards. He hit the ceiling with such force that it triggered his shielding, and the resulting repulsion sent him into an awkward spin on the way back down. The black widow's control over him was broken, and in mid-fall, he hit the activation button on his gravity belt.

The chamber was actually oriented sideways relative to the moon, and so the moon's gravity caused him to dramatically change direction in mid-fall by 90 degrees, causing him to land on what was technically the wall.

Gabriel landed on his back and opened fire, but the black widow had resealed her helmet and her shields easily swatted his bullets aside. How could a figure that thin have shields that pow-erful? Thanks to his belt, Gabriel was safe from her gravity glove, but he would need a different weapon to kill her.

But the black widow didn't give him time to re-arm. She swerved and danced as he continued shooting, as if pure agility were enough to defy his bullets. As she bolted back and forth with preternatural speed, she drew a tactical baton from behind her waist, flicking a switch which caused the tip to glow electric blue.

Defying the chamber's topsy-turvy gravity, the black widow then used the gravity glove on her free hand to boost herself off the floor and land on the ceiling opposite Gabriel, then propel herself back down again in order to land on top of him.

Gabriel switched to concussive shots and fired at his airborne opponent, but his shots barely slowed her descent as she extended the glowing tip of the baton towards him like a lance. Gabriel slid to one side to avoid her as she fell, but was too slow to avoid the baton.

The tip brushed Gabriel's foot, sending a bolt of electricity surging through his armour. The energy-absorbent layers redi-rected the power surge across the suit's systems and sent some of it arcing out from his limbs, but it was enough to temporarily short out the exoskeletal motors in his suit. Had it made contact with his flesh, he would have been fried to a crisp.

Gabriel crumpled to the ground in mid-dive as his suit mo-tors were briefly paralysed. System alarms flashed in his helmet HUD, warning him that his exoskeletal motors were non-respon-sive. As if he couldn't already tell from the fact that his armour felt ten times heavier.

Before he could get up, the black widow pounced on top of him and planted her boot on his chest. Standing over him like a dominatrix, she flipped the baton around in her hand and flicked another switch. This time, a long spike emerged from the oppo-site end of the baton, and she raised it with both hands like a stake, ready to deliver the killing blow.

Gabriel swung his left fist, the clenching motion causing his remaining three combat claws to extend. He caught the death spike in between the curved claws as it descended towards his neck, and twisted it out of its wielder's grip, sending it clattering across the floor – or the wall. Then he knocked the black widow's leg out from underneath her.

With the agility of a gymnast, the black widow turned her sideways-fall into a backward somersault, but by the time she was back on her feet, the regenerative systems in Gabriel's suit had kicked in, restoring his exoskeleton to functionality. Gabriel pushed himself off the ground, returning to his feet, and drew the alien sword from his back, activating its energy field.

The black widow extended her palm towards her baton and used her gravity glove to pull it back towards her. A clever trick, but by the time the baton was back in her hand, Gabriel had already closed the distance and brought the sword to bear, severing her arm at the elbow before bringing the blade back around and striking her neck.

The black widow stood for a moment like a tottering, one-armed statue. Then she fell to her knees and then to the ground, her helmeted head rolling off her shoulders and across the floor like a badly designed horror prop.

At that exact moment, the column unexpectedly retracted back into the ceiling and the squad's comm. signals returned to sensor range as they all came flying out of the gravitic tunnel. All three men, apparently alive and well, alighted on the ceiling of the chamber.

"*Seems like you didn't need our help with that one, Colonel,*" Bale remarked, noting the freshly decapitated black widow.

"*Actually, I probably could have used it,*" Gabriel replied.

"*That fucking observer,*" Cato cursed.

"*I know,*" Gabriel answered, "*It split us up on purpose.*"

"*And almost got us killed in the process,*" Viker added.

The giant black column re-emerged from its slot and resealed the gravitic passage, and the members of the squad jumped back down to the floor of the chamber. Gabriel disengaged his gravity belt and joined them.

"*Two blocks, over there*," Gabriel pointed to the two 'keys', still lying on the floor where he'd dropped them, "*the black widow called them 'keys'.*"

"*Sounds like superstitious ramblings to me*," Bale suggested.

"*Probably*," Gabriel conceded, "*but I'm not so sure we should put them back, now.*"

"In fact," he continued, this time speaking aloud, "I'm not so sure that you aren't at full functionality already, or that you can't hear us or talk back."

Silence.

"Fine, I'll do the talking," Gabriel shouted at the chamber, "I think you want us to believe that these columns are a power source without which you can't help us, and I think you've avoided helping us until we restore the keys in order to make us think that one requires the other. Why the charade of pretending that you're less capable than you are?"

More silence.

"*Maybe it really does need those columns to speak*," Viker suggested.

Without warning, a section of the floor beneath them and the ceiling above glowed, and a gravitational force hoisted them into the air. It felt like a far more precise version of the black widow's gravity glove, with minimal strain on the limbs; and they were only being suspended a few feet above the ground.

Nonetheless, they were trapped and helpless.

"The observer underestimated you," the observer noted.

"So you did intentionally split us up," Cato said.

"Correct," the observer admitted without apology, "The deception was necessary to induce you to accomplish your assigned task as quickly as possible and provided that you did so, there was no serious danger."

"What do the columns do and why do they need to be restored?" Gabriel demanded.

"They are, in fact, power sources," the observer explained, "but the observer's own systems are not dependent on them. Rather, they provide energy to a containment shield. Perhaps you recall seeing it when you first entered the central chamber?"

"It's for containing the Swarm?"

"Correct. Although with all six columns disabled, the containment shield was barely functional and unable to prevent the Swarm from entering an organic host."

"How strong is the containment shield, exactly?" Gabriel asked.

"Clarify your question with context," the observer requested.

"You know what a 'joule' is from listening in on the researchers here, correct?"

"It is a unit of measurement that your species utilises with respect to energy," the observer replied, "Do you wish to know the maximum amount of energy that the containment field can contain without failing?"

"Yes."

"The maximum pressure which the containment shield can theoretically exert is equivalent to five multiplied by ten to the fourteenth joules. Which is itself approximately 1.39 times greater than the explosive force of the device you are carrying."

The rest of the squad collectively blinked, thinking they might have misheard.

"*Uh…Colonel,*" Cato said tentatively on behalf of the rest of the squad, "*with all due respect, what the fuck is he talking about?*"

"*My 'command module' is an antimatter bomb,*" Gabriel replied matter-of-factly, no longer seeing the need to keep it a secret, "*It has an explosive yield of 86 kilotons, hopefully enough to destroy the observatory and the facility above with it.*"

There was another round of stony silence on the comm. channel.

"*So when were you going to tell us this?*" Viker asked, his voice trembling with rage.

"*When it became necessary to tell you, and no sooner*," Gabriel answered calmly, unmoved by Viker's anger.

"If in the course of your private deliberations, you have devised an alternative plan for destroying the Swarm, the observer desires to be informed of it," the observer interjected.

"Yes, the plan consists of the following," Gabriel said aloud to the observer, "phase 1: restore the containment shield to full power–"

"Which you can do immediately," the observer interrupted, deactivating the artificial gravity holding them in place and dropping them back to the floor.

"Phase 2:" Gabriel continued as the squad collected the remaining two oblong keys, "lure the Swarm back to the central chamber."

"Phase 3:" the observer finished as the last two keys were reinserted, "trap the Swarm and its host inside the containment shield and use your antimatter device to annihilate both."

"Wait a minute," Viker interjected, "what about Ogilvy?"

"Clarify."

"Our squad-mate," Viker clarified, "isn't there a way to force the Swarm out of him?"

"No," the observer replied bluntly, "not unless the Swarm departs of its own accord. And even if there were such a way, the effects of neural fusion are irreversible. Even after the Swarm is destroyed, he would remain enthralled to it."

"He knew the risks when he signed up," Gabriel said grimly, "and so did we."

The squad was silent, but out of sombre agreement. From the moment they had sworn the oath and put on the armour, all of them had accepted death as a hazard of duty. Ogilvy's fate was horrible, but he was no exception.

"This is an armoury," Gabriel noted, "check your weapons and armour, and stock up on anything that looks useful. Then we'll head on to the central chamber."

The entrances to the chamber were suddenly blocked off by energy barriers.

"The observer advises haste," the observer said, "the Swarm's thralls have identified your location and are converging on this chamber with speed. The protective barriers will pose only a temporary obstacle."

"Let's make it quick, then."

The squad began to scavenge through the armoury, unearthing a specialised storage case for spare ammo blocks. Gabriel checked his own light machine gun and found he only had a few dozen shots left out of about fifty thousand possible shots. He began dismantling his weapon in order to replace the ammo block with a fresh one.

"Do you value your continued existence, voidstalker?" the observer asked.

The squad paused their work, caught off guard by the question.

"*Keep working*," Gabriel ordered, then replied, "What makes you think I don't?"

"You have a high yield explosive attached to your armour," the observer pointed out, "of a kind which must be actively prevented from detonating. Either you were coerced into carrying it in spite of your sense of self-preservation, or you volunteered for reasons which transcend the self-preservation imperative."

"I volunteered with full knowledge and complete freedom to decline," Gabriel stated.

"Why volunteer for a mission with near complete certainty of death?"

"Because there are tens, if not hundreds of millions of lives at stake," Gabriel replied resolutely, "and if no one is willing to step forward and put their own life on the line for them, they would all be extinguished."

"You sound as committed to your objective as the Enthralled are to theirs," the observer replied, "Unless there is a mechanism for safely detaching the device?"

"…There is," Gabriel confirmed reluctantly, then added over the comm., *"thirty-minute timer post-decoupling, with an anti-tampering fail-deadly mechanism."*

"The concealment of crucial information is not conducive to trust," said the observer.

"Neither is splitting us up against our will," Viker pointed out.

The observer was silent for a moment.

"True."

"And just as an aside," Cato added hostilely, "none of us are totally convinced that you aren't somehow connected to the Swarm itself."

There was another pause.

"That inference is logical but inaccurate," the observer replied, "The Swarm's nature and origins are unknown, but since its motives are malevolent, its destruction is paramount."

"On that, we can agree," Gabriel answered.

They had no choice but to trust the observer, for now.

* * *

The owner of the club had been furious when one of his servers had panicked and called Civil Security instead of him first. His anger was assuaged, however, when the ACS officers pointed out to him that concealing a suspicious death in his establishment would count as criminal complicity, whether or not he had anything to do with it.

The body was lying sideways, knees bent as though he had been kneeling when he died, with a single entry wound through his right temple. The cheap, black market handgun he had presumably used to take his own life was still clutched in his cold, dead hand.

The forensics drone hovered over the body, bathing the corpse in sensory light as it scanned the body from head to toe and back again. Several patrol officers stood guard outside the room whilst two other officers, a forensics specialist and a supervising detective, stayed in the room itself to examine the crime scene.

"Suicide looks like the obvious verdict," the detective concluded.

"Really?" the specialist asked, raising a sceptical eyebrow.

"Well, look at him," the detective pointed to the body, "he clearly blew his own brains out. What other explanation is there?"

"A murder set up to look like a suicide," the specialist replied.

"How?"

"Well, why would someone go to the trouble of renting out a private room at some nightclub in order to take his own life?" the forensics specialist asked rhetorically.

"One last fabulous ride before ending it all," the detective replied, "Seen that before."

"Which hand did he prefer?" the specialist asked.

"Why does that matter?" the detective asked, puzzled.

"Tell me and I'll tell you."

The detective had already reviewed the footage, but he duly pulled up the video from the club's security cameras. As a Civil Security officer, he enjoyed automatic access.

"Looks like he favours his left hand," the detective said, "at least, he does in this video."

"Which raises the question," the forensics specialist pointed out, "why would a left-handed person hold the gun with his right hand in order to shoot himself?"

The detective was silent, realising his colleague's point.

"Maybe we should swap jobs," the forensics specialist quipped.

"Maybe he was ambidextrous?" the detective retorted defensively.

"No evidence for that," the specialist countered, "It's more likely that someone forced the gun into his hand without knowing that he was left-handed."

"And what's the evidence that someone forced the gun into his hand?"

As if on cue, the forensics drone completed its post-mortem scan and displayed a life-size, holographic recreation of the body in the air. Highlighted in red was the fatal wound through the skull, appearing as a red-shaped cone with the entry wound at the tip and the exit wound at the base. However, there were also uneven blotches of brown on the elbows and wrists as well as on the backs of the knees.

"See those," the specialist pointed to the parts highlighted in brown, "subcutaneous bruising. Likely caused by applying substantial pressure to the skin."

"He was physically restrained?" the detective asked.

"That's what it looks like," the specialist confirmed.

"So our victim comes here to meet someone," the detective pondered aloud, "and even though he looked agitated in the security footage, he came alone; so he probably wasn't expecting his contact to betray and murder him."

"At least two suspects forced this guy down to his knees and put their feet on the backs of his knees to keep him on the ground," the specialist explained, "Then one of them forced the gun into his hand and bent his arm until the muzzle was touching his temple, hence this area of bruising in the crook of the right elbow."

"A murder made to look like a suicide…" the agent mulled it over.

"Exactly as I said," the specialist concluded, "probably a professional hit."

"Not very professionally done, actually," the detective replied, "a professional killer would never make sloppy mistakes like this."

"Then who would think to do it this way?"

"Someone who wanted to make sure the job was done in person," the detective surmised, "with accomplices, but without the expertise to do it properly."

"Well that leaves motive," said the forensics specialist.

"Masterminds know what the motive could be at this point," the detective replied, "But a DNA match and a name would be a good place to start."

The forensics specialist scanned the body, coming up with a profile almost instantly.

"Dr Felix Kessler."

THE TRAP

Whoever the observatory's architects might have been, they had clearly been immune to motion sickness. So was the squad, thanks to their physical enhancements; but even though the gravitic tunnel network shaved an hour off their journey, Gabriel couldn't help but think that most people would rather walk.

After the insane, high-speed journey through the bowels of the observatory, one by one the squad dropped down through the ceiling into one of the many sub-chambers. Several of the Enthralled saw the squad drop in and were shot dead before they could raise the alarm. Once they had secured the room and made sure there were no enemies hiding there, the squad took stock of their surroundings.

Having abandoned the original facility, the research staff had also abandoned all the labs they had been using before becoming enthralled. But they had taken with them as much equipment as they could move into their Temple, and this particular sub-chamber had been converted into a substitute lab. The walls were lined with all sorts of machinery, including surgery tables equipped with robotic medical suites, and fluid-filled growth tanks; some with live subjects and others lying empty.

Upon closer examination, the term 'live subject' seemed like a polite exaggeration. The subjects were mutilated and deformed, their skin turned pale by exsanguination or darkened by injuries, the victims of revolting experiments to enhance their bodies and minds. Some had had their chest cavities opened, and half-finished cybernetic components were visible inside them, while others sported cybernetic limbs or other implants.

Life signs were still visible on some of the monitoring screens, but even if the test subjects weren't dead, they might as well be.

"What were they doing in this place...?" Cato said with disgust, inadvertently talking through his helmet speakers.

"This chamber is one of several which were requisitioned for experimentation by the Enthralled," the observer explained, having overheard his question, "All surviving test subjects have since been 'elevated'. The rest were abandoned."

At the far end of the chamber was another fluid-filled growth tank, much larger than the others; in fact, the top reached all the way up to the chamber's ceiling. It was also the centrepiece of the lab, with a constellation of computers and other equipment connected to it, still churning out results.

The specimen inside the tank wasn't Human.

"What about this tank?" Gabriel asked.

"A leftover from the experiments your kind were conducting prior to falling under the influence of the Swarm," the observer replied, "It appears that they were attempting to create a clone using DNA extracted from fossilised remains discovered within the observatory."

The squad looked up in a mixture of fascination and disgust at the strange creature housed inside the tank. It had shrunken, stunted-looking limbs and claws like a lizard as well as an elongated tail. Its skin was egg-white pale, and its eyes were glossy black; it looked like an alien embryo grown to adult size.

"This thing looks like a half-grown mutant," Bale observed with disgust.

"The DNA sample had already degraded to a fraction of the number of original base pairs," the observer explained, "The experiment ultimately failed."

"You said the DNA they used was based on fossilised remains," Cato pointed out, "was this alien part of the original crew?"

"The observatory does not require an organic crew," the observer replied perfunctorily.

"Well if there was no crew needed, then what was this thing doing on board?" Viker demanded, "What kind of 'observatory' was this place?"

"'Observatory' is an imperfect translation," the observer replied, "The term might be better translated as 'observational facility'."

Gabriel activated his gravity belt. Seeing his action, the squad did the same.

"You have activated your...*untranslatable*...devices," the observer noted, "Yet the observer does not detect any nearby...*untranslatable*...threats."

"We call them 'gravity belts'," Gabriel replied, "And before I explain why, how quickly would it take the Swarm to reach the central chamber?"

"From its current location, approximately ten minutes."

"*Viker, get behind me,*" Gabriel ordered, turning his back, "*I need your help.*"

Viker paused for a second, then stowed his weapon and stood behind Gabriel.

"*There's a slot on the underside of the command module,*" Gabriel said, "*open it.*"

Viker did as instructed, and the slot opened, revealing a turnkey with a small keyhole in the middle. The light around the key was glowing a dangerous red.

"*Turn the key 180 degrees counter-clockwise,*" Gabriel continued, "*and be prepared to catch the module when it detaches.*"

"*I hope you're not about to blow us all up, Colonel,*" Viker quipped wryly.

"*Do exactly as I say,*" Gabriel replied with deadly seriousness, "*and we might just survive this suicide mission after all.*"

Viker turned the key. The complicated set of mechanical latches holding the device in place unlocked simultaneously, and the 'command module' detached cleanly from Gabriel's armour, dropping into Viker's hands.

As soon as the bomb detached, a timer appeared in the corner of everyone's HUDs.

30:00:00...29:59:03...29:58:08

"*Now, attach it to the back of my belt,*" Gabriel instructed Viker.

Viker duly pressed the bomb against the back of Gabriel's waist, and the magnetic clamps on Gabriel's belt latched onto the deadly payload, fastening it securely behind him.

"I have a theory," Gabriel said aloud to the observer, "You were built in order to study how the Swarm influences organics, which is why you don't need an organic crew."

The observer was silent.

"The original alien from which this thing was cloned," Gabriel continued, confident in his conclusions, "and probably hundreds of others, were used as lab rats for you to observe while the Swarm enthralled them one by one. And when you lost control of the experiment, you deliberately crashed into this moon and waited for the test subjects to die."

"Come to think of it," Cato added, expanding on Gabriel's accusation, "you probably weakened the containment shield on purpose in order to let the Swarm corrupt the researchers and watch what happened. Except this time the Swarm was smart enough to figure out how to disable the shield indefinitely until we restored it for you."

Another round of silence.

"The observer has greatly underestimated your species' deductive capabilities," the observer noted backhandedly, "And it seems you do not trust the observer's intentions."

"Of course we don't trust your intentions," Gabriel answered, "Aside from the fact that you split us up against our will and hid the true nature of this place, you're an alien artificial intelligence, and our primary mandate is to protect our species from alien threats."

"So you wish to guard against any ulterior motive that the observer might possess by triggering the antimatter device's countdown? That is logical," the observer responded, "However, the

Swarm does not know your current location, and the time estimate is based on the assumption that it heads immediately for the central chamber."

"Well then I suggest you get its attention, and quickly," Gabriel replied, "Because one way or another, this bomb will go off. Whether you're destroyed along with the Swarm depends on getting it into the containment field along with the bomb."

"If we fail, you will also be obliterated," the observer pointed out, "Does the voidstalker truly possess no sense of self-preservation?"

"I have five…technically six reasons to leave this place alive," Gabriel answered, "but if I have to die to make sure they can live, so be it."

* * *

The doorbell sounded and the intercom lit up with a video image of the caller. Roused from her anxiousness and self-pity, Aster walked over to the intercom and saw an Asgard Civil Security officer on the other side, flanked by two support androids. The intercom's holographic display identified him as Detective Timothy Bell.

"*This is Detective Bell from Asgard Civil–*" the ACS officer began.

"I can see who you are," Aster replied impatiently, "what can I do for you?"

"*Is Aster Thorn available?*" he enquired, ignoring her impertinent tone.

"You're speaking to her now."

"*Open the door,*" the detective ordered, "*I need to speak to you, urgently.*"

"Why can't you just talk through the intercom?"

"*Refusing to cooperate with the authorities is a criminal offence,*" the detective warned her, "*Open the door and I'll tell you exactly why we need to talk.*"

The maganiel android was still standing guard in the hallway, and Aster gestured for it to come over. Then, reluctantly, she opened the front door.

The ACS detective was dressed in a regular uniform with light body armour, whereas the two armed support androids accompanying him were equipped with submachine guns; a fact which put the maganiel android on alert.

"Do you know a Dr Felix Kessler?" Detective Bell asked.

"Yes," Aster replied suspiciously, "I work with him at Jupiter Engineering Co."

Aster was sick to her back teeth of being interrogated by authority figures, uniformed or not; but she knew better than to be overly rude to him.

"When was the last time you saw him?"

"This morning, at the labs," Aster replied.

"Yes, you were suspended this morning pending an internal investigation into a security breach there," Detective Bell noted, consulting his wrist-top computer, "is that correct?"

"I'm not at liberty to discuss the details," Aster said legalistically.

"Neither were your employers," the detective noted, "After you were suspended, did you come straight home or did you go anywhere first?"

"I came straight home," Aster responded, "What happened with Felix?"

"You haven't seen the news?" the detective raised an eyebrow.

"No," Aster answered, her stomach tightening.

Detective Bell pulled up a set of images on his wrist-top computer's holographic display and flipped the display around for her to see. Aster looked at the screen, and the colour and feeling drained from her face.

It was a slideshow of a set of crime scene photos, showing Felix lying dead in some kind of private room. He was slumped on his side with a gunshot wound through the side of his head. She could tell it was him from his dyed black-and-gold hair, and from his steel grey eyes, now blank and lifeless.

"He was found dead about an hour ago," the detective explained, "Bruising on his arms and legs indicates that he was physically restrained by someone, or something, much stronger than himself. Something like the maganiel android you have there."

Aster was in complete shock, too much shock to register the veiled accusation.

"Has your maganiel android left the house at all?" the detective asked.

"…No…" Aster replied falteringly, "no it hasn't."

"*This unit has not departed the house since it was reactivated approximately twelve hours ago*," the maganiel android volunteered helpfully.

"We'll need to confirm that by accessing your maganiel's logs," the detective replied, "And I'll need you to come in for further questioning as well."

"You heard what it said," Aster said defensively, regaining her resolve, "the maganiel hasn't left the house since I activated it."

"And how do I know you didn't tell your maganiel's to say that after ordering it to kill Felix Kessler?" Detective Bell asked.

"Are you fucking kidding me?" Aster demanded angrily, "I've known Felix for years, you seriously think that I killed him?"

"Dr Kessler went missing in the wake of a suspicious power failure at your place of work, a power failure that *you* were suspected of causing," the detective pointed out, "Then you were suspended from work and claim to have come straight home afterwards. Somewhere in that sequence of events, Dr Kessler was murdered; so if you know what's good for you, I suggest you come with me immediately."

"Unless you have an arrest warrant, you can fuck off," Aster said defiantly.

"Verbal harassment of an ACS officer or obstruction of justice, which would you prefer to be arrested on?" the detective asked.

"Again, if you don't have a warrant, have a nice day," Aster said before attempting to shut the door in the detective's face.

The detective stuck his foot in the door, preventing it from shutting, then tried to force his way inside the apartment. With reactions faster than any Human could match, the maganiel drew its sidearm and stuck the barrel in the detective's face, pushing him back with the gun. The officer backpedalled immediately as the two ACS support androids, in turn, raised their weapons, taking aim at the maganiel.

"*This unit has been authorised to employ lethal force in defence of the residents of this home,*" the maganiel politely informed the detective.

"Oh, you're definitely my prime suspect now," the detective said menacingly, reaching for his comm. device, "this is Detective Bell requesting armed backup at my location. One hostile suspect and one armed android present."

"Would you like to explain to your backup how you tried to force your way into my home?" Aster said gloweringly, taking cover behind the maganiel.

"If you had nothing do with Dr Kessler's murder, then why don't you just come in and explain everything?" the detective challenged her.

"Because I'm sick to death of being interrogated over things that I'm not fucking guilty of!" Aster raged, her composure dissolving, "and after being suspended from my job, you come to my door to tell me one of my friends was murdered and that *I'm* your suspect!"

"Well, sorry for your loss," the detective replied without sounding too sorry, "but unless you have any information that can point us in the right direction, at best you're a person of interest, and at worst you *are* the prime suspect."

"You needed backup?" said another voice.

Everyone turned to see another uniformed individual approaching, also accompanied by his own team of armed support androids. But the newcomer's uniform was plain and dark, without any insignias, let alone ACS markings.

"Who the frick are you?" the detective demanded.

"Scan me," the unidentified person replied.

With a glare of suspicion on his face, the detective approached the newcomer and flash-scanned his eyes. His suspicion evaporated when he saw the ID and organisational affiliation.

"That's right," said the newcomer, "The acronym for authority here is 'DNI'."

"This woman is a person of interest in a murder investigation," the detective protested.

"Yeah, that's why I'm here," the DNI agent replied, "we know for a fact that she's not your culprit. We have the evidence to prove it and I'll be accompanying you back to your HQ so we can clear all this up."

The detective's suspicious glare returned, but he duly turned away and reached for his comm. device, presumably to contact his superiors.

"Dr Thorn," said the DNI agent to Aster, "we received your communication."

"It was Jezebel who killed him," Aster asserted in a hushed tone, "I know it."

"That may or may not be the case," the agent replied, "I couldn't possibly comment."

"Who else could it be?" Aster insisted, "She took my children home with her from the medical centre, which has to be a massive security breach, and then she tried to–"

The DNI agent raised a finger to silence her, his expression turning serious.

"*Never* talk about confidential matters out in the open," he said sternly.

"Well, you saw what I sent, didn't you?" Aster demanded.

"That's not for me to say," the DNI agent answered, "I came down here because the ACS officer was going to arrest the wrong person."

"Ok, but...Felix was a close friend of mine," Aster explained, her voice shaking a little, "can you at least promise me that you'll get whoever killed him?"

"It's all being sorted out," the agent promised.

* * *

From a gentle glow, the containment shield had brightened into a translucent ball of light, bright enough to illuminate the entire cavernous central chamber. Standing on the raised dais at the edge of the scaffolding platform stood the self-styled leader of the Faithful, facing the containment shield with his hands raised as if in prayer.

Some distance behind him, eight figures were crouched down in a semi-circle around the prophet like a gathering of bodyguards or attending priests. They were the same type of surgically mutilated scarecrows that the squad had encountered earlier – the remains of their J.E. Co. security uniforms still visible on their monstrously deformed bodies.

A squad of enthralled foot soldiers stood further back at the edge of the platform, watching the prophet as he presumably listened to the Voice in his head. They were meant to be guarding the entrance to the central chamber but were standing in visible awe of the spectacle before them.

Derelict in their sentry duty as they were, none of them noticed as the four remaining commandoes appeared from one of the sub-chambers and executed them from behind. Their comparatively weak shielding failed to deflect, or even stop, the commandoes' bullets, and they crumpled to the floor, their faces blown out by the exit wounds.

The gunfire alerted the honour guard of scarecrows. They turned around and stared at the squad, their cybernetic eyes glowing electric blue, highlighting the congealed blood stains on their cheeks. Without any signal from the prophet, they howled like rabid attack dogs and charged, pouncing forward on limbs enhanced with synthetic muscle tissue.

The squad switched to concussive shots and fired at the charging scarecrows. The creatures' surgically implanted shield emitters rippled and flashed as most of the pellets were deflected. Some made it through the scarecrows' shields, punching through their cybernetically enhanced flesh but barely slowing them down.

Bale tossed a frazzler grenade into the path of the charging scarecrows. Detonating in mid-air, the device emitted a powerful repulsive field similar to the shielding of its targets. The resulting interaction of discordant energy fields produced a violent and instantaneous feedback loop. The pack of scarecrows was sent flying like a collection of ragdolls in a windstorm, their shields frazzled out by the explosion.

The squad switched back to automatic fire and executed the scarecrows with precision bursts before they could get up again, aiming for their torsos and heads. The creatures screamed in fury – they probably couldn't feel pain – as the hail of bullets riddled their bodies, punching through vital organs, or fracturing as they penetrated bionic components.

Coloured liquid leaked from the scarecrows' wounds – a mixture of red blood and clear mechanical fluid – and their muscles twitched and spasmed as they died. It was a nastier way to go than the other four, but no one doubted that they were better off dead.

"Your blasphemous schemes are transparent to me, even without the Voice's guidance," the prophet's voice boomed through a vocal enhancer.

The prophet turned around to face the squad. He was still dressed in his makeshift priestly robes made out of a hazmat overcoat covered in bloody symbols and glyphs. The micro-emitters in his skin glowed faintly, ready to swat aside any incoming projectiles, but the look of zealous superiority on his face was crinkled with frustration.

"So what do you think our plans are, then?" Gabriel asked, hoping to keep the prophet talking until the Swarm arrived.

"You have successfully reactivated the prison in which the Swarm was held," the prophet replied, "No doubt with the assistance of the entity which inhabits the Temple, seeking to prevent others from partaking of the knowledge that the Voice of the Swarm imparts."

"Entity?" Gabriel opted to feign ignorance, "what entity?"

"The lying voice that speaks from within the walls of the Temple, enticing you to reactivate the containment field in order to re-entrap the Swarm and its anointed host!" The prophet bellowed with righteous anger, "The entity which has attempted to thwart the Faithful by erecting barriers and tossing machinery to and fro like toys! You have ignorantly chosen to whore yourselves out to its blasphemous schemes!"

"If we noticed, I guess they would too," Bale mused.

"It is an evil spirit making craven and desperate attempts to thwart the re-ascendance of a power far greater than itself!" the prophet thundered away, "The Swarm is a power which it can merely observe, but not confine; one which has granted unto *me*, and unto *my* Faithful, secrets unfathomable to the narrow minds of the greedy and wretched corporates or the evil, fricking government!"

"You're out-n-out brain-fricked," Viker retorted in Undercity dialect.

"Am I?" the prophet asked rhetorically, "or is it really your superiors at the Directorate of Naval Intelligence who have been deluding you all this time, sending you into the carnivore's den to protect Humanity from the supposed threat of xenotech research whilst secretly pilfering the fruits of that research for themselves?"

The squad collectively blinked.

"Do you believe that to be mere supposition?" the prophet asked.

"No, we think it's a bollocks conspiracy theory," Bale retorted.

"Of course you do," the prophet sneered, "Why would slaves be curious about their masters' plans? I certainly wasn't, harvesting all the data that Dani could gather and sending it back to my false masters."

The squad blinked again.

"Has it dawned on you at all?" the prophet continued, "how could the DNI possibly be so ignorant of the existence of such a vast and illegal research facility a few hours' spaceflight journey away from a major hub-world for so many years?"

The squad blinked a third time as the pieces of the puzzle assembled in their minds.

"Jupiter Engineering thought they had pulled the wool over the eyes of the DNI," the prophet continued, "Hah! The DNI sees and hears *everything* that happens within Human space, and far beyond it too! They let it happen so long as they could steal for themselves whatever discoveries J.E. Co. made. *That* was my assignment."

There was a fourth collective blink of disbelief.

"Lawrence Kane?" Gabriel asked incredulously.

"The one and only!" The Prophet Lawrence Kane declared.

"But you're dead!"

"Do I look dead to you?"

"But we found the body in the medical bay!" Viker exclaimed.

"You found *a* body," Kane pointed out, "no doubt with the ID tag still attached to the corpse. If the DNI's dogs are this easy to throw off the scent, perhaps I needn't have worried."

The squad blinked again, but this time at their own sloppiness. It had never occurred to them to scan the corpse's DNA and make sure it really was Lawrence Kane.

Their motion trackers flashed red.

"I would tell you more," the prophet said with a grin, "but it seems you are out of time."

The prophet's eyes and head rolled back as he entered some kind of trance, and the squad turned their guns around to face the threat.

In fact, the threat was all around; they were pouring in from every entrance, and spreading across the walls of the enormous spherical chamber. Enthralled foot soldiers were joined by jumpers with their jetpacks and shotguns, and scattered amongst them were more black widows in their lithe, black body armour. All of the Faithful's remaining manpower had converged on the central chamber for the final showdown.

"*One way or another*," Gabriel said to everyone, scanning the assembled horde for the Swarm-possessed Ogilvy, "*this bomb will go off.*"

"*Yeah, we don't need to be Masterminds to remember that, Colonel*," Viker replied sarcastically, tracking targets in his HUD, "*We can all see the countdown.*"

"*That's not what I mean*," Gabriel said grimly, "*I mean that my death will kill us all.*"

* * *

The penthouse never felt as homely as it did when coming back from doing one's own dirty work. Madam Jezebel entered the palatial living room and settled into a couch, heaving a sigh of partial relief at being home. The two androids who had accompanied her stood to attention, waiting for further instructions.

"Self-destruct," Madam Jezebel ordered the two androids as she pulled the red chip out of her pocket, "No recovery of data or recycling of components."

"*All logs and information stored on these units will be permanently lost*," the androids informed her in their digitised voices, "*are you sure you wish to initiate self-destruct?*"

"Yes," Jezebel replied, "Do it."

The two androids nodded and departed the room. In a side room of the penthouse, there was a special disposal chute for robotics and electronics leading down to an incineration unit far below. Nothing would be left of them to recover.

Jezebel pulled out a tablet computer, wafer-thin and flexible with intricate nanocircuitry visible through the translucent body. Laying it on the small table in front of her, she made sure to disable the tablet's wireless capabilities first. Even though her penthouse was equipped with counter-surveillance technology – 'garblers' as some people liked to call them – it was always possible that someone had found a countermeasure.

She placed the data chip in the reading slot, micro-magnets holding the chip in place as the tablet established a connection. Once the connection had been established, Jezebel accessed the chip's contents and furrowed her brow in confusion: there were no data files of any kind on the chip, at least none that she could see.

She disabled protected file concealment. Nothing. She performed a deep probe of the data chip's memory. Still nothing. She double-checked that the chip connection was actually functional. It was. That meant that either the data chip had been completely wiped…

…Or there was nothing on the chip to begin with.

Jezebel ground her teeth in fury. The simplest explanation had to be incompetence or sloppiness: a stressed and frightened Kessler might have just grabbed the first data chip he found and hoped it had something useful on it. But he'd always been a reliable source, it was hard to believe that he could slip up at this point.

Had he double-crossed her? Possibly. Kessler had never been happy about working as a mole in the first place, maybe he'd been looking for a way out this whole time. But if that was the case, he wouldn't dare do such a thing if he didn't think he could get away with it. He would have needed outside help.

Jezebel snatched the tablet off the table with the data chip still attached. If her hunch was correct and Kessler had betrayed her, the chip could very well contain spyware or some other means of tracking her location; a paranoid leap of logic, to be sure, but better to be paranoid and free than naive and in prison.

With the tablet in hand, Jezebel rushed into one of the side rooms where the androids had obediently leapt to their destruction. The disposal chute was still open and Jezebel tossed the tablet in, sealing the chute after doing so. Now that all the evidence had been destroyed, she needed to skip town.

The security alarm sounded, a harsh beeping klaxon alerting her to intruders. Whoever they were, they had somehow forced their way through the front door. Jezebel threw open a storage closet and rummaged around, pulling a handgun out of a hidden compartment. Then she returned to the living room to confront the intruders.

As Jezebel aimed her gun in the direction of the main hallway, an entire squad of figures clad in night-black body armour entered the living room with far more firepower at their disposal than she had. One member of the assault team, apparently the squad leader, lowered his weapon and stepped forward, activating his helmet speakers.

"Madam Jezebel Thorn," said the squad leader, "put the gun down."

"You've broken into my home and are pointing guns at me," Jezebel pointed out, still pointing the gun squarely at him, "why should I put mine down?"

"We have orders to bring you in," the squad leader replied coolly, "whether we bring you in dead or alive makes no particular difference."

"So I'm guessing you're not Civil Security?" Jezebel asked.

"Of course not," the squad leader replied, "Now are you going to surrender, or do we have to shock you or kneecap you first?"

Jezebel was ruthless, but not reckless. She activated the safety and tossed the gun across the floor, placing her hands on top of her head. But she wouldn't get down on her knees, not for them or anyone else, even as members of the armed squad approached to detain her.

"Who did you say you were with again?" she asked as her wrists were bound.

"You'll find out soon enough," replied the squad leader as Jezebel was led away.

* * *

The squad opened fire and the Faithful fired back. Viker activated his wrist-shield, protecting the squad as best he could from the incoming fire, but they were exposed and the storm of bullets was raining down on them from all around. If they wanted to survive, they had to get out of the open and right into the thick of it.

Jumpers swooped down on them like mythical harpies, and Cato and Bale turned their guns skyward, firing concussive shots at their fast-moving opponents. The jumpers were wearing cuirasses made from bulletproof nanotube plating in lieu of shielding, but the bullets struck with enough force to pulp their targets' innards, causing some to tumble from the air.

Those jumpers who evaded the incoming shots landed cleanly on their feet and opened fire with their shotguns. The squad's shields were strong enough to slap the spray of pellets away, but at point blank range some made it through with reduced energy, clattering against their armour like a shower of tiny pebbles.

Cato and Bale returned fire with more concussive shots. Again, the pellets failed to penetrate the jumpers' armour but struck with enough force to send them flying back across the floor. They switched to automatic mode and fired at the jumpers whilst they were down; this time the bullets penetrated their targets' armour, punching clean holes through their organs.

While Viker covered him with the wrist-shield, Gabriel provided sniper cover as best he could. The Enthralled foot soldiers stayed put behind barricades, taking turns to shoot. One of them fired a projectile from his weapon which bounced off the floor at an awkward angle, exploding at head height and splattering burning plasma in all directions.

Dodging the explosion from the poorly aimed grenade, Gabriel picked off the enemy who had fired it with a high-velocity shot. The bullet screamed through the air, punching straight through the target's skull, and continuing out the other side.

Another grenade detonated nearby. The squad's shields absorbed the impact of the shrapnel, but it was enough of a distraction for another jumper to dive in with sword drawn. The blade missed Viker's head as the jumper landed and took another swing at Gabriel, the tip of the blade narrowly missing his stomach. Viker deactivated his wrist-shield and fired a burst into the jumper's chest, cracking the jumper's ribcage with the force of the impact.

An empty crate came sailing through the air, striking Cato and knocking him off his feet. A black widow appeared, using her gravity gloves to bounce from surface to surface and drawing an electric baton in mid-pounce. She landed on top of Cato, pinning him to the ground and bringing the deadly spike down on his head.

The slanted angle of Cato's faceplate deflected the spike to one side, saving his life; and Bale fired a burst of bullets at the black widow's head to defend him. The material used to manufacture the black widow's helmet was strong enough to stop the bullets, but they were fired at point blank range, too close for her shields to deflect them. The force knocked her head violently sideways, breaking her neck.

As Cato got back on his feet, a sinister, buzzing cloud appeared in one of the doorways. The Swarm-possessed Ogilvy entered the chamber with a commanding saunter, looking around the chamber with an evil stare from eyes as black as smouldering coals. The Enthralled standing nearby backed away out of reverence and fear.

"*There's our boss fight!*" Gabriel shouted as he gunned down another target.

The Swarm-possessed Ogilvy raised a fist and let out a piercing scream that no Human vocal chords could mimic, causing the remaining Enthralled to freeze up as if in a trance. The possessed Ogilvy pointed at the squad, and the Faithful charged, howling with fanatical fury as they rushed forward to tear the squad limb from limb.

This was an altogether different enemy. The Faithful screamed hysterical oaths as they attacked, all sense of self-preservation erased by whatever the Swarm had done to their minds. Some of them kept their weapons in hand, firing madly in the general direction of the squad. Others dropped their weapons in a mad rush to bring their bare hands to bear.

The squad sprayed bullets on full automatic, mowing down as many as they could. The front ranks of fanatics crumpled and fell, but the ranks behind simply charged on forwards, literally tripping over one another to get their hands on the squad and tackle them to the ground. Gabriel's weapon was knocked out of his hands as a dozen enthralled fighters pounced on him, dragging him down to the floor and trying to beat him to death.

Being assaulted by a fanatical swarm pounding away at nigh-invulnerable armour was a bizarre experience. Gabriel flailed ferociously, swinging his fists and kicking violently at his attackers. He felt his foot connect with someone's gut, and the combat claws on his left gauntlet punctured someone else's neck. But this was hardly standard combat; it was a frenzied brawl, with his assailants' knuckles turning red as they beat their fists bloody against his armour.

A rifle butt connected with Gabriel's helmet and he swung his arm around in retaliation, swatting the weapon out of his attacker's hands and uppercutting him with his armoured fist. His helmet protected him, but amidst the pounding and brawling the next weapon could be one of the jumpers' xenotech swords, and he wouldn't survive a wound from a weapon like that.

"*SHIELD, OVER-PULSE, NOW!*" Gabriel enunciated into his helmet's mic.

His armoured suit's onboard computer registered the voice command and triggered the over-pulse mechanism. Instead of merely halting or redirecting incoming projectiles away from the armour, the shield emitters could also emit a one-off repulsive field, forcibly pushing nearby matter away in all directions as a defensive last resort.

The over-pulse violently threw the attacking mob skywards in a spectacular cloud of flying and flailing bodies. Because Gabriel was on his back, the over-pulse pushed against the floor beneath him, launching him straight up into the air along with his attackers as if he had been bounced into the sky by an enormous trampoline.

A warning flashed in Gabriel's HUD – the over-pulse had temporarily shorted out his shield emitters – but he was more concerned about falling back to the ground. As he ran out of momentum, he felt inertia tug his innards the other way as gravity pulled him back down again. Gabriel grabbed a flying body in mid-air and twisted around, hoping to break his fall with the body of the flailing foot soldier.

It worked.

The Enthralled's body hit the hard floor of the platform, breaking Gabriel's fall and the Enthralled's back with a sickeningly audible crack. As Gabriel rolled away, he rose to his feet in the same motion and drew the xenotech sword from his back. He flicked the switch to activate the energy field and looked around for the Swarm-possessed Ogilvy.

Another black widow appeared to confront him, and Gabriel swung the blade at her. She ducked and swung her baton around to strike the back of his knee before jabbing the electrified tip into his shoulder. The million volt jolt shorted out the motors in Gabriel's suit again, triggering more warnings in his HUD as his armour suddenly felt ten times heavier.

Gabriel swung his sword around in a defensive arc as he crumpled to the floor, slicing clean through the black widow's body in mid-pounce and instantly cauterising her flesh. Part of her chest and shoulder fell to the ground and her upper half twitched for a few seconds before the trauma of being bisected killed off her mind.

Still holding the sword, Gabriel rose to his feet with great effort whilst the exoskeletal motors in his armour recovered. He was strong enough to move without assistance, but the entire suit weighed more than 50kg, making it difficult to move with speed or agility. That fact almost proved fatal as yet another jumper came at him with a sword of his own, aiming for his head. Gabriel raised his own sword to block the attack just in time.

When the two energised blades connected, they rebounded from one another in a spectacular flash, releasing a metallic keening sound. Gabriel stumbled backwards from the clash just as the motors in his suit rebooted, whilst the preternaturally agile jumper performed a backward roll before righting himself again and charging at Gabriel a second time.

Swordsmanship wasn't taught in the military, but with his exoskeletal motors restored, Gabriel could make up for lack of technique by moving at least as fast as his opponent and swinging with much more force. Using the swords' rebounding effect to his advantage, Gabriel deliberately swung at the jumper's own sword, forcing him onto the defensive before closing in and driving the tip of his sword through the jumper's faceplate.

As his opponent keeled over dead, Gabriel looked around and saw that the over-pulse had scattered the Faithful all over the chamber, with many of them falling to their deaths. Their broken bodies lay scattered across the platform, some stirring with agonising effort, hardly able to move due to their injuries, but mostly immobile and lifeless.

His squad members' bio-readings were all still visible in his HUD and green, but they had been thrown clear by the over-pulse. Besides, with an antimatter bomb behind his waist and a possessed former squad member to kill, he couldn't worry about them now.

Gabriel turned around and saw one of the Enthralled who had survived the over-pulse pointing a gun at him. In fact, it was *his* gun: the LMG knocked out of his hands during the brawl, now being pointed at him by an enemy grinning triumphantly even as he strained to hold the enormous weapon aloft. Gabriel didn't try to take cover or even move as the foot soldier took aim at him and pulled the trigger.

Without Gabriel's DNA, or the array of biometric transmitters in his gauntlet to relay that information, the gun wouldn't fire. Instead, a set of microneedles, each as thin as a Human hair, punctured the target's skin, injecting a cocktail of specially designed nanobots into his hand which began rapidly killing off nearby cells, before retracting again.

Gabriel deactivated his sword's energy field, replacing it on its magnetic sheath before approaching his foolish enemy. The Enthralled foot soldier could do nothing but stand there with a look of horror and agony frozen on his face as his blood vessels slowly turned black from the nanotechnological venom flowing through them.

Gabriel carefully detached the man's rigid fingers from the handle of the gun and took back his service weapon. By that point, the deadly serum of nanobots had completely paralysed the man's muscles, leaving him as still as a statue. Gabriel didn't deign to put the man down, multiple organ failure would do that for him.

Gabriel turned around and was immediately struck in the chest by an armoured forearm. He caught a glimpse of a whirring cloud of particles around the armoured figure of Ogilvy as he went tumbling head over heels back across the floor. Even with a bionic exoskeleton, there was no way Ogilvy should have been strong enough to bring that much force to bear.

Gabriel's armour protected him from being winded, let alone actual injury, but it was pretty clear he wouldn't stand much of chance in a hand-to-hand fight. He scrambled back to his feet and prepared a high-powered shot, taking aim at the gravity belt around Ogilvy's waist and squeezing the trigger.

He should have known better from their first encounter. The bullet travelled towards its target at atmospheric escape velocity, but the Swarm's shielding slapped it back at him like a rubber ball hitting a wall. The bullet lost momentum from being deflected, and lost even more as it was slowed by Gabriel's partially recovered shields, but struck him in the chest plate.

Multiple layers of carefully forged metallic alloy and nanotube plating interwoven with shock absorbent materials prevented the deflected bullet from penetrating Gabriel's armour – saving his life – but it still struck him with enough force to knock him off his feet, and to knock the air out of his lungs.

Gabriel tried to get up, but the possessed Ogilvy got to him first, wrapping his fingers around Gabriel's neck. The gorget armour protected Gabriel's throat from behind crushed, but he found himself hoisted into the air, dangling like a puppet. He struggled to prise the fingers away from his throat, but the grip was unfathomably strong, too strong to undo.

The demonic Ogilvy stared at him with his burning coals for eyes as he tried to choke the life out of his former squad leader. Gabriel could see that the capillaries in his eyes had been darkened by whatever the swarm of alien particles had done to his body. Gabriel couldn't help such attention to detail, even though it didn't really help him.

In the corner of his HUD, Gabriel noticed his squad member's position markers approaching. A figure came up behind the Swarm-possessed Ogilvy and jabbed a black rod into his back. The electric jolt shorted out the motors in Ogilvy's armour, causing the possessed Ogilvy to stumble forward, dropping Gabriel in the process.

The enraged Ogilvy whirled around and swung his fist at Bale, getting up to confront him as Bale used the black widow's baton as a club to fight back. As they fought, someone came up behind Gabriel and unlocked the clamps securing the bomb to his waist. With Bale distracting the possessed Ogilvy, Viker took the bomb and rushed up behind him, diving forwards and planting the bomb behind Ogilvy's waist.

The clamps on the back of Ogilvy's armour automatically snapped around the bomb, locking it in place. The Swarm-possessed Ogilvy wheeled round again in fury, smacking Viker in the side of the head. His helmet and neck armour protected him from having his neck broken, but he was knocked unconscious by the blow.

As Viker collapsed, Ogilvy turned back to Bale who tried to stab him with the spike end of the black widow's baton. Ogilvy caught the baton and twisted it around to stab Bale through the weak point in his shoulder armour, impaling him. Bale's bio-readings turned orange as the possessed Ogilvy took the baton by both ends and used it as a handle to lift Bale up, swing him around, and toss him into the air like a ragdoll.

Losing two squad members in as many seconds turned Gabriel's vision red. Before Bale hit the ground, and before his opponent could react, Gabriel charged forwards and shoulder tackled Ogilvy around the thigh, leaping into the air in the same motion. Gabriel's own genetically enhanced strength was superhuman and combined with the strength provided by his armour, he was able to toss Ogilvy skyward the same way Bale had been thrown.

The possessed monster roared in fury as he went sailing through the air. Yet somehow he twisted in mid-air, landing on his feet with a preternatural agility that no Human could achieve. Gabriel didn't give him a chance to recover, drawing the sword and flicking the energy field switch as he charged forwards. The possessed Ogilvy snarled like a feral beast as Gabriel swung the blade at him, attempting to force him backwards off the edge of the dais.

The Swarm's energy shielding didn't merely block projectiles, it could also guard against the deadly energy field around Gabriel's sword. Every time the blade came close, it was slapped back again with a flash of energy, protecting the host from being sliced apart.

But it had the desired effect; Ogilvy was forced on to the back foot, backing away from the relentless attacks all the way back to the edge of the dais.

However, the Swarm had no intention of being forced back into the containment shield, and without warning, Ogilvy grabbed the xenotech blade between his palms. The Swarm-generated shielding protected his hands from being cut to pieces, and also generated a violent feedback loop, causing a sputtering whining sound as the two energy fields clashed.

Gabriel strained against his opponent's superior strength, but the Swarm-possessed Ogilvy was literally pushing the blade back at him. Then with a ferocious scream, Ogilvy snapped the blade with his armoured gauntlets, scattering the shards in all directions. Before Gabriel could react, Ogilvy had shoved him back down the steps of the dais and landed on top of him, unsheathing his combat claws before bringing them down towards Gabriel's neck.

Gabriel put his hands out at the last second. With his left fist clenched, his remaining combat claws locked with Ogilvy's claws whilst he grabbed Ogilvy's other fist with his clawless right gauntlet. Gabriel was pinned on his back, locked in a two-handed grapple as a much stronger opponent bore down on him.

Gabriel lashed out with a kick to Ogilvy's gut, hitting the button on his gravity belt and deactivating it. Ogilvy hardly flinched, instead pushing down even harder, trying to force his combat claws through the weak points under Gabriel's gorget armour. The swarm of alien particles began to whirl even faster, forming a screaming, silver maelstrom that seemed to reflect the aggression of its host.

Even with the assistance of his strength-enhancing exoskeleton, Gabriel was straining to keep the deadly claws away from his throat, and without much success. His armour was an added layer of protection, but with enough force applied to the weak points, it could be pierced. Gabriel's strength was starting to fail.

It felt like trying to bench press an armoured vehicle with a deadly incentive to lift closing in on his throat.

Was this how he was going to die?

11:09:73

The timer was ticking down towards zero, and they would both be annihilated when it did. So why not bring everything to a close right now? Just let the claws slide through armour's weak points and into his neck? Once his jugular and carotid were severed, it would take about a minute for him to lose consciousness from blood loss, and a few more minutes for his heart to stop. Once his pulse ceased, the bomb's timer would skip to t-minus 00:00:01.

They would die together.

Through the swirling silver cloud of particles, Gabriel could see the ghostly pale face of his former squad member, his eyes turned black by the Swarm's possession, and his mouth slowly twisting into a sickly, triumphant grin. Gabriel could hardly make out the face of his soon-to-be killer, but he could vaguely make out the grin.

It reminded him a little of Rose's grin.

For some reason, that memory was what flashed through his mind whilst staring his own death in the face: his daughter's mischievous smile when she'd poked him in the nose on his way out the door. If he died, would she understand why he wasn't coming home? Would Orion or Violet or Leo understand?

Of course they wouldn't.

The pain in Gabriel's muscles was subsumed by a much more biting pang of emotion: the vision of four pairs of bright green eyes, identical to his own, brimming with tears at being told that daddy was never coming home. Aster would be grief-stricken, but at least she would understand; the children wouldn't.

In fact, it would be worse than that. When the antimatter bomb detonated, the energy released by the explosion would annihilate all matter within a cubic kilometre or more. There would be nothing left of him to bury, no remains to be collected, not even a piece of his armour over which Aster and the children could mourn. All trace of him would be obliterated, with nothing but an empty casket at his funeral.

Ogilvy's combat claws made contact with Gabriel's armour, pressing against the weak points in his neck armour. If he was going to survive, he had to fight back now. His muscles were on fire from the effort of pushing back, and he had very little strength left to resist.

But he did have one last trick left to play.

"*Override. Lieutenant Ogilvy, root access,*" Gabriel said through gritted teeth, straining to pronounce the words into his mic, "*Victory. Sovereign. One. Seven. Zero. Seven.*"

The pain in Gabriel's muscles made it a challenge just to enunciate clearly enough to be acknowledged. But it worked; a command link was established remotely from the computer in his suit to the computer in Ogilvy's suit.

"*Override. Shield…over-pulse…*" Gabriel could barely get the syllables to leave his mouth clearly, and he felt Ogilvy's combat claws find the weak points in his armour and the cold sting of the claws starting to pierce his flesh.

"*NOW!*" he screamed.

Gabriel's voice command remotely triggered the over-pulse mechanism in Ogilvy's armour, violently repelling all matter around him. Gabriel was already on the floor and was knocked flat again, but the Swarm-possessed Ogilvy was catapulted straight into the air.

Ogilvy's flailing body travelled straight upwards in a steep parabolic arc over the dais, crying out with a keening scream of thwarted rage all the way up and all the way down again until he fell through the top of the containment shield.

The timer jumped to 00:00:01.

THE TRUTH

Sitting in a cramped and windowless interview room with her wrists secured to the table, Jezebel Thorn was outwardly silent and calm. Inside, she was fuming with impatience. Since it was the DNI who had detained her – apparently, on the ACS's behalf – she wasn't technically under arrest, and hence couldn't be formally questioned. Instead, she had to sit there and listen as the details of her alleged guilt were discussed right in front of her.

"So this data chip she took," the ACS detective said to the DNI agent, "you said it was some kind of tracking device?"

"Oh, it was a lot more than just a tracking device," the DNI agent replied, "it's a shame she tossed it down the chute; otherwise I could have given you a live demonstration."

"I still have no idea what either of you are talking about," Jezebel lied.

"The chip was part of what we call a 'MacGuffin trap'," the DNI agent explained, ignoring the suspect, "it's a kind of sting operation where we plant something supposedly important, make it out to be really valuable, and then see who comes to collect it. That way, we can lure out suspects, moles, and other people of interest."

"I hate to presume to lecture an ACS officer on the law," Jezebel interjected with a slight sneer, "but I believe it's illegal to speak to a suspect without legal counsel present."

"Good thing no one's speaking to you, then," the DNI agent retorted, "Now as I was saying, the data chip was also covered in a very fine layer of biometric sensors capable of scanning the DNA of whoever touched it. We were able to record not just where the chip was, but the identity of everyone who touched it as well as when and where they touched it."

The DNI agent produced a holographic display on his wrist-top computer, displaying a list of dates, times, and faces. Jezebel saw Aster Thorn's face displayed, followed by Felix Kessler's face. She found it hard to keep her composure when her own face appeared.

"See right here?" the DNI agent pointed to Jezebel's face, "She took the chip from your murder victim shortly before he was murdered, in the exact same place where he died."

Jezebel was silent. Assuming the DNI agent wasn't bluffing, there was no conceivable explanation or answer that she could give to make that fact go away, and opening her mouth to try would only make things worse.

"What about the other suspect?" the detective asked.

"She was blackmailed by Madam Jezebel," the agent explained.

"For which I presume you have evidence," Jezebel interjected with lofty sarcasm.

"Indeed, I do," the agent replied, "Take a listen."

The DNI agent pulled up another file – an audio file this time – and pressed play.

"*And by coming, you're officially complicit. Unless, of course, the real reason – the one you'd like me to corroborate if the investigators ask – is that you simply came to pick up your children from their grandmother's home.*"

Jezebel remained silent. There really was no explaining that away, assuming they had the whole recording in their possession.

"By the way, yes, we have the whole recording," the DNI agent said, closing the audio file, "Which we can give you, along with the tracking logs from the data chip."

"None of that proves that I had anything to do with Felix Kessler's murder," Jezebel said unconvincingly, "or that Aster Thorn wasn't the one who killed him."

"Aster Thorn was at home around the same time that the victim passed the data chip to you," the DNI agent replied, "we have data to show that too. Bottom line: you're fricked."

* * *

Within a fist-sized containment bottle forged from material suitable for starship hulls, an electromagnetic suspension field was deactivated, and a globule of antimatter weighing precisely 2 grams dropped under gravity and inertia until it touched the side.

The resulting mutual annihilation of matter and antimatter resembled the life and death of a star compressed into a single blinding flash. The observatory's containment shield barely held against the force of the explosion, sparing the witnesses from obliteration, and releasing energy only in the form of light.

As suddenly as it began, the explosion was over. A blaze of astral light that had lasted for a twinkling in time was gone, leaving the retinas of those who witnessed it bleached by the sight. The containment shield continued to glow faintly, but no trace remained of the Swarm or its Human host. The chamber was as silent as a tomb.

Gabriel lay sprawled on the ground where he had been pinned, lying as still as a corpse. He resembled a life-sized toy soldier, or a circus prop discarded on the ground to gather dust and dirt after the show had packed up and moved on.

He stirred.

The muscles in his arms were burning, and he could feel a set of stinging wounds in his neck where the combat claws had started to push through into his flesh. And yet, even though the bomb had detonated early, he was alive. Even though his arms hurt, his legs felt fine, so he kicked his feet into the air, lifting his ankles over his head and using the momentum to roll backwards onto his feet.

His armour had seen better days. Most of his shield emitters had been shorted out by the over-pulse he had triggered, as well as by the energy required to protect him from being crushed by the over-pulse from Ogilvy's armour. Parts of his suit had taken physical damage as well, with the redundant motors in his exoskeleton picking up the slack for the ones which had been overloaded by electrocution.

But more importantly, he was alive, something which could not be said for most of the swarm of brainwashed zealots. Thankfully, the remaining members of his squad were also still alive. The bio-readings of Viker and Bale were orange, but they were alive and conscious, and Cato's bio-readings were green.

Someone else was still alive. A figure kneeling motionless on the dais, dressed in a white hazmat overcoat covered in symbols and glyphs written in blood, his overgrown hair and beard covering his face. From the righteous and triumphant image he had projected earlier, the figure he now cut was miserable and defeated.

Gabriel approached the erstwhile Prophet Lawrence Kane, rage steadily building in his chest at the insanity and death this little coward, this one sad little traitor had unleashed. Gabriel had lost his LMG again, his xenotech sword had been broken into pieces, and the combat claws on his right hand had been sliced clean off. That left only the claws on his left hand, his sidearm, and the combat knife on his shoulder.

Gabriel drew his knife.

He gripped the man's hair and pulled back his head, looking the false prophet in the eyes. The microdots in his skin were still visible, but they were only useful against bullets and blast force, they could do nothing against a blade. Gone was the look of smug triumph that had been smeared across his face; now his expression was blank, and his eyes were wide and dazed, like a man who had just discovered that the world around him was a lie.

"All hail Lawrence Kane," Gabriel sneered, his helmet speakers turning his voice into a deep and demonic snarl, "Leader of the Faithful. Prophet of the Voice."

"You…" the prophet stammered, "…don't know…what you've done."

"I destroyed an alien threat to Humanity," Gabriel replied.

"…Destroyed?" Kane murmured, then his voice became filled with anguish and rage, "you have destroyed NOTHING! What you have inflicted is a mere pinprick upon a god! The orb we found; it was an atomistic part of a far greater whole, a vessel for aeon's worth of knowledge! Knowledge gathered from countless civilizations long extinct! Knowledge that could have been ours to wield!"

"What are you talking about?" Gabriel demanded.

"The Voice," Kane continued, his own voice trembling, "It was the voice of an entity more ancient and more powerful than you could possibly imagine. I know because it touched my mind, just as it touched the minds of my followers and the mind of your comrade."

Hearing Ogilvy referenced gave Gabriel the sudden urge to slit the self-styled prophet's throat, but he resisted for the moment.

"The Voice speaks cosmic truth beyond the comprehension of creatures of mere flesh," Kane continued to blabber, "it can bestow the knowledge to manipulate the building blocks of the universe at the quantum level, and the knowledge to construct world engines that can create and destroy planets and stars. All this and more!"

His rantings were getting more unhinged, and yet more fascinating.

"The Voice spoke, and I listened," Kane's ravings continued, a deranged smile starting to curl the corners of his lips, "the Voice spoke through me, I became the voice of truth! So much truth which I recited to my Faithful, and which I can recite for you!"

"I don't want your recitation," Gabriel replied coldly, "I want you silenced."

Gabriel flicked the switch on his knife, flash-heating the blade. Then he sliced carefully across the top of the false prophet's neck, directly above the thyroid cartilage. The incision was just deep enough to open up a slit without actually cutting his throat, and the flash-heated blade instantly cauterised the wound.

As the dying prophet reflexively choked and gagged, Gabriel deactivated the blade and replaced it in its sheath. Then he stuck his fingers into the wound. The dying Kane's eyes turned wide as Gabriel wormed his fingers inside his neck and upwards, closing his grip around his tongue. Holding on tight to Kane's head with his free hand, Gabriel yanked the false prophet's tongue out through the slit in his throat.

There was a sickly series of tearing noises as Gabriel ripped the entire organ out through Kane's neck, snapping it free of the muscles and tendons which held it in place. The prophet keeled over backwards, choking and gurgling blood from his now tongueless mouth and the crimson maw in his throat. And he wasn't actually dead yet; the shock might cause him to lose consciousness, but blood loss would take several minutes to kill him.

It was a fittingly poetic end and a deservedly gruesome one at that.

Gabriel stared at the mutilated corpse of the dead Lawrence Kane, wanting to feel satisfaction, or better still, vindication. Instead, he felt troubled.

He had no qualms about executing an enemy of Humanity, or the macabre method by which he had carried it out, but the dying words of the erstwhile prophet and the numerous implications they carried were what troubled him. What was the Swarm, and what did Kane mean that it was part of a greater whole?

There were countless other questions swirling around his head; fortunately, some of them could be answered immediately.

"Observer!" Gabriel called out through his helmet speakers.

"THE VOIDSTALKER IS TO BE CONGRATULATED ON HIS SURVIVAL," the observer acknowledged, its voice booming out across the giant chamber, "PERHAPS YOU WISH TO KNOW HOW IT WAS THAT YOUR DEVICE DETONATED EARLY?"

"That's one question I have!" Gabriel shouted in reply, turning away from the dais and walking back towards the rear of the scaffolding platform.

"The Swarm's thralls – your kind – utilised primitive radio technology to communicate across distances," the observer explained, adjusting the volume of its booming voice lower as Gabriel approached the wall of the chamber, "easily detectable and easily intercepted."

"What about it, then?"

"*Your* communication system is far more sophisticated," the observer continued, "It utilises extremely precise gravitic waves transmitted in the form of precisely timed quantum pulses. These pulses produce minuscule, but measurable, distortions in the... *untranslatable...*, which the observer can detect, but cannot intercept."

"That doesn't explain how the bomb detonated early," Gabriel pointed out.

"Recall that when you were separated from your subordinates, you were unable to communicate," the observer explained, "The observer has the ability to block the transmission of these quantum pulses. When the device was detached from your armour, the observer detected a similar signal from your armour to the device. The observer concluded that your life signs were directly tied to the device's triggering mechanism."

"So you disrupted the signal once the Swarm was inside the containment shield in order to detonate the bomb prematurely," Gabriel guessed.

"Correct," the observer confirmed, "There was no guarantee that the containment shield would retain enough power for long enough to wait for detonation. Furthermore, the observer could not guarantee that the voidstalker would survive further combat."

Cato had found his way back and was tending to Viker's head injury. Viker had his helmet off, revealing a grizzled face with the pale complexion of an Undercity dweller and the buzz cut of a marine. His eyes were brown and still slightly dazed from being smacked on the side of the head. Bale was sitting nearby, nursing the hole in his shoulder where the spiked baton had been rammed through, having survived being tossed into the air.

"*Good to see you're alive, Colonel*," Bale said as he attempted a salute. The muscles in Gabriel's arms were still burning, but he managed to salute back.

"There is no need to keep any further secrets," the observer said politely.

"You said you wanted to guarantee my survival," Gabriel called out, "Why?"

"The observer has three priorities: containment, observation, and self-preservation, in descending order of importance. Now that the Swarm has been destroyed, there is nothing left either to contain or to observe, leaving only self-preservation. Whatever authority sent you is evidently prepared to take extreme measures to neutralise perceived threats. In the interest of self-preservation, the observer wishes not to be perceived as a threat."

"You want to use us as bargaining chips?" Gabriel asked.

"No, rather as emissaries," the observer clarified, "threatening or terminating your lives would not engender goodwill from your superiors, and would most likely result in the observer's own destruction. Whereas releasing you alive and unharmed would produce a chance of goodwill from your superiors."

The squad members looked at each other. They wouldn't have managed to defeat the Swarm without the observer's help, but they still didn't trust it.

"What are you offering in exchange?" Gabriel demanded.

"Knowledge," the observer replied, "Without the insidious requirement for neural fusion or mental enslavement to the observer."

"What kind of knowledge?"

"The observer has existed for over 610,000 local solar years," the observer answered, "the observer has thus accumulated 610,000 local solar years' worth of observations as well as a wealth of scientific knowledge above and beyond your species' grasp."

"You want to trade information in exchange for survival?" Cato concluded.

"Correct. The observer cannot impart knowledge if it has been destroyed."

There was silence as the squad considered the proposal. In fact, it was Gabriel who considered it, since the offer had been extended to him.

"We would need to consult with our superiors first," Gabriel replied.

"That is acceptable," the observer replied, "As a further gesture of goodwill, and so that you can contact your superiors, the observer will guide you to the exit."

"Bout' time we get out of this fricking place," Viker muttered as Cato finished salving his head wound, "and it's good to see you shut Kane up for us. Literally."

Gabriel saw that he was still holding Kane's severed tongue in his fist. He dropped the bloody trophy on the ground and went to retrieve his LMG.

"*Is everybody well enough to move?*" Gabriel asked as he picked up his service weapon, "*Or do some of you need carrying?*"

"*I can barely move my shoulder,*" Bale answered, standing up as best he could, "*but that spike missed all the major blood vessels, and I survived the trip downwards.*"

"I got whacked in the head," Viker responded as he put his helmet back on and retrieved his gun, "*but otherwise I'm good to move too.*"

"*I got blasted off the edge of the platform by the over-pulse, and then got jumped by a bunch of fucking Faithful,*" Cato replied, packing up his medical kit, "*but no injuries here, either. Can't say the same for them though.*"

"*Lucky you, play-fighting downstairs with the skinny little cultists whilst the big boys handle the monster,*" Bale joked.

"*Oh yeah,*" Cato retorted sarcastically, "*Because being impaled and then tossed into the air like a sports ball is SUCH hard work.*"

Everyone laughed, even Gabriel.

* * *

It was a long trek back through the sepulchral alien labyrinth to the exit and an even longer trek back to the loading bay where the Wolverine was waiting for them. From the loading bay all the way across the canyon network, there was nowhere suitable for the DNI vessel to land and pick them up; so Viker had to drive everybody back to the landing pad.

There was very little talking on the way back, and the surviving squad members were all out of jokes and backslapping by the time they were back aboard the ship. The mission was a success, but they had still lost one of their number to an alien enemy they knew nothing about. In any case, they were exhausted; the most they could manage was to drain some energy drinks and get out of their armour.

Doran had made it back safely, at least. His casket had been packed aboard one of the automated freight trucks and then driven back to the landing pad. His transponder had alerted the DNI vessel to his presence, and he was already on board by the time the squad got back. Once they were back on Asgard, he was quickly transferred to a DNI medical facility.

Ogilvy's helmet and service weapon – the only items left of him – were returned to the DNI. The weapon would be returned to the armoury, and the helmet would be prepared for a funeral service; his family would need something over which to mourn.

Whilst Viker, Cato, and Bale were debriefed and treated for their injuries, Gabriel was summoned to speak directly to the director-general. No doubt she would have already reviewed his helmet footage by the time he arrived and would have further questions to ask.

And he had questions of his own.

* * *

"Excellent work," the director-general said from her throne-like chair.

She had always looked cool and professional before, someone exerting dispassionate control over an enormous network for the good of Humanity. Hundreds of thousands of subordinates reported to her and ultimately entrusted their lives to her decisions, and Gabriel had long been one of them.

But looking at her now, Gabriel's impression of her had changed drastically. Now she looked like a smug and manipulative black widow, tugging on little strands of silk from the centre of her web, watching everything around her with that bionic red eye of hers.

"Thank you very much," Gabriel replied professionally, before adding, "'Dani'."

A flicker of surprise passed across the cool and dispassionate look on Red-eye's face.

"It would have been greatly appreciated if the Director-*Admiral* of Naval Intelligence had informed us that there was already a DNI mole stationed at the Loki facility before we deployed," Gabriel said less-than-coolly.

The accusation was implicit in the phrasing.

"'Director-general' is a very ancient civilian title," Red-eye explained, attempting to duck the accusation with trivia, "it refers to someone with general responsibility for the running of a large organisation. Since this is the Directorate of *Naval* Intelligence, 'director-admiral' was the technical division's idea of a joke, hence the codename 'Dani'."

Gabriel's normally impassive face was crinkled ever so slightly into a scowl. He had figured that out for himself on the journey back and wanted an explanation – perhaps, even an apology – for his being sent in without 100% of the available intelligence.

"The short explanation is that Kane was written off as an expired asset," Red-eye said, using the polite intelligence euphemism for 'hung out to dry'.

"So you didn't think he was worth mentioning because you had no further use for him and expected us to kill him anyway?" Gabriel's tone began to rise in volume.

"Actually, no," Red-eye replied, unfazed by Gabriel's tone, "Kane stopped sending us data from the Dani spyware shortly before J.E. Co. lost contact with the Loki facility. When J.E. Co.'s security team didn't return, I concluded that the team and the staff must be dead, including Kane. If I had known Kane was the cause of the incident, I would have told you."

Gabriel remained silent. That was a start, now what about the rest of her explanation?

"As for the long explanation," Red-eye said at length, "how exactly do you think we stay at the cutting edge, ahead of Humanity's enemies?"

"You think stooping to the level of corporate espionage is worth 'staying ahead'?"

"'Stooping'?" Red-eye raised an eyebrow, "the corporate sector's highest loyalty is to their balance sheets – as you well know – which is why they steal secrets from one another and gamble with Humanity's survival through reckless xenotech experimentation. The secrets *we* gather, however, are put to use designing and building the next generation of technology to keep the fight going, including the armour and weapons that *you* take into battle."

Red-eye's voice was disarmingly level. There was no defensiveness, no anger at being taken to task by a subordinate; just calm explanation of her reasons. And yet, her logic was a hair's breadth away from the corporate sector's own arguments for doing the same thing.

"So it's justified so long as someone else gets their hands dirty, is it?" Gabriel spat in contempt, his composure breaking down, "is that what you told Kane when you recruited him or did he just want you to treat his blood disorder?"

"Kane didn't have a blood disorder," Red-eye answered, "That was just part of the cover story required to exfiltrate data from the Loki facility. The important thing is that the intelligence he provided will bear fruit for years, if not decades to come."

"Even more so if you take the observer up on its offer," Gabriel added cynically.

"That's another discussion for another time," Red-eye replied, "But the fruits of *that* arrangement will be thanks to you. So I don't understand why all this bothers you so much."

Gabriel did something he had never dared to do before: he stepped forward, walking all the way up to the dais and planting his hands on Red-eye's desk. The director-general wasn't visibly moved, even as Gabriel narrowed his luminescent green eyes into a furious glare, locking with the impassive, heterochromatic gaze of his boss.

"I will not be lied to," Gabriel said with a barely suppressed note of menace in his voice, "either directly or by omission. Not even by you."

"Do you think that Ogilvy might still be alive?" Red-eye asked without even flinching, "Or that Doran might have been uninjured if I had told you about Kane?"

Gabriel had no answer. He couldn't know how the mission would have turned out differently had he known about Kane's status as a DNI asset, let alone how that information would have saved Ogilvy or Doran from death or injury. But he felt blindsided, nonetheless, and the apparent deceit and manipulation infuriated him.

"Or do you think I risked your life unnecessarily?"

"You risked *all* of our lives unnecessarily by not telling us about Kane!" Gabriel shouted, the remains of his composure dissolving.

"If I wanted to do that, I would have sent you in alone," Red-eye replied simply.

Gabriel was silent again.

"Did you seriously believe I foisted a squad on you in order to slow you down?" Red-eye continued, "The point of voidstalkers is to be able to act alone *if necessary*. Providing you with a squad increased your combat effectiveness dramatically, and probably saved your life. Otherwise, it would have been you who went tumbling over the railings instead of Ogilvy."

Gabriel's fingers curled into fists. Red-eye simply stared back at him, maddeningly indifferent to his anger. She knew he wouldn't do it.

"If there's nothing else," Red-eye said, breaking the icy staring match, "I suggest you go home and reassure your family that you're still alive. And you'll also want to reassure Aster that she's no longer in trouble."

"What kind of trouble?" Gabriel demanded, baring his teeth in a wolf-like snarl.

"Whilst you were on deployment, we raided J.E. Co.'s offices and labs, and prepared a MacGuffin sting operation," Red-eye explained calmly.

"Of course, we don't want the 'competition' stealing from us, do we?"

"The 'competition' turned out to be your mother," Red-eye continued, "and the mole was initially believed to be your wife."

Gabriel's snarl vanished.

"The ACS also labelled her the prime suspect in the murder of her colleague, Dr Felix Kessler," Red-eye added casually, "who turned out to be the actual mole."

Gabriel was speechless with rage; even more so because all she did was stare back at him with one Human brown eye and one bionic red eye. She looked more like a cold-blooded machine than a person.

"In any case, it's all been cleared up," Red-eye said, "So go home and get some rest."

Gabriel turned on his heel and headed for the door.

"Gabriel," Red-eye called after him.

He paused at the door, wondering if he was about to be reprimanded for his attitude.

"Anger makes you Human."

* * *

Gabriel was still angry when the chartered sky-car arrived to fly him home, too angry to parse Red-eye's cryptic pseudo-profundity about anger making him Human. He had been prepared to sacrifice the whole squad, including himself, for the mission. But doing so on the basis of incomplete intelligence was a different matter entirely.

Ogilvy might well be alive, and Doran not in critical condition, if it weren't for Red-eye's lie by omission. He couldn't know that for certain, but something in his gut made him feel it, and anger was the only way he could express it.

Before departing, he was handed a report containing a summary of the events that had transpired while he was away. His face and mood darkened the more he read, and by the time the sky-car touched down at the landing pad, he was absolutely livid. His mother was lucky she was in custody – because he wanted to kill her.

Gabriel paused in front of the apartment door, his scowl relaxing even though his anger hadn't abated. He couldn't be angry at a family reunion; at the very least he couldn't look angry, not in front of Aster, and certainly not in front of his own children.

The biometric sensor flash-scanned his eyes and the door opened for him. The maganiel android was standing guard in the hallway for some reason, with its sidearm primed and attached to the magnetic plate on its thigh. It nodded its head politely at Gabriel as he headed to the bedroom, shutting and locking the door behind him.

Aster was already there, lying on his side of the bed. She rolled around to see who had come in and sat up abruptly when she saw him. Then she leapt off the bed and rushed over to embrace him. Gabriel reciprocated the embrace, squeezing her tight against his chest.

"Your bosses sent me a message saying you were back," Aster purred with relief.

"It's good to be back," Gabriel replied.

"Gabriel, they accused me of–" Aster began to say frantically.

"I know, I was told," Gabriel interjected reassuringly, "it's all been taken care of."

"What, so you know I was caught up in some kind of sting operation?" Aster asked.

"Yes, the DNI told me everything," Gabriel said, then he added, "including about the trap into which you walked."

The warm reunion suddenly became cooler.

"Excuse me?" Aster said with a marginally harder tone.

"You're a brilliant engineer, but an absolutely terrible spy," Gabriel said matter-of-factly, "Not only did you get recorded snooping around a place by *three* separate groups, but one of them was able to find out your personal override code by surveilling you with a simple camera that he made in the lab."

"I know all that, thank you very much," Aster said defensively, "so what?"

"So," Gabriel continued, "you opened yourself up to being blackmailed *and* framed by a supposed friend and colleague, not only as the mole, but as the saboteur *and* as his killer."

"Fuck you!" Aster snapped, Gabriel's words had hit a nerve, "Felix *was* a friend, I've known him for years! He couldn't have been a mole, and he would never frame me!"

"Really?" Gabriel said with a hard glare, "how well did you know him?"

"Well enough to have been invited over for lunch countless times," Aster responded, "He and his partner are two of the nicest people I've ever met. You would've been invited over too if you were ever home!"

"So you knew the two of them well enough to know that Kessler's partner used to be a shipboard engineer?" Gabriel asked pointedly.

"Of course I knew that," Aster shot back, "he worked for twenty-five years on deep-space mining voyages before retiring."

"And during his career, he must have been exposed to an awful lot of cosmic radiation," Gabriel pointed out, "Treating and repairing the cellular damage caused by long-term radiation poisoning must be very expensive, even with medical insurance and two salaries."

Aster was speechless with shock and disbelief.

"It's almost impossible to get an already loyal agent to infiltrate somewhere," Gabriel continued, "It's much easier to recruit someone who's already on the inside, and bribery or blackmail – or a combination – are the two best ways to do it."

"You think he betrayed his employer…and his colleagues…to pay medical bills?" Aster asked, her voice quivering with disbelief.

"I don't 'think' that," Gabriel answered, "I *know* that because that's what the DNI discovered during the investigation which cleared *you* of responsibility."

"And you seriously expect me to happy about that?" Aster demanded bitterly.

"Happy about being exonerated on charges of corporate espionage, criminal complicity, xenotech possession, and first-degree murder?" Gabriel shot back, his normally level tone hardening, "I would have thought so, yes."

"One of my best friends was murdered this morning," Aster said, angry and hurt, "*and* I've been suspended from my job. How the fuck am I supposed to be happy?"

Aster punctuated the last word by punching Gabriel in the arm. Of course it didn't hurt, but Gabriel's face twitched into an angry scowl at being hit, nonetheless.

"Oh, you don't like that, do you?" Aster goaded him.

She followed up with a second punch, and in retaliation he grabbed her wrists and pinned her to the wall, baring his teeth at her in his typical, wolf-like snarl.

"Nice to see you drop the strong-and-silent pretence," Aster said mockingly, unafraid of him, "anger makes you a little more human than normal."

Gabriel had had enough of women manipulating him.

He abruptly released Aster's wrists and reached down, hooking his hands behind her knees and hoisting her into the air. He carried her to the bed and tossed her down onto the duvet without ceremony, pouncing on top of her like a predator. Aster pretended to struggle back, then slapped him across the face just to show that she could. Gabriel snarled angrily and Aster laughed, daring him to go further.

He tore her clothes off like a primaeval savage while trying to get out of his own uniform at the same time. Aster cut to the chase by ripping open his shirt. That rekindled his frenzied anger, and he pinned her back down to the bed and entered her.

She yelped at his forceful entry and wrapped her legs around him in response, hooking her legs behind his thighs and holding him in place as she ensnared him with her arms. He closed one hand around her throat and choked the pillow with the other, taking his anger out on her with a vigorous rhythm while she moaned her delight that he was home.

* * *

Gabriel finished with a climactic snarl, and Aster responded by raking his back with her nails like a feral cat, locking her limbs around his body and denying him the power to leave. They lay together as they coasted down from their mutual high, savouring the touch of each other's skin and the satisfaction of their reunion.

After a while, Gabriel pulled out and rolled over. Aster rolled over with him, snuggling up against his chest and resting her chin on his shoulder. He pulled the covers over their hot and sweaty bodies, scattering the shredded remnants of their clothes across the floor.

"Welcome home, sweetheart," Aster murmured sweetly.

"I'm sorry about everything," he said, reciprocating the embrace and stroking her hair.

"You don't have anything to apologise for," Aster replied.

"Actually, it was a sympathetic sorry," Gabriel clarified.

"Oh, I definitely don't want that," Aster answered, "The past day or so has been bad enough without other people's sympathy."

"Well, your day wasn't as bad as mine," Gabriel replied grimly.

"My career is on life support, my colleague was murdered, and I got blamed for it," Aster said pessimistically, "You're telling me you can top that?"

"You were accused of killing a colleague and then cleared of blame," Gabriel answered stoically, "I actually had to kill a colleague."

Aster looked up at him in shock.

"Did he deserve it?" she asked.

"No, but it had to be done," Gabriel replied, "And if our positions had been swapped, I would have expected him to do the same for me."

They lay together in silence for a while.

"Why does anger make me Human?" Gabriel asked Aster.

"You're so emotionally repressed all the time," Aster explained, "It's hard to know what you're thinking. At least when you get angry you show your feelings."

"I don't mean to be," Gabriel answered, "it's just that…"

"I'm guessing the DNI did something to you to make you as strong and silent as possible," Aster said, resignedly, "and that what exactly they did is classified."

"It keeps me focused on the mission at hand," Gabriel replied.

"I'm sure it does," Aster said sceptically, "And I'm sure it's not just a way for the DNI to make sure that its tools don't answer back."

Gabriel was silent for a moment.

"There was a point when I thought I might die," Gabriel said eventually, "and I would have been ready to die to make sure you and the children could be safe."

"What made you want to live?"

"Wanting to come back and see you all again," Gabriel replied, "and to spare you the burden of having to explain to the children why daddy wasn't coming home."

"Very considerate of you," Aster answered wryly, "Although, if anything did happen, we'd have to stop at baby number 5."

Gabriel flinched.

"Relax," Aster flicked him playfully under the chin, "I'm not pregnant."

"Good," Gabriel replied simply.

"Why 'good'?" Aster asked, suspiciously, "You don't want a fifth one?"

"I'm lukewarm about having another one," Gabriel answered, "Four seems enough."

Aster snuggled closer into his embrace.

"In that case, we'll need to find another outlet for all that aggression."

* * *

The Spire never slept. Tens of thousands of analysts, technicians, operatives, and agents worked in rotating shifts around the clock. It was, after all, the centre of all military intelligence operations in the entire sector, coordinating the activities of dozens of DNI stations and sub-stations, each of which, in turn, coordinated numerous smaller operations at the fringes of Human-controlled space and beyond.

And the aftermath of one such operation needed a lot of explaining.

"*I have never believed you to be someone who takes unnecessary risks,*" said one of the speakers in the holographic teleconference, his face concealed and his voice electronically altered, "*so to say that I believe this technical intelligence operation you were running in the heart of a major star system is 'out-of-character' would be a gross understatement.*"

"If you read my report, as I assume you have, you will know that the operation was ultimately a success," Red-eye replied, unfazed by the criticism, "Which, by definition, means that it was not an 'unnecessary' risk."

"*Indeed,*" said a second digitally altered voice, "*and now, apparently, this 'observer' wants to trade its knowledge in exchange for a stay of execution.*"

"You would rather I destroy it?"

"*Far be it from me to presume to tell you how to run operations in your sector,*" the second voice replied loftily, "*but if I discovered an active alien AI in the home system of my sector, I would have ordered its destruction sooner rather than later.*"

"If this 'Swarm' is as malevolent as the reports indicate, I suspect we will need all the resources we can muster," Red-eye replied, "Even including the support of an alien AI."

"*On a separate note, the performance of your voidstalkers continues to impress,*" said a third voice, "*even though one of them apparently threatened you.*"

"I should hope so, considering that the Masterminds themselves commissioned the programme," Red-eye responded, "and as to your second point, he did not threaten me."

"*His anger would indicate emotional instability,*" a fourth voice noted airily, "*an undesirable trait in a field operative at any level.*"

"He is anything but unstable," Red-eye answered calmly, "and in any case, if the voidstalkers were meant to be that docile, they would be an army of robots. They are not."

"*Robots lack the capacity to second-guess their superiors,*" the first voice remarked.

"They also lack something much more crucial," Red-eye replied.

"*Which is?*"

"The spark of Humanity," Red-eye explained, "The Void-stalker Programme has long-term purposes which transcend its immediate utility as a tool of deep-space intelligence operations. They hinge on the long-term survival of Humanity as a whole, and it is therefore vital that the voidstalkers actually *be* Human, anger and all."

"*How very cryptic,*" remarked the first voice, "*And uncharacteristically poetic.*"

"No doubt you will all be ordered to initiate satellite programmes modelled on my own when the time is right," Red-eye responded.

"*I would not be surprised by that,*" said a fifth voice, "*Projects of this sort are routinely allocated to each of us individually, and the reasons are entrusted to that person exclusively until the time is right to divulge the full explanation to the rest of us.*"

"In that case, fellow directors-general, does that conclude our call?" Red-eye asked.

"*I believe it does. Farewell until the next Terran year.*"

The various callers terminated their secure, trans-stellar comm. links, ending the conference call and leaving Red-eye alone on her throne.

She turned back to a set of four medical reports on her desk, scrolling through the reports and absorbing the positive results with silent approval. When she scrolled back up and saw the grinning faces with their father's emerald green eyes, she couldn't help but smile.

THE END

About the Author

I'm not a full-time author, few of us are that lucky. I have a five-day-a-week job which pays the bills, including the book-related bills. I enjoy writing and science fiction as a hobby and an escape, and the result of unwinding at the end of every day, and over every weekend, are the stories I write.

By the way, if you enjoyed Voidstalker, be sure to read the second book in the series, Krakenscourge.

Made in the USA
Coppell, TX
26 January 2021

48863868R00152